THE HOPPING BIRD

GRANT ALEXANDER DOSSETTO

To my amazing parents, Richard and Ginger Dossetto. God took you too soon.

Special thanks to Jonah Goldberg whose writing inspired the title of this book and a key passage therein.

Grant Alexander Dossetto

THE FIRST HALF

CHAPTER ONE

"You're going to have to go get Three Way," The Walrus said.

"Yeah, I know. Just want to see him cool down a bit before I take the ball from him." I gazed out through an ever-moving curtain of moisture. The late spring storm was coming down hard now, pooling on top of the dugout and washing over the flat roof edge that separated the protected haven of the home dugout from the elements and the field beyond.

"He's given up ten again in three-plus innings and there's been another three errors behind him in the field. I know the bullpen is thin but you let him get shell shocked the last two times out. You have to go get him and I don't think waiting is gonna make that any easier."

"You seem to think I had another option. What choice did I have? Who is left to go to in the bullpen, Wal? Detroit's already called up my top three relievers because of injuries. First year on the job and they have to raid their farm team by the middle of May. My luck just never stops running out, does it?" The last part of my outburst was rhetorical and my bench coach was smart enough not to answer. I spit out tobacco juice onto the cracked concrete floor below me. The tarry substance didn't slide toward the drain, instead it clumped there in all of its brown, phlegmy glory. Baseball had outlawed the stuff years ago, kowtowing to the politically correct, but I was too damn old to care. Besides, the Mud Hens couldn't draw five hundred fans to a game right now. There wasn't anyone here to feign outrage at my habit. My misery should have welcomed the company of apathy. Staring at the blob of poison I had spit, the opposite reaction stirred. If someone is yelling at you, you know you still matter. When those who seem to make a living out of haranguing you stop, that's rock bottom. I spit again just to further my point. Maybe I should stop, I don't even taste it anymore. A long time ago, tobacco just became a craving, an empty desire that never seemed to satisfy. "He's so mad, he's gone pale. It's like his body had to shut down or he would have popped a couple of capillaries in his cheeks."

"If looks could kill, The Latin Lover would be dead," joked The Walrus.

"Jesus Christ, why does every player on my team have a sexual nickname?" I asked heatedly.

"A group of twenty five young men, I can't possibly see how that could wind up in a bevy of off-color sex jokes. Besides, Three Way isn't sexual at all, I actually think it's a pretty decent pun."

"Yeah, you'll have to enlighten me as to why they call my hand picked anchor for our rotation 'Three Way' then."

"Easy, he throws a four seam fastball with the speed of a two seamer, straight as an arrow at ninety miles an hour if he's lucky. He throws a three seamer. Hence the nickname Three Way," The Walrus recited, chuckling to himself when he finished. Each guffaw pulled the rolls of fat that had replaced cheeks, already droopy with age, toward the ground. It was a pretty decent joke, if you like baseball that is. I was unsure why I never got it before. Managers are always the last ones to understand their team. It is a wonder any of us are thought to be good.

"It's really raining. Cold too. Why don't they just call this game?" I mused.

"Columbus is in first place this year, a rarity. Were you really expecting them to throw away a sure win over their rivals?"

"No, not really. And God forbid a team attached to the Indians doesn't get their way. Think they'll care about shrinkage?"

"I think thirty-something soccer moms in Toledo are pretty easy to please on that front," said The Walrus.

"Let's hope so." I rose from the pine bench and attempted to bound effortlessly up the steps to field level but my left knee weakened in protest. My cleats burrowed into soft dirt before displacing the shallow roots of the immaculate grass, and I waited. I could feel the ligaments and bone shift before settling back into a tenuous peace. I felt the familiar knot tighten and breathed a sigh of relief when it popped as I began to walk again into the driving rain.

Three Way was glaring at me over the top of the webbing of his glove like Andy Pettite in his prime. I could see the muscles at the corners of his eyes flickering, pulled by a jaw that was assuredly throwing cuss words into the worn leather. Silently I waited from a safe distance but it didn't abate. A couple of steps and I was now close enough to hear what he was saying, even worse than I thought it might be. I could do nothing but wait out his burst of creatively massaged expletives strung together just well enough to make you believe it might mean something.

"You done?" My palm laid upwards at the end of an extended arm for far too long. Three Way's eyes began to soften and the rim of his glove slowly moved from his nose until it came to rest just above his waist.

"No. What the fuck are they making our uniforms out of these days? It rains and all of a sudden we look like tawdry Chippendale dancers out here." He finally cracked a smile.

"Yeah, quite a show for those left in the stands, huh?"

"First they added those stupid vents under the arms, as if I wasn't going to sweat throwing a hundred pitches because of it. Now they've messed with everything and our white pants stopped being white a couple innings ago. Christ, I can tell you aren't wearing any underwear Skip. Funny that Majestic makes these damn things, the view is anything but."

It was true, I hadn't worn any under a uniform since high school. I don't remember why I found myself in that particular predicament but I know that the first game with me commando I went four for four with power. Out of all of the superstitions I tried during my career, that one was the only one which stuck forever. Hell, here I was as a manager and it was still a thing. Of course when I played I had a jock strap to provide a bit of privacy if the worst happened. Now I didn't even have that. I looked down as if it couldn't possibly be true without me checking first. Yep, everyone knew what my sixty year old self was working with. Good thing I kept in decent shape or it would be more embarrassing than it already was.

"Well, who said the Mud Hens weren't worth the price of admission this year?"

That did it. Rick gave a hearty laugh that belied the embarrassment still evident in his features and his posture before handing me the ball. He began to walk off toward the home dugout, stoically enduring the cat calls of the Columbus fans huddled in the sections immediately behind the visitor's dugout. I realized that I hadn't made a signal to the pen and had become the sole focus of attention. The home plate umpire pulled his mask up and away from his face to yell at me but I recovered fast enough to head off his throaty command. Three Way is right-handed so Columbus had a lefty heavy lineup and, being up 11-3 already, didn't have much incentive to shuffle their card. I made the signal to bring in Mendenhall, the only southpaw with enough stamina to pull middle relief duty and eat up some innings. I sure as hell didn't want to have to come walking out here again flaunting everything a second time. Maybe Wal could do it...

Mendenhall didn't charge to the mound out of the pen, instead choosing to do his normal slow walk. He thinks it is intimidating. To his credit, it worked. One of the few pieces of the patchwork bullpen I could rely on. When he finally got to the mound, I handed him the ball and stood and watched his warm up tosses. Mendenhall stopped throwing, looking at me conspicuously, silently telling me that I needed to head to the dugout. I just stared past him, my gaze aimed at nothing in particular. A shadow grew darker in the corner of my eye.

"Hey Harold, what the hell are you doing?" The Ump's

6

voice was stereotypically gruff. It must come with years of arguing balls and strikes. It's funny though, deep down they kind of like it. I think that they secretly want to see what we'll think of next. Stealing first base like Lloyd McClendon is a bit much, kicking dust is better but that was passé when Weaver did it. Those are actions though and baseball is a strategic game, any ump wants to know how we'll creatively insert the magic word to get the heave ho. I've had some good ones. Poor sap. I knew today needed to be no-frills, just waste some time until the rain's intensity matched the blackness of the clouds rolling in from the west.

"I didn't know we were so close Kelly." The guy has been doing International League games since before my major league career ended. Using the first name of the elder statesman of minor league baseball, he'll like that.

"Since when did you get permission to use my first name on the job? I was just trying to be nice, thought you might be having a stroke or something. You were just staring into space and I still have some semblance of manners, it's basic politeness to be cordial during a health episode. Won't make that mistake twice. Get the hell off my field Freeman."

"You thought I was having a stroke?"

"Yeah. Now if there is something you want to talk about, spit it out or get off the field."

I erupted. "What's going to send me to the ER is continuing to play this game in a downpour, Kelly. I know ump's are God damned blind but I figure one of your worthless fucking senses worked." His arm was motioning

7

that I was tossed before I finished the sentence. "Mendenhall here throws ninety-eight when it suits him and he can't even feel the seams in this weather. It's on your head when he loses one at the side of some poor Clipper's bean. You ready to send flowers to a funeral? 'We are gathered here today to celebrate the death of a great young man. Deceased, crew chief's incompetence.'"

"That's enough Freeman or you're going to force me to write you up for a fine. Couple of games' pay isn't worth it. None of us make enough to throw it away."

Damn it, they usually play to the crowd and get animated. He was just standing there. Minor league hockey games always have the opening minute fight to get the crowd worked up, minor league baseball has the ump/manager confrontation. It works a hell of a lot better than Disco Go Kart Night, unless the other side is figuratively turtling. "Don't worry about my pay, I've got a couple of tips coming my way when I go do a little routine on top of the dugout." I stuck out my hips towards him. "One hell of a bachelorette party, huh?"

That brought out the fire in him. "Enough!" Another ejection motion followed by him closing the gap between us. "I am not going to see you make a mockery of my game. We're going to play this thing to completion even if Noah's fucking flood sits over us for the rest of the afternoon. You, and you're fucking embarrassing prick, won't be a part of it. Now get the fuck off my field before I remove you myself."

I turned on my heel like I was truly offended. The cheer I got for my effort was meager but, considering the sparse attendance, somewhat gratifying. It sure beat the Bronx cheer my transparent uniform would have gotten me alone. If the eyes are the window to the soul, I don't quite want to know what transparent pants on a card carrying AARP member are the window to. The pinstripes were the only thing providing any modesty, clinging tightly to my front and back sides. They looked like jail bars, framing a pornographic scene. Mia Malkova (don't ask why an old man knows who that is) might like that but I sure as hell didn't.

I doffed my cap for reassurance, the cheers got louder in response. As I made my way down the steps and through the dugout towards the locker rooms I cracked a smile. It may be bad form to offer your own curtain call but I needed to know that I was the only one who was thinking about Dennis Franz and *NYPD Blue* during the whole sordid affair.

CHAPTER TWO

There are few places more isolating than the clubhouse after you have been thrown out of a game. People laugh at him but I sympathize with Bobby Valentine. It is almost worth trying to don a fake moustache and some shades and attempt a poor man's *Spy Vs. Spy* routine to sneak back to the dugout without being noticed. I sat with the closed circuit television turned off, as well as the set with cable. I wasn't in the mood for the inanity of daytime soaps and watching your own team's broadcast is obviously bad luck. That's two superstitions that have stuck with me.

My water logged uniform seemed to cling to me tighter as I sank into the chair behind my desk. With nothing to think about, I suddenly realized how chilled I was. I curled my arms and legs as tightly against my body as it would allow anymore, trying to warm myself back up. Compressing my body didn't help, it actually made things worse. I couldn't really figure out why that is, it seemed counterintuitive, and it probably was. Much like a child wants to climb out of a cold pool, only to find the warm air is anything but, I had to accept my condition. I unwrapped my legs but kept my arms draped around my chest. In a bit of stunning news, the desk before me, my menial kingdom, was a shoddy mess and the constant drip from my hands and sleeves would only make it worse for the hodgepodge of scouting reports, performance evaluations, and correspondence with the Tiger's roving talent instructor. Who am I kidding? All of those things were probably expendable but today brought the newest edition of *Baseball America*. Few things in life created greater anticipation than opening up its glossy pages. Coke, apple pie, Chevrolet, and BA; the only constants in American life. It may be a guilty nostalgic pleasure but in this modern world where I need to understand Twitter and Instagram because they can ruin careers, it is a figurative grounding wire for my leathery hands to hold.

I couldn't hear anything in my bunker, no crowd noise. Guess that means there wasn't a comeback in the offing. The dull thud of rain grew to a roar, steady in its drumming of the stadium above me with a seemingly random backbeat that was also intensifying as wind added edge to Nature's melody. Finally a strong *crack!* pierced the air, followed by a long, deep rumble of thunder that vibrated the floor. It was turning into a hell of a storm. Men, my men, began to be heard through the door of my office as they streamed thankfully into the clubhouse as fast as they could come. I turned on the closed circuit television, a graphic spread across the bottom of the screen showing the offensive output for each inning. Columbus was batting in the top of the fifth when the game was called, less than an inning until the result became official. This unofficial game told the story of our season. The other team had big numbers in the runs and hits columns while we dominated the errors column.

The lightning strikes came quicker and the thunder rumbled longer as the storm had now begun in earnest. The men sat silently in the clubhouse, waiting for news of a true postponement before they began to pack up and enjoy a rare off day in the middle of a homestand. No travel, just fifty hours without playing baseball. I planned to enjoy the time away given how bad of a stretch we'd been going through. I hadn't bothered to check the radar, my gut knew we were in for a long soaker, and besides, I couldn't have done anything even if the game was restarted. I headed for the showers and let the hot water run over me for hours.

I turned the knob and the water slowed to a trickle then a drip as the leaky shower head protested my decision. I dried myself, meticulously rubbing cotton over my nearly translucent skin. Prolonged exposure to the jets had left my skin saturated, the cells just under the epidermis ready to burst. I paused to laugh at myself, epidermis. Never would I have used such a word but Gail's melanoma last year made it so even a man who has only been involved with a game his whole life started to think about old people problems and adult terms. Maybe I should shoot myself before I make it to Depends.

Now that the shower was off I could hear loud latin music echoing from the clubhouse. The Tigers franchise has more Hispanics than most organizations but I still didn't know much of the language. Who could blame me though when ojo, oso, and oro mean everything from eyes to gold. Maybe English was like that if I ever thought about it but I didn't think about it. I found out a long time ago to make sure that philosophical questions remained above my pay grade. My wife made sure to elevate everything else to the same status.

Whether it makes a lick of sense or not, it does have the nice advantage of being upbeat. I'd take it over what passes for rock today and don't get me started on rap. I stood at my locker unsure of what to wear home. On one side of the locker was a victory suit, ready for me to strut myself around with my chest out like the God damn President. On the other was my loser sweats, as if me dressing like a hobo would keep people from recognizing me after a loss. Okay, that's three superstitions. I never had to worry about pressing the sweats but the suit was always the preferred postgame wardrobe. At one time, my habit got me a lot of haranguing. Poor guy from the Commissioner's Office used to become apoplectic at the sight of me in a ratty sweatshirt being anywhere near his logo. No one holds their logo in more reverence than MLB. If it was indeed modeled after Killebrew, he deserves a lot more than he got for it. Then football coaches started to look like dumpster divers even in victory and baseball stopped being so concerned.

I decided on the sweats, we were losing after all. No, we were getting our ass kicked and luck, plus a bit of crooked pool on my part, got us out of it without taking a loss. Suddenly the salsa music felt out of place, there is something to be said for being defiant in the face of adversity but the rah rah spirit of the songs sounded a lot more like embracing failure. I couldn't hear any movement outside of the music, which wasn't unusual, the players always seemed to leave it on for me to turn off when I closed up. An annoying habit has a funny way of turning into a grating display of sloppiness depending on a man's mood. I was still cold, even after the shower, and today I had definitely stopped being happy.

I pushed open the office door with more force than was necessary, especially since no one was left to see my displeasure. Uniforms were left in disheveled clumps in front of lockers. A stench pervaded the room that resembled that of a high school football team rather than a professional organization that contracts out for laundry and cleaning services on a daily basis. It had been getting worse but familiarity had brought acceptance. No more. I jotted a note in the pad I always carry in my back pocket or I'd probably forget to demand a locker check. I could already see one of the culprits, wine was leaking out of the bottom of Andre's locker. The seal on his keg was going. Who drinks wine out of a keg? When you're a mountain of a man, it isn't as big of an achievement as you might think. The man sure can down it and I've never seen him drunk. Unfortunately the poor bastard can't field a lick even when sober.

My hand was beginning to return to its normal state of wrinkliness, which isn't anything to sneeze at, as it pressed the off button on the stereo. I was expecting silence but instead heard sobs. Strong bursts of breath rolled across skin like wind on a sail. There was only one man I knew who possessed enough skin to billow.

CHAPTER THREE

It didn't register but I know I must have appeared shocked to see The Walrus in turmoil. We had known each other for decades and whenever I got the stupid notion in my head to manage a team he was my only choice for bench coach. He also had the distinction of being the happiest man I had ever known. Given his rolls, if baseball was in season during the holidays he'd probably have a more flattering nickname. The year I did the rounds as manager for the Arizona Fall League and Winter Ball, all the Dominican players called him Sin Barba de Santa or something like that. I'm told it translates to the Beardless Santa. He'd probably get called Buddha if we ever made it to India to manage Cricket. It was just the first year for me in Toledo. Only Gwinnet was worse last year than the Mud Hens in all of the International League, so I should have had a decent honeymoon, but it always feels like a noose is around the neck of a losing manager. We definitely did a lot of that these first five weeks. It wore on me, or so I thought, but it never seemed to get to him.

What was more surprising was that The Walrus didn't seem surprised when I caught him in his moment of weakness. It was as if he wanted to be caught. His puffy eyes seemed to firm first and the heaves slowed down until they only intermittently broke his breathing. "Hey Harry, remember what Spark-," a sob tried to rise from inside his diaphragm but it petered out halfway up, "what Sparky said about me the first time he saw me down at Camp in '81?"

"Wal, you sure you want to do this?"

"Why shorten it? Just come out and say it, call me Walrus."

"Or Wally."

"C'mon Har, no one calls me Wal because of my name. I've been The Walrus for decades, even the radio guys say it when I have to fill in for you on the pregame interview. Walrus, Walrus, Walrus. I asked you a question. Remember what Sparky called me back in '81?"

"Yeah, Wal I do. He called you the Alpha Male," I responded sullenly. Me and The Walrus were similar in age but I was the better player, having cracked the 25 man roster in 1978. Not that I got all of the headlines, those were reserved for The Big Wheel, Sweet Lou and Tram. When the hell did I do anything wrong in the conversation? For some reason it felt like I had.

"Now look at me."

"Easy there, big guy." I stopped, wincing at the poor choice of words. The Walrus eyed me but seemed to let the incident pass without a new stream of tears. "None of us look like we did back in our playing days. It's a fact of life that things never stay the same, especially our youth."

"You've stayed in shape." He was almost a whisper now.

"Well I go commando so I have to," I tried to joke. It didn't seem to work. "What's going on Wal?"

"I never hear about your sex life?"

"What?!"

"I always hear about Gail and the family vacation to

16

Aspen in the winter or how much the kids have grown. Sometimes you tell me about a joke she made on the phone. I hear about your relationship. I never hear about the sex."

"Gee Wal, I wonder why? And I don't think you are going to hear about it any time soon. You are crying in the locker room hours after game time because I don't go boasting about my sex life? I didn't do that in my twenties, I probably won't start now at sixty. What the hell is going on, Wal? I'm not going to ask again." I too had lowered my voice, my posture now resembling that of a snake who was done rattling and was ready to strike.

"No, you aren't understanding me Harold."

"That's because you aren't making any sense." I coiled further.

"You know what they say, in a bad relationship the sex is everything." He stopped and eyed me, waiting for me to finish the adage.

"And in a good one, it is nothing." I still wasn't sure where this was going.

"I always hear about Gail and the kids, it is so obvious how much you love them and how strong your relationship is. I never hear about the sex. It isn't everything for you." He paused, tears now streaming over the saturated levee of his eye lids accompanied by two strong sobs. "She left me Harold. Kim is gone."

I sat down, not knowing at all what to say, "Walter...I'm sorry." Yeah, it was a cliché, an inadequate one at that, but sometimes those work. The Walrus leaned over and hugged

17

me. Thank God none of the players were around.

"I need to get back into shape," he said.

"I think we can manage that."

"Was that a pun?"

"What?" I was legitimately confused but seeing him smile again was worth it.

"You know, manage and manage? I never know with you."

"Oh." I laughed. "If it was, it was a bad one."

The large man rose, taking a deep, uninterrupted breath. He opened his locker and out of habit checked his phone. I didn't need to have ever owned an iPhone to know that the display wasn't going to show any missed calls or new texts. The Walrus's resolve wavered for a minute, culminating in another rolling, yet sporadic, sigh that traveled all the way to his feet. Without looking at me, he stoically said, "Three Way's still in the ice bath."

I watched him walk to the exit door before stopping him. "Wal, you want to stay with me tonight?"

He didn't look back but his answer was the old Walrus, "Sorry Har, don't think I'm ready for a one night stand yet." Finally a heave was the result of a laugh and he was gone.

CHAPTER FOUR

The Walrus's description of the whirlpool machine as an ice bath was pithy but accurate. The metal sides had begun rusting outwards over a decade ago and had become thin, brittle even. The sides were crudely riveted at the bottom to the floor piece, warping just enough with age so that the leak was substantial but mostly unexciting. Someday it would finally go, collapsing due to the weight of someone inside and it would be explosive, like shooting an above ground pool.

The damn thing couldn't fill itself. A hose was connected to the tap at the other side of the trainer's room which carried the water to the whirlpool. The tap, which looked like it was first installed back when Toledo was still being fought for by the State of Michigan, had two modes, on and off. Turning the handle, either handle, just slightly elicited a blast strong enough to pass from a hydrant. Three Way used the thing more than anyone else. Even so, it was unusual for him to still be in it almost five hours after I took the ball from him. If you expect to spend more than thirty minutes in the thing you have to fill it back up. Five hours of soaking would be quite a messy process full of leaks and barely controlled aquatic explosions. The water which came out was so cold it felt like fire to a person's skin. I doubt even the waters of Lake Superior in winter could pull off worse. Faintly controlled liquid arctic and a makeshift fireman's hose…you could play a mean joke or two with that. Good thing the room was tucked away from the clubhouse. The only man who used it on a daily basis was the team doctor and he was a dreadfully serious man.

The tub had the distinction of having been made for men the size of sailors and Three Way didn't fit, none of the players did. I walked into the room to see just the top of his hairline sticking out over the lip of the side. I could imagine how stiff his neck was getting being craned so that he could get everything from the shoulder down under the water line. Splaying out the other side, over the metal was a lot of leg, all the way to his knees. It seems every pitcher these days is around six-five and Three Way was no exception. If the purpose of the ice bath was to dull your pain, I had no idea how this contortion served that purpose. It looked like he was in the gynecological chair from hell with invisible stirrups making sure his privates were accessible to the world. Luckily the view was pointing the other way. I could only imagine the difficulty it took to get out of, and reassume that position, and wondered how he managed not to split open skin on the rough metal that surrounded him.

I could feel water seeping through my shoes, several inches deep. It was a pitiable sight, maybe best that I talked to him from behind. "It's getting late, you about done?"

I could tell that he heard me, his head slightly cocked at the sound of my voice. It took him a long time to say anything though and the words came out melancholy, "Just hurtin' tonight, Skip."

"That's a lot of work you're doing just to keep the arm cold."

"Shit, it ain't just my arm. I'm no spring chicken anymore. When I throw a hundred pitches everything hurts. Hurts more on a last place team when I don't get out of the third inning."

"What hurts?" I really should be more understanding of my players. Expectations had been blown to bits by all of the call ups but that didn't excuse me for phoning it in. Me and Three Way had a long history and I was completely clueless about his physical condition. Hell, most of the time I just spent my time watching him with pity that at thirty-seven he was still playing AAA.

"Wish I could say it was my arm, it's mostly dead. My fastball's got no giddy up, less than normal and the joke about me throwing a three seamer isn't exactly undeserved. How'd Jamie Moyer do it until he was forty-six? Everything else is what hurts. My back no longer wants to fully rotate and my sides won't stretch. Jimbo, the pitching coach that is, keeps railing on me letting my arm trail my body and that's got the ball up in the zone. I'm so creaky I have to fight in the first inning just to keep my delivery repeatable. Can't get a consistent arm slot."

"How about a brace? Or maybe cortisone?" I asked.

"It's not just my back and my obliques. Coming out of a full wind-up, my right hip, where my weight shifts to, it erupts until I see stars in my eyes. And my kick leg blows up at my shin, just above the ankle, when it reaches the landing spot. Not to mention the plantar fascism or whatever it's called in the foot itself. It's only slightly better if I use a slide step and then I need to rely on my dead arm to generate some power which it seems incapable of doing."

"I didn't know Rick." I've had to use people's real names too much today. I knew now that the day off I thought I had earned was going to be spent at the ballpark. Rick was giving me more than he had left and I was hanging him out to dry with one of the worst defensive teams I had ever seen.

"You didn't ask Skip." That hurt. "This is it for me, the last year. Youth is wasted on the young, right? The kids on this team think they'll play forever but it doesn't work like that. I can almost forgive them for backsliding through another year in last place. There is certainly the excuse for it with all the guys we've lost. I could talk to them 'til I'm blue in the face about how it is over faster than you think. Tell 'em to savor it because it is special but they wouldn't listen. So many don't know what they have until it is gone. I don't understand you though. When you were in Baltimore you were so close. Toronto, and then the strike, were all that stood in the way of a World Series in '94. Being in The Show at the top. The way you lost your shot, greed and everything that doesn't matter, getting in the way of what did. They fired you and fell apart a couple years later. They were wrong. When I got to play for you, I've never seen a guy who loved the game like you. Why are you coasting through this season, Skip?"

That hurt even more but a long relationship allows for candidness. I stood there saying nothing, feeling the water rise just a bit further, creeping towards the bottom of my ankles. He was sitting in a half empty tub now and my feet were freezing. I had a chill in my gut as well. His words cut into me, honesty to a loser is a terrible thing. I should have left but I knew he wasn't done speaking yet. I wasn't mad at him, nor what he had said. A man over twenty years younger than me had just educated me on leadership. My pride said to lash out but my heart said to listen. I realized only now that we were in the dark, the only light shining in from the hallway behind me. The shadow I cast crept all the way to the whirlpool. Tom Landry once said that leadership isn't getting someone to do something they didn't want to do, it was getting someone to achieve what they wanted to achieve. I had brought Rick on to be a mentor to a bunch of guys who were so close to being key components of major league staffs. I had thought I was doing him a favor by simply letting him play another year. How wrong that thought was. Rather than being a light to the right path, I had darkened his last shot at a championship. My shadow cast itself across the room, it was fitting and heartbreaking. Rick finally began to speak again.

"To be a pitcher in baseball must be one of the stupidest ideas God ever devised. First they put you sixty feet from a guy who is trying to hit the ball back up the middle at a hundred miles an hour. You're one of two guys who touch the ball on every defensive play and they put you on a pedestal they call a mound so that everyone has no choice but to make you the center of attention. You can throw the perfect pitch, splinter some guy's bat into a thousand pieces, and he might still flare the ball weakly down the line for a double. Or you could have one bad inning that turns you into a goat seemingly on demand. I think I'd like to be a manager over that."

"I don't know, managing comes with it's own kinds of regrets Rick." The nausea that had formed in my stomach was now crawling up my esophagus and I was sure was plastered on my face. Esophagus, another medical term. Today had been too much of an adult day and now it was bringing up old memories I'd rather stay buried. Maybe it was a good thing he was looking the other way or I'd see his face, not as it was now, but as it was at 21. He was a top flight prospect then, got a cup of coffee in The Show the September before. Durham was loaded with high first-round draft picks but none were progressing like expected. The parent club, the Devil Rays, were still convinced that running out a squad with washed up veterans like Conseco or McGriff would work if they just had one ace to build a rotation around. Rick was supposed to be that guy. It was my third year there, first gig since the Baltimore debacle, and he had a hell of a first half. Then the elbow problems started and a Tommy John surgery later I was out on my ass and he was doomed to the minors forever.

Rick seemed to ignore my comment, starting back up on a different tangent. "I was watching Sportscenter the other day and here they are going on about whether colleges should be paying their athletes. Fucking journalists pontificating about how evil it is that kids have access to world class facilities, an endless supply of gorgeous girls who think they are smart enough to disguise being a slut for the jock with some tired bromide of female empowerment."

"'Bromide of female empowerment.' That's a hell of a

phrase Rick," I mused, legitimately impressed.

"What?" He asked, annoyed that I had interrupted.

"Never mind, just pretend I wasn't here."

"They were talking about football, the teams play twelve times a year. That's it. Most of them couldn't find the campus if you gave them a map, every game is on national television it seems and when they sign with the NFL they get a first contract that any baseball player would pull out his back molars for. Go top ten in the first round like I did and rookies are looking at $20 million guaranteed in football. I got a little over a million and so many were hacked off I got that. On top of everything, they usually come from out of state to the big programs so their scholarship is worth about $120,000. It's unbelievable to me how they can't see what a great deal they've got."

"Things sure have changed since I was a kid." My attempts to interject into the conversation were making me feel smaller every time I did it. I needed to just shut the hell up and let him finish.

"Remember where you were when Tom Browning broke his fucking arm?"

I said nothing and he said nothing, maybe he actually did want me to talk to him. "Yeah, never seen anything like it. Broke his humerus but it sure as hell wasn't funny. Thing didn't explode like a bat. That bone is never supposed to be able to break like that, it snapped clean through. Sounded like a starter pistol went off and he was screaming before he hit the ground. Instantaneous, incredible pain. He was on the ground before the ball got to the catcher's mitt in 0.6 seconds. He still threw a strike. I've seen it before."

"How often?"

"It's rare," I said. "Only ever seen it happen to lefties."

"It terrified me. Thought that was how I'd go. That or I'd take a comebacker to my skull and it would scare me so bad I'd never have the wherewithal to pitch again. Thank God I was already washed up when I saw Rick Ankiel forget how to pitch. Funny how you fear the crazy stuff and dismiss the routine."

"I understand. I never thought I'd tear up my knee on astroturf getting picked off of third base. My career as a Tiger ended on a play that I still think is the worst moment in my life. We had done all that work chasing down Toronto in one of the great playoff chases ever and I wasted all of it by fucking up against a Twins team that had barely made it to .500," I drearily reminisced. Always at the front of my brain on bad days. Nearly thirty years later and it still hurt. I should probably have never rejoined this franchise. Like visiting your hometown, some experiences are bound to come back to you with force if you return.

"I got signed at 18 out of high school and got to ride a bus around the Florida State League playing in front of hundreds, maybe a couple thousand if we were lucky. Double-A wasn't much bigger. I think our good start in Durham was the first time I played a game in front of five thousand people. Pitch counts were already a big deal back then but inning count hadn't been thought of yet."

"Rick, I know, I was there."

"I threw about 70 innings my senior year of high school. I threw at least double that every year in the minors. It started at the end of my second year, just a dull throb in my elbow. It didn't affect my stuff at all so I threw through it. Did it again the next year and the year after. Funny, a perpetually sore elbow never scared me, it was always the one-in-a-million stuff that kept me up at night. Then one day, the sore elbow became the useless elbow and I got acquainted with Mr. Tommy John," Rick spit out.

"Rick, I feel bad about that, to this day."

"It wasn't you Har, you just took the fall for it. I'm not trying to relitigate the past either, I'm just thinking out loud. Baseball takes players who love it and grinds them down in dusty sandlots a hundred and forty times a year for peanuts. It's all worth it, even the injuries, just for a couple week stint in the majors on a team that was out of playoff contention on Opening Day. Hell, this game is so beautiful it's worth it if you never make it out of Scranton or Lakeland or Clearwater or Erie or whatever other hole in the wall town has a team across this country. That scene from *Eight Men Out*, at the end, where Shoeless Joe is playing in Jersey under a fake name because he's been banned from the game for life but can't think of something better to do? That doesn't happen in football. I'm not here Har to get a charity check. Minors pay like shit and you know it. I've never won a championship, when you convinced me to give this thing another year, it didn't take much to persuade me but I've lost enough for a lifetime. I want to go out a winner."

"Ok Rick. We'll get you that championship." I walked out without waiting for a response. The hour drive to my Brother and Sister-In-Law's just outside Detroit, where I had a bedroom and cooked meals that come from somewhere other than a can, would be a long one tonight. I wouldn't bother thinking my usual thoughts, the ones about whether Rusty Chevrolet would make it home or just pass out on the side of the road like a dog that had curled up to die. No, for the first time in weeks I had remembered why I was here.

CHAPTER FIVE

The old Malibu hated spring. It was the time when concrete and asphalt buckled under the weight of heavy trucks, outward sturdiness belying structural damage that had occurred as the snow and ice of winter thawed and refroze, expanded and contracted in every crack and sliver of pavement until it gave way. Pot holes opened up, big enough to swallow entire front ends, threatening tire alignments and, on occasion, disrupting the electronics. This spring had been a cold one making the roads worse than normal. The increasingly familiar drive up Monroe Street to 14th to I-75 was easy enough to navigate but it got dicey after that. It is only eight miles from entrance ramp 202 to the Michigan state line but that is forever when it transforms into a minefield.

Like so many Ohio freeways, 75 through Toledo bloats and returns to normal as it merges with other freeways. Two lanes splitting off to 280 or 475 or some Ohio highway towards Bowling Green with two lanes continuing north towards the Motor City. It seems that these bottlenecks are always the site of the worst potholes, stretching from end line to end line like a gaping maw. The three semis around don't seem to notice but Rusty Chevrolet always did. I slowed down, causing a long line of traffic behind me to lay on their horns, only to wince as the corroded undercarriage of Rusty vibrated to its core as it pushed through the rough asphalt mouth. I imagined the thick caking of oxidation trickling into the abyss like an appetizer and thanked God that the muffler didn't go with it.

I knew my mechanical *Charlie Brown* tree was sick but it was still only dropping needles. The end was near but against all odds she kept kicking. I snuck a peek at the odometer, 290,000 miles and fifteen years old. I had picked her up on a used car lot to log the unforgiving miles of a roving instructor. After five years, the brass had finally decided to give me another manager's gig. And what had I managed to bring to Mud(Hen)ville? These were the thoughts running through my head when the flip phone sitting in the driver's side cup holder began to buzz. I stared down at the display and smiled. She always made me smile. I answered her call just as I passed the Pure Michigan sign, "Hey babe."

"Is there a good reason why *ESPN* has footage of you running every fifteen minutes blurred out from the waist down?" Oddly, she didn't sound mad. They say men mellow with age but women do as well. What would have been an embarrassment a decade ago was now the cause of mock interrogation.

"Attendance hasn't been so good. I'm guessing that our see through jerseys aren't getting the reaction everyone was hoping for?"

"Au contraire. They seem to be going over quite well. I just wish I got to see it uncensored. It has been too long since I got to see you like that."

"Just tell me they aren't looping footage of the grenade guy with it."

"No. Lindsay Czarniak actually seems pretty impressed. Doesn't seem fair she gets to ogle over your crotch and all I get is to deal with the fallout tomorrow. It's hard enough to teach high school kids as it is, now I have to contend with them teasing me about my husband being practically naked on the one cable channel every teenage boy is sure to watch. School year ends next week so detention isn't a threat anymore."

I laughed, "Sorry Hon, your mom told you I was no good before we got hitched. Guess you should have listened to her."

"She was right. Why do you think I kick you out of the house for half the year? The best times of my marriage are you out on the road and you can't even get that right." I didn't have to be able to see her to know that her tongue was sticking out at me through the invisible connection spanning thousands of miles.

"You've got a good paying job, just divorce me."

"Oh, I see what you're trying to do."

"What's that?" I teased.

"Reverse psychology. Throw out the Big D and I can't help myself but to come running back to those big strong arms of yours."

"You got me babe, is it working?"

"Kind of." She took a deep breath and tension formed in my gut. She wanted to talk about something big but had been putting it off. I had learned from experience that was rarely a good sign.

"Babe, can I ask you a question?"

She didn't respond immediately, confirming she was lost in her own thoughts. "Uh, sure. What's up?"

"Have you and the mailman managed to have a

miraculous bastard child together? It is obvious you want to talk about something other than my theatrics, what is it?"

She roared on the other end and I would probably have joined her if I didn't need to stay focused on the road. "You got me, no fertility clinics or anything. I figured the sweats a decade ago were menopause but I guess I was wrong." She barely made it through her answer without suffering from another bout of laughter. It died down and she became quiet for a moment. I listened to her breathing return to normal. "Was it that obvious?"

"That you've had an immaculate conception? No, that was a lucky guess. If you meant is it obvious that you want to talk about something, then that answer is yes."

The words came out in a rush, as if Gail would forget them as soon as her stream of consciousness shifted to another train of thought. "I think I'm ready to give up teaching. It has been a decade since the kids moved out and the house finally feels empty. Cleaning isn't my favorite thing in the world and I can't think of a room I want to renovate right now. Summer in Phoenix means I don't need to do much yard work. It's quiet here and I have given you to others; as a player, a coach, a manager, an instructor for so much of our lives together...I want us to be together for whatever time we have left. I know I can't tear you away from the dugout so I won't try. I know you won't want me with you on road trips but I want us to have a life together all year."

"Hon, I can't think of anything I'd rather have than that. Especially after a day like today, you being more than just a voice over the phone would be a great thing."

"We've got time, what's up?" Gail's favorite thing to say in the world. I loved it the first time I heard it and will probably enter the ground feeling the same way. 'We've got time,' as if the world was still all opportunity. If happiness is opportunity then I can't think of a more contentful phrase. Is contentful a word? It was now, driving through Carleton on I-275, there was a half hour until I was home, maybe longer as the closure of I-96 had caused everything to back up in all directions though rush hour had come and gone. I started telling Gail about The Walrus's pending divorce just as Rusty Chevrolet passed one of the many Ford Plants down this way. Fix Or Repair Daily. I had always been a GM guy, bailout and all. Hard to think any other way I guess. That day off that had been so sought after this afternoon, now was filled with a tight schedule of baseball activities. The Latin Lover and Andre were in for an early morning surprise.

CHAPTER SIX

Baseball managers have always had authority to keep a tight leash on their players while the team is traveling. It really has to be that way. While there may be some resentment from the players, it would be hard to come up with an alternative. There is no other sport that requires such a specific skill set. Physics says that hitting a round ball with a round bat that is being thrown downward with movement from sixty feet away should be impossible. Just the ability of a player to recognize the grip of the pitcher and the spin of the ball to determine whether it is a fastball or a breaking ball, and the adjustments needed, should never be possible in the split second a batter has to make contact. A Hall of Famer may get a hit only three out of every ten times he steps to the plate, the difference between him and a utility player being that he can do it with power. Baseball demands you fail and then stew on it for innings or days at a time. There is no next play to erase the thought of looking like a fool in front of the world. The game attracts men with thick skin and makes them legends.

It isn't much of a leap to go from thinking of yourself as a great ballplayer to thinking of yourself as a God. Such hubris never ends well for a man in his twenties. Add in a stipend just big enough to open some doors and the possibility to fritter away your nights on alcohol, women, or some other weakness means that curfews are strictly enforced at the team hotels. Worse yet is when the player begins to think that the amazing has become routine, that it isn't something that requires constant discipline and attention to detail. It is those players where the manager receives a call from jail. To lose appreciation for his gifts so that a career which is the dream of nearly every red-blooded American or Latino boy in this hemisphere, the stimulation needed to make that man care about anything at all is spectacular and almost always disastrous. The whims of Ruth and Mantle are but two that come to my mind when I forget this stuff is supposed to be above my pay grade.

Then of course there are the dangers when a player does all of the right things. Ever since Darryl Kyle was found dead in his hotel room from a heart attack at 37, teams have adopted comprehensive emergency contact policies that give managers and coaches the ability to find their players on days when they just don't show up for work. That information can come in handy at other times in less dire circumstances.

That is probably why Andre is tucked uncomfortably into the passenger seat of Rusty Chevrolet, bent like an accordion even though I pushed the seat back as far as it will go. Giants aren't meant to fit in supposedly mid-size sedans. Andre certainly fits the bill as a giant, hence the nickname based off of the 1980's WWF superstar. The man is a walking spectacle, the kind that would make Vince McMahon's eyes light up with envy. His hands are the size of my skull and his arms and legs are naturally thicker than many tree trunks. Andre's voice is a deep baritone that attracts the ear of whoever it reaches. Speaking in his customarily deliberate cadence always draws a crowd of enthralled listeners. I've never figured out if the epicness of the man helps us consider him more charismatic than he really is or if Andre's charisma is truly as large as he is. Maybe it doesn't matter, what really matters is that the man lives life to the fullest.

He drinks so much, without any effect, that it was once the subject of scientific inquiry. Last offseason Andre needed to be put under for surgery to remove his appendix. His large appendix. The anesthesiologist had never put someone under the size of Andre and was terrified that he would wake up in the middle of the procedure. She ended up calculating how potent the gas should be by backing out how much alcohol he could imbibe without effect. Such a lifestyle is not conducive to the early morning but he had been rather subdued in his response to my pre-dawn intrusion. On our way to The Latin Lover's studio apartment, Andre just gave the occasional bear growl in my direction. Hopefully he was just beginning to wake up. Or I had just made my first baseman feral which wouldn't endear me with the folks in Detroit. At 26, the prospects of Andre putting it all together had dimmed significantly the past year or so but no team ever gives up on potential. Power and left-handed pitching, just flash a little something and someone will give you a chance. Andre had been strictly a DH before I got here but many felt he'd have more value if he could improve in the field enough so that people didn't cringe at his defensive inadequacies. It was always going to be a project but it got me one more year out of Percy so I was okay with trying. Six weeks and twelve errors later it wasn't so much fun anymore. Twelve errors, and some of the scoring decisions were generous. It could have easily been worse.

I wasn't up and at it in Toledo often in the morning, I had never seen a sunrise over the blue glass of the Fifth/Third building until today. For a moment I felt at peace in the city which I had not yet learned to call my home. Like other industrial Midwest cities it had its scars. To the untrained eye they covered the city's charms almost completely and I had come to think of Toledo as just another victim of the Rust Belt. It was nice to focus on something other than Washington Avenue and the vacant buildings, crumbling brick with ads for St. Vincent de Paul or another charity for the large number of poor down on their luck. Pulling up to LL's pad, I hoped my contentedness would last. I knew I would need serenity today.

The key I wasn't supposed to be using turned in the lock and I entered the apartment, quickly pushing my way towards the back where the one bedroom was. I had never been here but it is odd how all apartments are laid out nearly the same. I didn't bother knocking, striding into the bedroom matter-of-factly. LL was passed out, snoring as he laid on his stomach, the physical embodiment of exhaustion. The reason for his condition was lying on her back, already awake, or maybe she never fell asleep. She didn't scream which was surprising, just stared at me dully. Dull, in a lot of ways that is the perfect description of an athlete groupie.

The sheets covered LL sufficient to protect his modesty but I could not say the same for her. Her amber hair framed attractive features against milky skin. The tresses curled at the ends, just above perky breasts which moved at a leisurely pace. Her nipples were engorged, as if she still was waiting for the action of last night to shift from foreplay to pleasurable intercourse. That or the Latin Lover was so good his nightly conquest was still ready for more. Given her apathy I guessed the former but didn't really care. She made no attempt to cover herself.

"He's all yours," she said half-heartedly.

"Uh, thanks I guess."

The Latin Lover began to stir, coming to a start when he realized another man was in the room with them. "Skip, what the hell?!"

"What, no hello? You seem unhappy to see me. C'mon, we've got to get to the field. A lot of work to do today," I said.

"It's our day off." He looked quickly at the clock on the small stand next to the bed. "And it is 7:30 in the morning!"

"Like I said, a lot of work to do."

"I'm tired, can't we wait until day actually breaks?"

"It has." I moved to the window and pulled open the blinds. Sunshine poured in, LL squinting, the girl barely reacting at all. She didn't cover up now that she was exposed to the world outside. "Let's go."

"Do I have to?" LL whined. "I'm serious, is that even required? I have rights, don't I?"

"Rights? Yeah, you've got those. That doesn't include you not showing up to the field during the season when your manager has so politely requested it."

"You didn't request anything. You broke into my house early in the morning and told me to go to work without any warning. That sounds like something I have a right to say no to."

"Andre didn't," I said. "He's waiting in the car. He really won't be happy if you say no and his getting out of bed was for naught. I'm not sure you want an angry giant to deal with."

The girl shook to life for the first time this morning. "Giant? How big?"

"Big enough for you, I'm sure. Everywhere." I winked.

She turned to the Latin Lover, "Rodrigo, you didn't tell me about this giant." Rodrigo, even his name sounded like that of a Casanova. Our Mud Hen Casanova. I was sure he had other bad mornings but he seemed to be taking her hostility poorly.

"Well no," he stammered.

"Why don't you join us? Andre is quite the personality. You'd be lucky to get to know him." I didn't smirk or make a comment about her suggesting LL had a small penis. There were more important things to tend to and I needed both of them out of this apartment five minutes ago.

"Skip," LL said sheepishly, "you don't mind stepping into the other room while I put some clothes on?"

I didn't feel like fighting the point so I excused myself to the kitchen and looked for some black coffee. LL was many things but he had never lacked charm before. He was always the type who could talk his way out of putting equipment away or some club house task. Most infuriating was when he managed to make you feel bad for asking him so that, without even knowing it, you had volunteered to do his job for him. This morning's whining and almost sheepish humility was not his trademark. Her apathy, whatever her name was, was also unique. Casanovas weren't known to engender indifference in their targets and LL was no different. On occasion his playboy ways got him in trouble and Ray the security guard would be put on lookout duty for a scorned heart still on fire. Usually, at least how LL tells it, he has his girls so wrapped around his finger that they would often make him breakfast or do his laundry for him. I had always wished that smoothness would make itself onto the diamond but it never quite did. In another reality, LL might be able to use his charm to get onto a NBA team where he could hide mediocrity coming off the bench but baseball, a game where I'm pretty sure statisticians have metrics to rate themselves, was too coldly scientific for him to break through to The Show. I didn't think his numbers could get much worse but the recent erosion of his charm seemed to coincide with a distinct worsening of his playing abilities.

Scouring the cupboards for some grounds turned up nothing. The only thing approximating a cup of Joe was a canister of International Brands. Foo foo shit that my wife drinks, the stuff you stir in and microwave. At least he went with the normal French Vanilla, it could have been worse. I stood there with my hand at the tab of the plastic top, paralyzed and unable to actually go through with it. I had stopped at a Speedway when I left Livonia two hours ago, downing their extra-large coffee, so I may have been able to get away with a second cup at girl strength but I couldn't bring myself to stoop that low. The thought of my father snickering at me in heaven gave me pause. The thought of my son, a cop whose beat includes some of the more eccentric parts of San Francisco, chiding me with, "that's pretty gay Dad," made it impossible. I would just have to stop at the little cafe north of the Convention Center.

Her name was Amber, pretty easy to remember assuming she didn't dye her hair. She had been excited to meet another player besides the Latin Lover but that excitement ebbed quickly when she realized that with Andre's seat pushed back, there was only room in Rusty Chevrolet to fit one in the back seat. The ensuing drive required her to ride sitting atop the Latin Lover, the seat belt forcing her tightly against his crotch. The position had a far different effect on her than on him. With a coldness that bordered on contempt she said, "Really?"

My eyes flicked up to the rear view mirror to make sure there wasn't going to be a scene. "Sorry, it's morning," LL said, that same uncharacteristic sheepishness from earlier seeping into his uncharacteristic apology.

"Would you two knock it off back there?" My stressed pun was almost cruel. I'm not sure how this was supposed to help The Latin Lover get back to where I needed him to be, maybe it wasn't. Ever since the conversation with Three Way last night animosity toward him had been building somewhere in my gut and his newfound meekness only seemed to make it worse. He looked, talked, fucked like a loser right now and somehow that made me consider myself one as well. In LL today I saw everything that last night I saw in me, looking into the mirror in the cramped half bath off of my rented bedroom. I desperately wanted him away from me and yet, I had forced him into my car to oversee a long session of fielding practice. I hated him, the fire that craved winning hated him.

When I stopped for coffee LL whined and Amber let out an impressive 'Ack!' followed by a stream of cuss words. She went from petulant, uncaring child to angry woman at the wrong time though. There was no sympathy left to play out of me. I stepped out of Rusty Chevrolet and slammed my door muffling their protests. Andre had stopped groaning and fallen asleep, oblivious to the world. I should have been mad at him but I could never stay mad at Andre. What can I say, the guy is enthralling.

After three steps I had made it from the curb to the door, grasped the handle and listened to the animosity from the back seat turn from me to each other. Amber demanded that LL control his erection as I stepped inside for coffee so black it might as well be a cup of dry grounds.

CHAPTER SEVEN

It is hard to complain about the Mud Hens stadium. Tiered seating of about ten thousand with a party deck for groups and corporate functions in left field as well as suites that rival anything found in the majors make it a great place to watch a game at a price that remains affordable. Looking at it in the early morning, the empty stands weren't much different than the attendance at yesterday's game. For that I was to blame. Cut down below street level, the stadium became like a Temple, the old warehouse that had been transformed into the team's corporate office and retail store wrapping around like a cocoon behind home plate. Monroe Avenue was hidden by the scoreboard, the Seagate Arena and Convention center framing the outfield view. Immaculate green grass and tan dirt became the only thing that mattered, even here in the city. What had been a late frost in Michigan had given way to heavy dew that seemed to make every blade of grass strain just to maintain poor posture. It was idyllic, reinforcing my newfound resolve to salvage this season. Sometimes the grind of the season makes you lose focus on the true meaning of the game. Like a writer who sits staring at a finished manuscript, I knew that even if no one came out for the rest of the season what we did between the chalk lines here meant something special.

Amber sat on top of the home dugout Indian style. Her momentary burst in the car had receded to docility again. Amber never looked out towards short where the Latin Lover was finishing up his stretches. Her eyes faced in the general direction of first base but had glossed over, large pools of doe brown that failed to change with sensory perception. Her pupils were dilated, only periodically interrupted from their nothing by a blink of heavy lids. Even they acted passively, slowly closing then reopening in a languid fashion that seemed to suggest they wouldn't bother with the task except for the urge of instinct.

I pulled my vision from her as I gripped the tape and rosin that coated the handle of my trusty bat. I'm no Roy Hobbs, I didn't carve it out of the remains of a tree that had been split by lightning, but it had been with me a long time. I traced my index finger and thumb where the old Louisville Slugger nameplate had lost its black paint. As it had chipped away, all that remained were the ridges of the logo. Eventually they were lost too, eroding bit by bit as I hit grounders with a heavy dose of top spin thousands of times, maybe tens of thousands, to players over the many stops of my managerial and instructing careers. Respect the bat and it will respect you.

Taking my first ball from the industrial white bucket that sat where a catcher would normally be crouched, I thought back to the winter after Durham. I had sworn I would never give this game another minute of my time. Gail seemed happy with the idea and every weekend the honey-do list got a bit longer. The weekend just after Valentine's Day, when pitchers and catchers were first reporting to camp, and it had fully sunk in that I was really going to be at home all year round, Gail got ambitious and asked that I clean out the garage. Poking around dusty boxes had led to a lot of trips to

Goodwill which sure as hell beat having a yard sale. You didn't really have yard sales in the neighborhood we lived. Sweaty sandbox sales was closer to the truth.

It was also the first time I had come across my bat. For a week I had let the urge to swing it again eat at me until I couldn't take it. The thermometer had already touched eighty that year in Phoenix and the papers were filled with columns on the then eight teams that were in the Cactus League. I snuck out to the batting cage, got a helmet and a roll of quarters. My knee even felt good that day.

I stepped through the fence and faced the black hole that, according to the panel to my left, could simulate a major league fastball and might throw in a curveball every now and then when set to 'All-Star.' Giddily I had slipped in four quarters for thirty pitches and set into my stance in the right-handed batter's box, the pose sliding over me like a warm memory. The black mouth began to shake with controlled fury, whirring at a higher pitch until the ball popped out with a *shoomp* as if it had escaped suction. It came fast but didn't explode at the plate like a major league pitch would. It was a robot's fastball, not a human being's. My lower body tensed but I watched it go by, counting every fucking seam and unable to believe that I almost swung Old Reliable at such garbage. Respect your bat. Ok, we're up to what, four superstitions now? Gail was remarkably understanding that night when I told her I had to go back to the game. It was like she knew it was coming. I couldn't get a referral from the Devil Rays, whose front office was sacked only a year later anyways, so I had to start over at fifty years old coaching the local community college. My life was patchy Bermuda grass, lightning quick infields, and thin air which made every game into a slugfest. The winter of '08 brought my first contact with the Tigers in too long, organizing the golden anniversary of the World Series team ironically proved the foot in the door to get back to the minor leagues. I guess the bat knew what the hell it was talking about.

The ball skittered through the wet grass, the lack of friction giving the grounder a surprising amount of speed. It was obvious that The Latin Lover misjudged it as his motion stunted. Caught in no man's land, he jerked his glove upwards as if to protect himself. Even after the ball reached stamped dirt it stayed down and found the outfield through his wickets. It was the defensive play of an amateur, rule number one for the infielder is to always keep your glove down and bring it up when the hop dictates. If you are to make a mistake, let it glance off the heel of the glove. You will look far less foolish adjusting upward than if you pull a Buckner. I told myself that an impromptu fielding session meant a lot less than the '86 World Series but it didn't help.

LL pounded at his glove and said something in Spanish that I couldn't make out. "That wasn't much of a start, torpedo number two is in the hole," I yelled as the ball looped upward and I swung, aiming back up the middle. LL should have seen the direction the bat was aiming as the head dragged slightly through the hitting zone but it looked as if he was caught flat footed. LL scrambled to his left, towards where second base would be if it had been staked into the ground rather than sitting somewhere in the groundskeeper's shed under the outfield bleachers. His glove stabbed at the ball at full extension, the full pocket nimbly coming to his waiting throwing hand as he did a three-sixty and set his feet. His delivery to Andre was at a three-quarters arm slot but it didn't tail. It wasn't the dreaded two-seamer that would pull Andre into the path of the oncoming runner, the ones that so often ended up in the dugout and the runner at second base with an error on the scoreboard. In a lot of ways, LL's throw may have been worse. The ball didn't snap out of his hand with life, it was hesitant, as if LL was throwing a shot put. He was guiding the ball and it hung like a wounded duck flying against a stiff western breeze. Time seemed to slow down, a little over a hundred feet stretching into a country mile.

If little *Danny Torrance* had thrown his red ball down the elongating hallway of the Overlook Hotel, it would have gotten to the far wall faster than LL's throw got to first. It was baseball's version of a horror scene, the type of throw that might make Steve Blaser wake up in night sweats. The ball was, perhaps remarkably, on target entering into Andre's glove at slow motion. It didn't pop into the leather mitt, more like a thud. I looked out at LL, even he seemed to think the end result was a mistake. "Ok," I paused unsure what to say next, "that's something to build on. Just, you know, have a bit of faith in yourself there LL."

I aimed the next ball straight at him, afraid of what might

happen if I sent one into the hole between short and third. LL stayed down on this one and his motion was fluid again until he went to throw the ball across the infield. He was aiming the ball, his arm motion slowing down like a pitcher who couldn't find the strike zone. It was something I just couldn't explain, it lacked confidence. Whatever it was, I couldn't tolerate it in my shortstop.

The shortstop is the captain of any defense. No position has more demanded of it. Every game the shortstop must exhibit good instincts and positioning, he must be able to range in both directions, make a tough throw across the diamond and be accurate with relays from the outfield as well as feeds to the second basemen for double plays. He is an anchor who stabilizes every other defender if he is playing well. Oh, and in today's game, he is expected to be a middle of the lineup caliber hitter as well. Fear or hesitancy from the shortstop bleeds into other players, an invisible flea hopping greedily from host to host.

The ball hit the pocket of Andre's mitt before falling out in a limp arc to the ground where it landed so softly that it didn't bounce or roll away. Andre looked down at his glove then to the ball in a similarly halting fashion to his fellow infielder. He looked to the Latin Lover, then to me. "I don't know what happened. I think I just had too much time to think about it Skip."

"Hey LL, I need you to take control of your field. How many errors did we have yesterday?" I asked.

The Latin Lover looked down at his shoes as he tried to

kick up some dust. It was too heavy yet and clumped together causing his cleats to catch like the wheel on a grocery cart that needs oil. "Three," he said without looking up.

"How many?" My voice echoed back to me from the scoreboard.

"Three. Tres. Three god damn errors. I personally fucked up on two of them." The words were raw, passionate finally but equally antithetical to LL's normal suaveness.

"How many runs did that cost us?"

"I don't know," LL yelled.

"You don't know!" I couldn't think of a worse answer from my defensive captain. "It was six, or it would have been if the rain hadn't come in. Six in three innings. I talked to Three Way last night, his arm is shot and so is the rest of his body. He came here to win a championship, something both he and I have been so close to before. He's giving you everything and more and you can't even tell me how many runs your errors are costing the team."

I threw another ball up in the air before I said something I would regret. I swung hard and aimed it for the hole. I swung so hard that my knee popped, but the adrenaline that was now coursing through hard veins made sure it didn't matter. LL ranged far to his right and dove, trying to backhand the ball. He didn't get there and the ball made it into left field, rolling significantly farther than the first error. Just as he had after the first, he got up and slammed his glove without brushing off his jersey.

A large block of gray sweats slowly huffed its way along

the gate next to Monroe, quick bursts of breath in the cold spring morning air signaling that even this was a struggle. I continued to hit grounders, varying where they were hit, their speed, and their spin. The infield was in great shape but on occasion it too yielded a surprise as the ball took an unusual hop. My bat produced five hundred ground balls by 11:30 in the morning. While things got better as the day went on, it was by no means a smooth exhibition by LL and Andre. I counted 39 balls that were booted. .922 fielding percentage without the pressure of a game; a runner burrowing down on LL at second, cleats up, a speedy left-handed batter out of the box crossing ninety feet in the blink of an eye, a simple throw that becomes difficult when it is all that stands between the team getting out of an inning unscathed and precious runs for the opponent. .922 fielding percentage, easily the worst in the International League for a shortstop and a first baseman if the fielding session had counted towards the stats book.

My eyes wandered from the disappointing display on grass increasingly to the sight in the stands. I didn't give LL or Andre any breaks and the constant fielding had left LL winded as well as frustrated. He didn't notice my attention moving elsewhere. The gray block snaked through the aisles weaving up and down rows of outfield bleachers until it was within my faded range of vision. It was The Walrus and he looked like he was going to die after doing the bleachers halfway around the lower bowl. His face was a fuscia tide of jowls with a rattling breath I could hear even down here at home plate that matched the stress that the white puffs in cold air had shown so long ago. He wasn't making any speed records but he was doing it. I had no idea how his old knees managed, the thought of cartilage grinding against bone where lubrication should have been, as would have happened in my own, made me wince. The pop I had felt earlier had made its presence known and acted as a constant reminder to keep tabs on my longtime friend. To his credit he kept going, his labored breaths providing a tense and dangerous soundtrack that ebbed and returned depending on where he was at in the stadium.

The Walrus ran for over an hour. He curled through the lower bowl until he had made it back into the outfield where I had first made eye contact with him. He started again, slower, but he kept moving. I thought a couple of times he was dead on his feet but then he'd manage to accelerate again. His second time around the stadium he added the upper deck as well, weaving one way then the other as he returned to the lower bowl. Amazingly, he made it five circuits around the stadium before melting into a seat near the concourse.

Amber had been shagging balls that made it to the outfield for us at my urging. Her docility briefly disappeared at the start of the session but Andre's regular drops of the ball had killed her enthusiasm towards him. She could always have left since her car was in the parking lot but I got the sense she didn't really have anywhere to go. Eventually that too got tiresome for her and she made her way back to the top of the dugout. She spotted The Walrus resting before she got situated and made her way up to where he was. Amber didn't seem to mind the smell, she brought her head in close and said something to Wal that made him laugh. Their conversation lasted about as long as it took for my last bucket to empty. I finally called an end to the session, LL and Andre making for the dugout as quickly as possible so that I couldn't change my mind.

CHAPTER EIGHT

I turned and walked towards the groundskeeper's gate behind home plate so that I could take the elevator up to the concourse. My knee was now killing me and the appeal of hopping the fence and walking up what had to be about 25 rows of stairs was close to zero. I never had figured out how this thing opened and truth eluded me once again. I cursed under my breath, or at least thought I had.

"It opens from the other side." The Walrus's bellow from above was accompanied by a timid laugh which got underneath my skin for some reason. Here I had been judging her as a groupie loser all morning but her amusement at my stupidity got to me. It didn't make much sense.

I followed the field railing towards the dugout until the black netting that protects spectators from foul balls ended. I eased down until my rear was enmeshed firmly into the foam padding that ran along the top of the railing. My right leg went up and over easily but I had to use two hands to pull my left from dirt up and over to sticky concrete. Even with the help my knee made its displeasure known. I wanted to say something but I figured the clairvoyants would find a way to hear it just like the mutter they picked up on earlier. I looked up to see them both watching me, glad to know that there was no merriment being had at my behalf anymore. Amber's eyes showed surprising depth now, maybe even pity.

At that moment I would have given up my athletic build for some flab and the ability to do what Wal had just managed. After pausing for a minute in a front row seat, thinking that extra leg room would have been nice, I made my way up. I clutched at air where a bannister should have been, cursing the architect's dedication to the sightlines of the paying customers. When I was within 7 rows of the two, Amber once again leaned in and whispered something into the ear of The Walrus. She smiled at me in a way that made me think she had been talking about me before she hastily headed around the concourse to the outfield gate that Wal had let himself in at. I think I was jealous. I made a note to keep that idea from Gail, she wouldn't have liked it.

"So…" I let my voice trail off, saying a lot with just a raise of my eyebrow.

Wal looked to make sure Amber was far enough away. "She's barely old enough to be my grandkid Harry. I may be a bit desperate at the moment but I assure you my rebound will be something closer to what is appropriate." He smirked, "Maybe." His voice was normal strength but it looked like he was having trouble with something as simple as moving the muscles of his mouth.

"How the hell did you manage to do bleachers at our age?"

"Easy, I didn't play enough back in the day to blow out my knee."

"I'd take that over the pity party the two of you just threw me."

"Pity party? Hardly. Amber is just looking for a guide right now. I don't know that I'm the best example but at least I didn't throw the righteousness of God at her." He paused to let that sink in for a minute. "Talking to me is probably better for her than to latch onto another jock until she is comfortable in her skin."

"It's good skin. I saw a lot more of it than you," I said in a clipped tone. I guess that Wal's delay had worked.

"Are you jealous that we are on better terms than the two of you?"

"No."

"She doesn't hate you. Can't say she was broken up about you hobbling like an old man though." He laughed. "And Gail would be pissed if I told her you were ogling a girl that was younger than your children."

"I didn't ogle her," I protested, with perhaps too much zeal.

"Easy. We are awfully testy today, aren't we?"

"You must have missed the high school level fielding display. I can't blame you as it sounded like you had pushed yourself to within a couple beats of a heart attack."

"I am tired," Wal said with understatement, as if the thought had just occurred to him. "Why'd you drag LL and Andre out here, exactly?"

I told Wal about my conversation with Three Way the night before.

"Yeah, we all let ourselves go a bit," The Walrus said, straining to get his eyes to look down at the flab which spilled out of the tiny plastic seat.

I told him about how it felt to be in the locker room all

alone after getting tossed, thinking about how I made a fool of myself to keep us from getting another loss and how the way we were going it wasn't going to make a damn bit of difference. "Gail told me yesterday she wants to join me up here. She's ready to retire and she said she knew I'd never walk away from the game. It seems I'm the only person who forgot that this game is important to me. Just like it is to Three Way. He wants a championship and I do too. It is going to be hard to turn this ship around with a defense that leaks like a sieve."

"Sieve? Isn't that a hockey term?"

"Yeah, I guess it is. Seems we spent too much time in the Midwest, the two of us."

"Don't look at me, I'm still a Georgia boy you hoser," The Walrus said.

"Not a big fan of the South, Durham didn't exactly treat us well," I said.

"No, it did not. Toledo might not be much more forgiving though."

There was no sense in continuing to avoid the crux of what I wanted to talk to The Walrus about. "LL has lost it."

"He never really had it. You think you can win a title with these guys? They were last in the division a year ago and Castellanos is up in the majors. Just ask Keith Law over at *ESPN*, the minors are dry right now."

"Triple-A stopped being a prospect's league years ago. We can win this thing with what we've got."

"Maybe. All of our best non-prospect filler, if that's what

you want to call it, is filling in at the major league level at the moment. I'm just warning you that will power isn't all it takes to turn trash into a championship Harry."

"A good shortstop will help. What do you think about Fiver?"

"You were the roving instructor who put him on Chad's radar. What do you need me to say, that I agree? If you can convince the head scout that this kid is the second coming of Tram at short and this franchise can get him back up to snuff at the plate, why would I disagree?"

"Do you want to do the paperwork, or should I?" I grinned as I asked the question.

The Walrus grinned too, "I'm tired Har. Who are you shipping out? LL?"

"No. I was thinking Cadiz."

"Thank God. I'm pretty sure it is his locker that reeks to high heaven."

"Really?" I asked. "I figured it was Andre's keg."

"Naw. Although that should probably go too. Or you could just let him start drinking again. He doesn't field any better sober."

"I know." I laughed, "I didn't tell him to stop."

The Rule Five draft is an anachronism unique to the game of baseball. Besides the 25 man roster that makes up the major league squad, another 15 players are given special protection by the club. Come September 1st, all 40 men on the expanded roster are eligible to be in the majors. It is rare that competing clubs take advantage of this but teams that have been out of the pennant race for months will often take the opportunity to call up their best prospects to test them and see if they will be able to address holes in the roster for the next season. Many players make it up for mere weeks, a cup of coffee. Most never make it back. Others, like The Walrus, may turn it into a stint as a role player coming off the bench. A lucky few will turn it into a long big league career.

In many ways, the decision on who is protected by the 40 man roster can be as important to a team's future as who makes the big league club. And, while 40 sounds like a lot, it is never enough. For those not on the 40 man roster, the franchise that they were drafted, or signed, by has the rights to them for six years before they become free agents. Before the last couple of option years they have, if a franchise decides not to protect them players are exposed to the Rule 5 draft. Operating from worst team to best based on the prior year's standings, teams have the option to draft eligible minor leaguers from other farm systems. The players taken often have potential that a team has never figured out how to unlock or doesn't fit a need for the franchise and isn't valuable enough to be part of a trade package. The only catch is that a player who goes in the Rule Five draft must stay on the major league team for the entire next season or he returns to the franchise he was drafted from and the drafting team pays a cash penalty. Nowhere else do players get treated like like something akin to chattle. Rule Five drafts occur at the Triple-A and Double-A level as well. For a player taken in the

Double-A phase, the penalty is $4,000. That tells you how important it is. Think of this headache as baseball's answer to the fact that teams can't trade draft picks like every other sport. Complicated? Yep. But considering that the mound is 60 feet and 6 inches from the plate because of an error in the original markup, it isn't the only unnecessary complication that traditionalists have clung to. Baseball is fucked up that way. The Rule 5 draft is infamous for gifting the Pittsburgh Pirates with Roberto Clemente. Its minor league counterparts have produced no such miracles.

As a manager, baseball provides more opportunities to obsess over "projects" than any other sport. The draft has nearly fifty rounds and a franchise consists of around seven teams in all. If you are a lefty and can throw a ball through a pane of glass, you'll get a contract. When I interviewed two years ago for a PCL gig in Albuquerque, a bit closer to home than my roving tour of the Tigers farm clubs in the east, I got to indulge in this fantasy. After my interview, I took a binder of newspaper clippings from the local library (before you ask I am able to use email and the internet but computers aren't my bread and butter) to my garage den and pored through stories and feature pieces on players up and down the Dodgers' farm system. Those who interested me got marked by a trusty highlighter and their article clipped and pinned to the tack board hanging across the long wall of the garage. Five names stood out to me and I kept up with them after I got the call that the Dodgers were going in another direction. Only one of those names was still floating out there last year: Alex Casillas.

The Dodgers consistently have one of the best farm systems in the game. Unlike some other franchises they aren't real big on trading away their future for pieces to compete today, or at least they didn't used to be. The glitz of LA and a tradition of success mixed with a popularity among casual fans that is exceeded by only the Yankees and Red Sox is a draw. The consistently beautiful weather doesn't hurt either considering how many players come from the tropical climates of Latin America these days. The Dodgers have always scouted well and maintain contacts that others have deemed passé. It was perhaps no coincidence that when Casillas got off of the plane in Vancouver with the rest of the Cuban National Team for an international exhibition in 2010 that Dodger executives were milling about at a hotel across the street from where the team was staying.

Without a shout, let alone a shot, the kid ducked the communist monitors and made what had to be a terrifying trip down twenty floors of the fire escape. It would have been certain to cut short his trip to freedom had he been found out. In all honesty, if he had been made Alex Casillas would probably never have been heard from again. The Castro Brothers are weakened but they still relish punishing those who forget to put country and Party before themselves. Casillas signed with the Dodgers in the lobby of a Courtyard by Marriott, not exactly the glamour of National Signing Day.

His glove proved as great as the back channel whispers had said it would be. In the second half of 2010 at low-A ball he hit .330 with good enough power. The Dodgers were sure they had their shortstop of the future and fast tracked the kid straight to Triple-A the next year where his first half caused such a commotion that it was a subject of much debate whether Alex should have gotten the starting job over Dee Gordon immediately. Inexplicably, for over a year the team's front office sat on Casillas while the press anointed him a potential savior. New ownership came in and shook things up, bringing in Hanley Ramirez in a big trade.

That was that, Casillas was stuck and the LA press stopped caring. At about that time Casillas's hitting disappeared. He had always had a unique stance and, once pitchers finally figured him out, he went a year and a half without a home run while his average fell to a level that flirted dangerously with the Mendoza Line. In 18 months, Casillas went from the next big thing to being on the outs. He got the stint in Double-A he missed on the way up as he slid back down the organization. By the end of last season, he was unprotected. I encouraged David Chad to take a chance and see if the guys down in Erie could turn a has-been into quality organizational depth. So far they hadn't done much, falling into the same trap of others and demanding he change his stance to something more conventional. With the fire burning again, my project was finally mine to tinker with.

It may sound weird to the rest of society but an opportunity like this is what managers live for. No one ever said we were normal. Or maybe it isn't so crazy. When Gail and I went to Oahu on our honeymoon I was content to sate myself on the pork at the luaus and spend my time up in the hotel room if you know what I mean. Her, being the history teacher, had other ideas and I wasn't so lucky. Most of the plantation tours and cultural mumbo jumbo from that week went in one ear and out the other. Hey, it's hard to think when you are celebrating your marriage to a beautiful girl. One thing stuck though, just like with Aloha, the Hawaiian word Kumu has two meanings. One is teacher...the other is lover. Who am I to disagree with an ancient culture that that there is no deeper bond between human beings than that forged on making others better?

CHAPTER NINE

There isn't a best practice when it comes to giving someone the heave-ho from the team. It is worse to cut a guy from the organization entirely, rather than just demoting them. For a while I tried to give the pep talk, just me and the poor sap who had found his neck on the chopping block alone in my office. That was a horrible idea. Even when they were expecting it, actually hearing it hit hard. I can't really blame them, if it had ever happened to me I would have bawled like a child. The vim of the pep talk, if it had been given by a great orator which I am not, was mauled to pieces by dark shadows of inadequacy. Drawing out the pain didn't soften the blow, it increased it.

Then I decided to be a tough son of a bitch and cut their legs out from under them. For a while the kids just got a terse, "you're being let go, best of luck in your future endeavors." I didn't mind that one personally if I didn't have to actually walk around my desk and push the kid out of the office before he became a blubbery mess. I don't have a heart of stone and the sound of sobs through my wood office door eventually broke me of this approach. Now I do what's best for everyone, break the kid's heart and then pass him off to The Walrus to handle the aftermath. He's good with that kind of stuff, being a beardless Santa and all. I had already called Casillas up so a new face was getting dressed in the locker room, it wouldn't take a genius to figure out that he had to be replacing someone.

I opened the door to my office and yelled for Cadiz. Sitting at my desk I couldn't see him, his locker faced the opposite wall and was on the other side of the L-shaped junction which cut into the middle of the room and acted as a divider. It would have been impossible not to hear the stillness that overtook every man in the clubhouse as they turned one by one to look at me. Even Casillas had stopped getting ready at his locker but he kept his back to me, trying to look like he was fascinated by the metal box.

The short Mexican reluctantly filled the door frame, his ridiculous *Speedy Gonzalez* mustache drooping more than usual. It was appropriately thin but never crisp. I had no idea why he couldn't get it right. "Si, Senor," Cadiz said weakly.

"Come on in and close the door," I said trying to walk the fine line between too somber and too dismissive. It's one thing to cut players breaking out of extended Spring Training, another to axe one of the Chosen Few. I had forgotten how much I hated to do this. You'd think it would be easier to do to a marginal player like Cadiz whose only distinguishing characteristics were his dark facial hair and the strain it took for him to converse in English, but it wasn't. Life really would be easier if I broke down and bought that Rosetta Stone kit. "I've got some bad news."

"I figured Boss Man. I may not be good with the language but I can count and there was one too many guys today."

"Then you know I need you to clean out your locker and be prepared to be off of the premises before game time. I will be happy to give you a recommendation but it seems that the

Tigers Organization is ready to move in a different direction Manuel."

"That it?"

"That's it." I wondered when his brown eyes would transform into pools but it didn't happen. He had already written himself off the team and I didn't have any idea. Managers really are the last ones to know what is going on in the clubhouse.

"My little one, Sofia, asked me to bring her back a present. Her birthday was a couple weeks ago and I couldn't get her anything before I left for Lakeland because money is scarce. Could you make sure that it makes it to the house?"

"A present? Is that why this locker room smells worse than the remnants of taco bell some frat kid puked up at three in the morning?" I'm sure someone would be willing to call me a racist but Taco Bell is the first thing I thought of when talking to a Mexican.

"I have no idea what that means but the smell, si, it is the gift. Estrada has a unique odor."

"Estrada?"

"My little baby named him. At least I think it is a 'him.' I'm not exactly sure how you, what do you call it, sex him. It? Her?"

"What exactly did your girl ask for?"

"Just be sure that he makes it home. I am sure that the Greyhound won't want him on board."

With that Cadiz turned and left the office. I followed in a hurry but he had grabbed his worn travel bag and was at the door before I caught up. He gave one look back then left without hesitation. How did he know he was getting cut? And what the hell is Estrada?

I cautiously made my way over to Cadiz's locker. Unlike the elaborate clubhouses in the majors, down on the farm doesn't look much different than the lockers found in a high school. I couldn't see inside, the only contrast to the navy blue painted metal was a small slit at the top which tried, in most cases in vain, to air out the hidden contents. Most of the time, their only use was when the laundry crew hung the players' jerseys from these slits when they were done cleaning them. The cleaning crew was responsible for everything else but the players were tasked with keeping things above hazmat level. That was sometimes a mistake with young men but, in all of the true horror stories I had seen over the years on cleaning days, I had never had a case where something in the locker was alive. Now that we had reached hazmat level, of course the slit was diffusing the fumes from inside the locker with appropriate gusto.

Standing at the locked threshold I yelled for the music to be turned off. As the locker room descended into complete silence I could hear it trying to get out of the locker. There was no roar, meow, or bark, just futile attempts at desperate escape. "Anyone know the combo?" Everyone assured me that they did not. "Ok then, Wal would you mind getting the lock cutters? Unless anyone here knows how to pick a lock…"

My words hung in the air as no one stepped forward. I didn't turn to face anyone, listening to The Walrus shuffle into

66

my office, probably glad to be away from the awkward silence. I heard someone shuffle their feet once, then twice before my centerfielder Jermaine Willis spoke up with anger. "Why's everyone looking at the black man? That's just racist."

The team laughed and broke into a menagerie of hoots and hollers. Andre's roars were loudest of course, followed by him saying, "Man, were just having fun with you. Don't go all Malcolm X on us. There aren't enough of you guys left playing ball for us crackers to get a good black joke in. We got to take our shots when we can."

"Really, that's how whites think?" Jermaine responded.

"Marquis got it," Andre said.

There was a pause before Jermaine ended the conversation with, "That's fucked up. You guys know that, right?" Another roar of laughter.

The Walrus tapped me on the shoulder just as it died down. I took the lock cutters, thanking God that I work in one of the few places where a groundskeeper would have these on hand. With hesitation I curled the sharp teeth around the shackle. Before I pinched down, rending metal through steel, I turned to either side looking for Cadiz's neighbors. He was an outfield replacement so his locker was next to Alston, the starting left fielder on one side, his right ironically, and Wampum, the right fielder on his left. "Any of you guys see Cadiz haul something in here?"

Wampum spoke up in mock Indian solemnity, "I have tracked no feral beasts in this urban jungle." Smart ass. Alston just shook his head no. I began to feel like Custer, oblivious to

67

the magnitude of the ambush I was walking into. I squeezed the handles of the lock cutter, surprised at how little resistance there was.

I had compensated too much and fell forward past my equilibrium point. Simultaneously, the beast that had been locked inside managed to break out of the locker without the latch being lifted. The door swung open and smashed into the bridge of my nose, immediately drawing blood. I went from leaning too far forward to being flat on my back with spots in front of my eyes before I could register what had happened. The blobs of purplish red floating in my field of vision kept me from focusing on the assailant that was now attacking my chest and face. Whatever it was, the muffled nature of its cries told me Cadiz had taped its mouth shut. A slender, but hard, head had taken to ramming itself into me repeatedly. I brought up my arms to protect myself, trying to throw it off of me. Groping through the tangled mass I found…webbed feet? What the fuck was Cadiz doing hoarding a bird?

The assault stopped long enough to allow the spots to dry up. For the first time in what felt like forever my focus was able to sharpen and my old eyes managed to filter a complete image to my brain for processing. Andre and the third baseman Fryer had corralled a Canadian goose inside their meaty forearms. His beak was taped like the handle of a bat and he was covered in his own droppings. "When did things start stinking in here?"

"It always stunk in here," some smartass yelled. I should have been able to recognize him by just his voice but I couldn't. He's lucky my bearings were still rattled or he would have been on the wrong end of an ass chewing.

"Been four or five days now," said The Walrus.

I peered into the broken locker, a pile of dried turds had now smeared everywhere. Looking at Fryer and Andre stains ran up and down the front of their jerseys. Looking down at my own chest and thighs painted a similar picture. "Hey Wal, we got any extra uniforms for tonight?"

"Not for the big guys there," The Walrus said, nodding towards the goose wranglers. I'd heard of stories about pig wrestling at county fairs, I'm not sure that wouldn't have been gentler.

"Damn it. Get that thing out of here and whoever is bravest rip the tape off his mouth. We'll figure out what to do with the uniforms when that's done."

Fryer and Andre wrestled the large bird through the exit while I tried to regroup. The blood was still coming from my nose and, now that the adrenaline was wearing off, it sure felt like a break. Aches from the focal points of the attack were sure to turn to bruises by game time which was now only two hours away. I propped myself up enough so that the blood from my nose went from trying to leak into my mouth to dripping down onto my chest and stomach. LL handed me a towel. This was possibly the only time I appreciated him sucking up. After yesterday, he needed to do a lot of it to keep from being the next Cadiz. Applying stiff pressure with the towel, it quickly saturated and LL was there with a second without me having to ask. Hell with calling him a suckup, I'm not too proud to admit that right then he was a God send.

With a nasally voice reminiscent of a bad cold I asked, "What is the deal with the Canadian goose?"

Percy, with his characteristic intelligence, chimed in, "el norte Skip."

"While it isn't unusual that I'm too stupid to figure out what you're talking about Al, today isn't a good day for being unnecessarily obtuse. Again, in English."

"Cadiz must have told his girl he was going north, norte in Spanish. She must have asked for a souvenir from the only northern country she knew."

"So she asked for a damn bird?"

"What else does Canada have named after it?"

"She couldn't have chosen a Celine Dion CD?" I asked. Percy had a good point. He usually does if he communicates in a way the rest of us understand. Canada is probably a lot easier to say than whatever the hell the good ol' US of A is in Spanish. Silly girl, at some point she'll learn about the proper name for the United States. No Mexicans sneak across the border into Canada. Now that was a racist thought, but I was pissed. There aren't many Mexicans playing ball, Cadiz had been my first in my career. I hoped then that he would be my last. Well, I'd probably take Joaquim Soria without much complaint. At the very least he could afford to ship his daughter a goose. Maybe when I cooled down I'd figure out something for Sofia. Right then I wanted to send coal and I didn't much care that that is a Christmas tradition.

CHAPTER TEN

The crisp, sunny air of yesterday morning hadn't changed much now that it was Friday afternoon. It was Memorial Day weekend but the long winter was still flaring up a couple of months into Spring. The high for today was forecasted to be all of 54 degrees, by the time we ended the game around ten tonight the weatherman was warning of a stray snowflake or two off of Lake Erie. I counted my lucky stars I wasn't in Cleveland. With great relish, I resumed my place at the plate with my trusty companion and started hitting balls at the new kid. He was good, really good. Not even the glare of LL from the dugout bugged him.

I expected Alex to be fazed by the thick Mud Hen infield. The Dodgers had moved to the Cactus League a couple of years ago, all of their affiliates now played out west in desert climates. Just ask a Tiger about the differences between Comerica Park and the Ballpark in Arlington if you think I'm blowing smoke about fielding on Bermuda grass compared to grasses used in the wetter north. Hell, Albuquerque Bermuda isn't much different from AstroTurf draped across cement if we're being blunt about it. Add in the variations of hops on soft dirt compared to hard, cracked infields and it should require a significant adjustment. Alex didn't flinch once, his throws precise whether his feet were planted or he was on the run. The transfer of the ball from his glove to his right hand was fast. He was even faster cocking his biological cannon. If Howitzers were built from human flesh, ligaments, muscle and bone they'd resemble Alex's arm. My Army brother liked to go on about how Howitzers are accurate assuming proper adjustments for wind and changes in elevation from 18 miles away, able to land within a football field of the target. I wouldn't bet against Alex given the same stipulations. He threw so hard that Andre had no choice but to catch the ball. If he didn't it might cost him his life. He caught every one, occasionally celebrating this fact by letting out a *Chewbacca*-like roar of satisfaction. When this would happen, I would take a look out to Alex and he'd meet my gaze with a shrug. The kid certainly had style. Through the cold, that blanket of antsy excitement that settled in my stomach like a shot of whiskey yesterday was growing. It pulsed emotional warmth to my extremities. I would have traded that for physical warmth but beggars can't be choosers.

For a long time it was just Alex and Andre on the infield, not much different than the off day workout. I hit balls as fast as possible but I was still cold, even with a team jacket on. Andre had on just a lightweight athletic turtleneck and a pair of sweatpants that didn't come close to reaching his cleats, exposing a good portion of his large calves to the western wind. His uniform, and mine, were still being cleaned. The Walrus said he'd handle it, I didn't ask. My more pressing concern was that I was dressed in my post loss sweats. I didn't have a superstition to guide me on this situation, it had never happened before, but my gut said it was ominous. The thought scratched at the back of my brain.

After getting stretched out by the strength coach and

completing some light sprints Fryer joined us. I started out with swinging bunts, testing his frozen hands by forcing him to charge and bare hand five in a row. Fryer glared at me. "At least I did it to you at the start," I said. My attempt at humor didn't impress the lumbering, reserved third baseman.

Alex had left his spot at shortstop but reappeared with gloved hands and a steaming cup of hot chocolate. I never paused hitting grounders to Fryer but I did give him a strange look.

"Got it from the vendor," Alex said. Then he gave another raise of his shoulders. That shrug was already becoming a staple. "It's cold out."

"Gates aren't open yet, who's selling already?" I asked.

"Oh, he wasn't selling anything. It was the beer guy. He ran across the street for me, guess there's a café nearby." Alex was already developing a rapport with the vendors. In a couple of hours he had them running errands for him. I doubted whether I'd get the same treatment and I had been here for a couple of months now. The kid sure had style.

"Alright, before you manage to get a girl's number get your glove back on. Let's work on the 5-6-3," I barked.

Trev Fryer talked to God more than anyone I've ever met but no amount of prayers could get him to backhand the ball down the line and make a nice feed to second base. They don't call third the hot corner for nothing, when a grounder's got some zip on it Trev only has time for a step and a dive if he wants to head off a double. By the time he had landed on the foul line with the glove in his hand a runner with a good lead

73

would already be halfway to second base. You wouldn't think he'd have time to think if he wanted to start the double play going around the horn, but he did, and the results weren't pretty. It should be a feed chest high on the near side of the bag. This allows the shortstop to use second base as protection from a sliding runner so that he doesn't get flipped ass over tea kettle. From a knee, Trev's throws were usually everywhere but where they were supposed to be.

Trev had to know what would be coming eventually. I let him fret first. I started hitting grounders straight at Trev, tailor made double play balls, and watched as my new infield executed the turns to perfection. I hit a high chopper to third and watched Trev simulate a look towards second before throwing across the diamond to Andre. It was the right play, no chance to turn a double play on that ball. I followed that with a swinging bunt that forced him to charge again and make the throw to first. Alex covered third to keep the invisible runner from trying to stretch the fielder's choice into an extra base and potentially a sac fly opportunity for the hypothetical next batter. I smiled at not having to say anything. Just nodded at Alex and tapped my temple with my free hand. He nodded back at me as he settled into his crouch, eyes scanning intently to find invisible clues about what was coming next. I threw the ball into the air and heard him moving up the middle before I made contact. The kid was damn good. He made the unassisted double play look easy, stepping on second base as he ranged that way before throwing to Andre.

My breath caught as I finally sent one down the line. I looked out to second base to watch Alex as he set up with his heel on the bag, waiting to receive the first half of the relay. He began his stretch high and toward the outfield before Trev had released the ball. His arm extended its full length and he caught it at the end of the webbing.

He had known where the throw was heading before it was out of Trev's hand and I had no idea how. They say that ESP and déjà vu, if that shit is even real, is just a person's ability to use more of their brain than the normal person. Alex must have possessed the fielding equivalent of ESP. Some might argue that it is luck, the ability to play a hunch. I'd dare you to watch him during a play and come to that conclusion. His body becomes cold steel, robotic, as if processing data we haven't thought to analyze and doing it at a speed others could never match. He never should have gotten to Trev's throw and have been able to keep his foot on the bag at the same time. He did though. The rifle-like throw to Andre using just his upper body almost looked normal by comparison. Alex had just made a play with a degree of difficulty around 9.5 look routine.

"I hope you don't expect me to do that," said Chuck Pzeulowski. My second baseman had finally joined us. Another 150 balls in, we had done some more 5-6-3 double plays, 4-3 putouts, 4-6-3 and 6-4-3 double plays, and some pop ups. After 400 balls, only 7 had been booted. .9825 fielding percentage. I could live with that.

CHAPTER ELEVEN

I sneezed. Again.

"Who does he think he is, Gary Sheffield?" asked The Walrus. I had put in so much fielding work with the guys I called off B.P. I hit Alex ninth and the game, as expected, was a pitcher's duel early on with the cold silencing our bats and those of the Syracuse Chiefs.

"Is this what I get for agreeing to let Rodney coach third base?"

"Who are you kidding? We both know you like my company." Wal was my bench coach and he moonlighted as the best third base coach in the league on the side. The exception being the rare occasion my hitting coach decides he wants to get a closer look at things or when I had been ejected. A new shortstop had raised Rodney's interest.

It was the bottom of the third before I got a chance to see him step into the batter's box. Unorthodox, that was the word everyone used to describe his stance and they were right. Rodney Young was a great hitting coach but he had never sniffed the majors as a player. He was living proof that those who can't do, teach and, as such, he hammered the fundamentals. Alex's swing was the polar opposite. There would be groans.

"I seriously doubt Alex tailored his swing after a black guy who retired years ago. Something tells me Cuba doesn't show a lot of American baseball games on their television," I shot back.

"Who else starts his hands up near his chin and swings the bat back and forth while he is waiting on the pitcher?" His 'I told you so' smirk said the argument was over.

I wasn't so willing to concede the point. "Yeah, but Sheffield is still with his hands cocked and ready to go by the time the pitcher is bringing the ball home."

"A fucked up Sheffield is still a Sheffield."

"Sheffield's back leg doesn't come off the ground," I said.

"No, it didn't. Say, does he have a nickname yet?"

"Not that I know of but I'd be the last to know. What are you thinking?"

"How about The Bird?"

"Why would we possibly call him The Bird?" Alex struck out on a fastball up and in. A big weak spot. The scouting reports had made it to the Chiefs already it seemed. The guys emptied from the clubhouse to take the field.

"He clucks his arms before the pitch and ends up pulling both of his feet off the ground during his swing. I didn't think that was possible. He looks like a bird trying to take flight. He's an emu that won't concede its fate is to remain on the ground," said The Walrus.

"We're not calling him The Bird. That name has been taken in this franchise, don't you think?"

"I doubt Fidrych would mind."

"Fidrych is dead Wal."

"Really?"

"Yeah. That's beside the point though, he played for one year essentially and we're still sitting here talking about it nearly forty years later. No need to saddle the kid with a legacy that big."

"How about The Hopping Bird?"

"No," I said.

"But he is more avian than the mascot. What the hell is a mud hen, anyway?"

"Who knows? Probably nothing. Considering he just came from a team called the SeaWolves it wouldn't shock me if it was a made up word. Maybe you should ask Amber for her program."

"Why don't you like that girl? Yesterday you were jealous and today all she did to you was pull emergency duty to get your jersey clean before the game," said The Walrus.

"She used too much bleach. I itch. Also, I'm sneezing which makes my face hurt."

I got up to go find some hot chocolate but the clubhouse guys hadn't set any out. I wished I had a gofer to track some down. I looked down at LL and he looked happy for the first time all night, he must have thought more about watching Alex fail at the plate than he did about watching Alex track a sure single down in the hole for an out like he did to end the previous inning. "Where are you going?" The Walrus asked.

"Need something warm to drink. These fossils are going to turn to dust if I don't get some blood pumping again."

"There's a pot of burnt coffee down the tunnel."

"As appealing as that sounds Wal, I'm going to pass. If I drink coffee this late I'll never get to bed."

"It sucks getting old, doesn't it?"

"Yeah. You want to sleep all day but don't get more than a couple of hours uninterrupted at night. Too bad there is no jeweler available to fix our biological clocks."

"There's probably a pill. Just be glad your bladder hasn't gone bad yet."

Dirk Bobbsey doesn't have a twin and he hates when you make the joke. Unfortunately his revulsion to the Bobbsey Twins didn't carry over to his opinion on vanity. Dirk Bobbsey could stare into a mirror and fall in love with himself if he wasn't careful. He was good looking, in a movie actor kind of way, but compared to LL he didn't come close in terms of the number of conquests. That would have taken away too much time from himself. He didn't have much time to develop a relationship with his teammates as I am sure Dirk saw them as beneath him. He viewed no one on the team with more preening contempt than our catcher Pigpen. Short, stocky, and hairy Pigpen was no self-styled Adonis. Even in today's cold he would be cloaked with a heady froth of perspiration from crouching on his haunches and being covered with pads, protectors and masks from head to toe. Later, when he would shower and change into street clothes Pigpen would brandish a couple more bruises from foul balls. Worse are Pigpen's bloody, crooked fingers that are the result of months of foul tips and wayward back swings. Dirk, a regular at the local spa for the weekly manicure special, would look at his polished clear cuticles and spit thinking of the dirt under Pigpen's cracked nails.

Dirk's high opinion of his looks and grooming habits carried over to his opinion of his pitching abilities. At 25, Bobbsey still had the stuff to make a major league roster but his raw potential had never matured into a finished product. He threw mid-nineties heat that was as potent in the late innings as it was in the first but his only complement to the fastball was a plus changeup. With two pitches, Dirk was major league bullpen material who wouldn't entertain the idea of pitching in relief. So, seven years after he was drafted as a first rounder, he was in his third organization (he was traded from the Red Sox to the Marlins in 2010, the prized prospect in one of the Marlins countless deals to offload payroll). Throwing curveballs caused his pampered fingers to blister which was an egregious sin to Dirk. The slider caused his elbow to flare up and he had been shut down at the end of last year as a precaution.

His numbers in the minors were good enough but he had yet to post a stretch in the majors with an ERA below 5. So far this year, Dirk was 2-3 with a respectable ERA at 3.20. It would be lower if he didn't fight Pigpen tooth and nail every game. There was hardly an inning that the two didn't have to conference on the mound because they didn't agree on location or pitch selection. There was hardly a batter where Dirk didn't vigorously shake Pigpen off as he stalked behind the rubber and kicked at the dirt. Almost unanimously, when the two were at each other's throats, Pigpen was right. Even when Pigpen stuck to his guns and called for the changeup against Dirk's objections, Bobbsey delivered a heater. Often it was right down the middle and rarely did it make it to Pigpen's mitt. A base runner and a smash and all of a sudden a commanding performance was soiled. I wondered sometimes if Pigpen didn't pull a *Crash Davis* and let the batter know what was coming. Of course, if we're being honest, the batter would be a fucking moron if he hadn't already figured it out.

After six innings of zeros, the same old story struck again. Leading off the inning, Syracuse's short stop, the number seven hitter, blooped a Texas leaguer into short right. Chuck Pzeulowski (I should just start calling him Chuck Jones after the old cartoonist as that name gets old) had a chance to make a basket catch over his shoulder but I can't fault him for having it careen off the heel. He read the ball well off the bat, sprinting with his back turned to the infield to a spot. The first time he would have seen the ball was when it was just inches from his glove. There wasn't enough time to make the last second adjustment and it bounced off leather, landing in the outfield grass, now slick with dew that more closely resembled frost. For anyone still dumb enough to watch the travesty that is *Baseball Tonight*, it was a web gem if he caught it.

I could see Dirk grumbling as he walked behind the mound. I should have gone out to calm him down, tell him that sometimes even good pitches fall in and that Chuck did his damndest making it close. I should have, but I didn't. Instead I watched him talking to himself as he toed the rubber. Just as he ran down Pigpen, he was running down Chuck. I couldn't hear what was being said but I was sure Dirk was not silent in his protests. He was berating his second basemen for all of the players, umpires, and the opposing team to hear. I liked a pitcher who scowled at his manager when the Skip came to take the ball out of his hand but this wasn't attitude and confidence, it was a temper tantrum.

Next up was the Chief's catcher. He reminded me a lot of Pigpen in stature and looks. Catcher has become the easiest position to get to the majors at and it shows. What was once a centerpiece of a team's lineup, the position of Bench, Berra, and Cochrane, catchers now were holes you tried to hide at the bottom of the order. Down here on the farm, they were even less. That's fine with me, I just want a guy who can call a good game and handle his staff. Those skills are mental more than physical. Catchers used to challenge corner infielders for power now they all seemed to manage between 10 to 15 home runs a year. That's pedestrian and as we continue to transition from the Steroid Era to whatever it is this game is going to, those numbers are probably sliding further still. A catcher can still hit a fastball though, including a good one, when he knows it is coming and it is right down the pipe.

The hit was flush but it wasn't majestic. It was too cold for a towering fly ball to get out, expending energy just to fight the air. Instead the ball cut horizontally across the sky wondering if it would stay elevated enough to get over the wall. It did, second row. Wampum didn't move, just observing it with a spin of his neck. It was poor form but if I had called him on it he probably would have given me some bullshit about channeling the owl mixed with enough esoteric mumbo jumbo about the Manitou spirits. I knew about as much about Native American religion as I do about the Spanish language.

Their catcher wasn't around third before I had hopped out of the dugout. Pigpen saw me coming and made to follow me to the mound, politely waiting for the Chiefs to cross the plate and exchange high fives. I shook him off. "You owe Chuck an apology," I said.

Dirk gave me a bewildered look. "The fuck are you talking about?"

"You ran him down publically, lost your cool, and cost this team two runs. Apologize."

"You're mad at me for expecting him to catch the ball?" Dirk asked.

"No. I'm mad because he went all out for you, hustled just to get to a ball that most second basemen in this league wouldn't have a shot at. It was one of the hardest plays any infielder could have and he almost pulled it off for you. He deserves your support, not your scorn," I lectured.

Dirk muttered under his breath, this time below the level that anyone could hear. He turned and walked slowly towards where Chuck was standing. I couldn't see Dirk's face but the pain of having to apologize must have contorted it in such a manner to make him look like a man with blood lust. Narcissus wouldn't have appreciated my punishment either. I saw Chuck begin to slowly back his way towards the rim of the outfield grass. He was afraid for his safety. "Hey Chuck, it's ok," I said in a manner that was both authoritative and comforting.

Chuck froze, eyes fixated on Dirk as he approached. Chuck was still unsure of Dirk's intentions and the tremor in his eye, something more than a tic, increased in intensity the closer Dirk got. Chuck's neck seemed to grow away from his shoulders, a man who knew the guillotine was coming clinging to the hope he could extend the time before the sharp metal made contact, even if it was just a fraction of a second. Dirk stopped about five feet away and I could hear him talking but didn't understand what he said. "Louder," I yelled.

"Chuck, I apologize for losing my temper and disparaging you in public," Dirk said. He forced every word out.

"That's better Mr. Bobbsey. Hug him."

Chuck begged me to call the hug off. I ignored him. Dirk turned and yelled back to me a lone word. It spoke volumes. "Really?"

"You better hurry up or it is going to seem rather insincere." The couple hundred fans who were in attendance were now laughing. Dirk turned red with embarrassment, Chuck turned green with queasiness. Dirk spun from me and quickly gave Chuck a hug that was all arms. It was over in the blink of an eye.

"This isn't a Catholic school dance. I am not requiring any room for the Holy Spirit. Give him a real hug."

This time Dirk's arms reached towards Chuck slowly, taking forever to reach around the second baseman's small shoulders. Andre gave me a thumbs-up from first base, accompanied by a huge smile, to let me know that Dirk's arms had locked together on the backside of the hug. Dirk pulled Chuck in until their chests were touching each other and held it. Chuck's arms didn't return the favor, hanging at his side with wariness. At five seconds Dirk began to release the hug to which I cleared my throat loudly. Another five seconds passed and the crew chief finally jumped on me about delaying the game. I was surprised that he gave me this long to make my point but I guessed he probably enjoyed it as much as the others. "That's good," I said and walked back to the dugout. The Chiefs began taunting Dirk with the childhood rhyme about K-I-S-S-I-N-G in the tree. They were silent when he struck out the side, all swinging, with changeups. We were still down 2-0 at stretch time.

In the first six innings we had two hits total. Both were registered by Gary Wampum. He was a left-handed batter who was expected to someday be major league caliber at the plate. Wampum hit for average but he hadn't developed enough pop in his bat to get an extended look in The Show. Most scouts projected his ceiling at around 20 home runs. He's already proven enough speed to get him to be a member of the 20-20 club; doubles, and stolen bases. I have struggled to get him to be consistent. Wampum's production is a bit hollow, in a given month he'll take three weeks off and go on a tear the other week. Much like clubs have a player who have a certain team's number, Wampum comes alive against a very specific set of nicknames. A proud member of the Seneca Nation, Wampum, has been an outspoken advocate against teams using Indian terms as mascots. The first expense I incurred as manager of the Mud Hens was to spring Wampum on bail. I still can't figure out why he called me as we had never met and that definitely isn't my fight. He had pushed through barricades outside RFK that had been placed in the far end of the parking lot for protestors of the Redskins. He had dressed in full war regalia, paint smeared across his face, and a Tomahawk hanging conspicuously from his belt. A man dressed for war and armed outside the "free speech" zone drew police attention in a hurry. He was lucky no one drew their tasers, or worse. The stunt worked, Wampum was hailed as a hero. That's probably a good thing as the bail was rather expensive. Being reimbursed with casino funds fairly quickly made me breathe easier.

Until I can find a way for Wampum to find motivation in some other way I'm stuck with waiting until we play the Chiefs, Braves, or Indians. Considering the International League has only 14 teams, that ratio isn't so bad. Tonight had been no exception to the pattern with Wampum putting two singles back up the box. With no runners on base, neither hit had led to anything though. I had moved Wampum up to the five hole to take advantage of his extra production and I had nothing to show for it. If we lost tonight, that is the type of thing that the fans never give a manager credit for. Funny game baseball, even when you're right you can be wrong. Not much else like it.

The number two hitter was leading off the seventh, Syracuse's DeLouise had faced just one over the minimum so far. As he finished his warm up tosses and stood behind the mound breathing on his hands, I pulled my best bat handler, Alston, the left fielder, in close. "We need base runners so that Wampum gets a shot to drive some guys in."

"I'll give you everything I've got Skip," Alston said with his characteristic enthusiasm.

"Put down a bunt on their third baseman. Grass is wet, if you make him charge and bare hand it, he'll never get a grip."

"You sure Skip, I'm not the fastest."

"Not the fastest, not the slowest either. And you've got a bad throwing arm, hence why you're in left. This isn't a player evaluation, none of that matters. The third baseman has been playing back all night and he'll never get the ball picked up cleanly if you make him charge. You'll make it."

"Good Hands" Alston dug in to the right-handed batter's box using his normal routine. Left foot found purchase first, then the other where it rested lightly on the back chalk line. His bat was set down, head touching the inside corner of the plate and handle on his belt buckle, so he could clap his hands together. He picked the bat back up and rested it on his back shoulder until DeLouise began the wind-up. Mark Alston pivoted on his foot until his chest was pointing towards the mound and his hands had separated from the normal grip near the handle. Delouise brought a fastball home that was going to be low but Mark had already tipped his hand, the third baseman was on the charge, still a long way from home, and he wouldn't be sitting that far back for the rest of the at-bat. Mark had one chance to get this right.

Mark's bat hung over the plate for what seemed an eternity as time slowed down. His bat adjusted downward, tracking the pitch trajectory around the middle of his shin. Bunting is a difficult art to explain, good bunter's need to almost catch the ball with their bat to deaden it down the line. A pitch out of the strike zone can be difficult to bunt, high or low, because it forces the batter to spear at the ball. Mark did it perfectly though, getting the bat head down early so he was waiting with a still 32 ounces of Appalachian ash. In the slow motion of anticipation, you could see the bat head actually get shifted backward as the ball crossed the plate. A dead thunk preceded a dribbler that stayed fair, maybe three feet inside the foul line. It nestled into the wet grass like a bad golfer's lie. Mark was fast out of the box, running so hard his helmet fell off on the way to first. He probably would have been safe anyways but the Chiefs third baseman lost any chance at the out when he ran past the buried ball, his fingertips unable to find a grip on their target.

"Atta boy, Good Hands!" I yelled, along with a majority of the team. It was the first time our leadoff man had been successful in getting on. Statistically that gave us a 42% chance of scoring. Few things look worse than a team that struggles to score. Whether the drought lasts a night, week or season it appears that no one is trying. Mark getting to first wasn't going to be featured in tomorrow's article in *The Toledo Blade* but it gave the team some pep. Even when Andre struck out next at-bat, you could feel something was in the air. Trev walked after fouling off six two-strike pitches and the tying runs were on base with DeLouise getting pulled for one of the Chief's vaunted set up men.

Syracuse had only lost one game when leading in the seventh inning or later all year. If they had a better offense they'd be challenging for a division instead of sitting around .500. We were in a bad spot, trailing with a need for a win. We had been just 1-4 so far on the home stand with a rain out. I caught Wampum's eye as he moved from the on-deck circle to the plate. Right then, I felt confident that something good was coming. I would have thought that if I was managing this rag tag group of minor leaguers in Yankee Stadium in October. When you've been around the game long enough, you learn to trust these feelings. It wasn't wrong. Wampum drove the 1-0 pitch deep to right center, all the way to the concourse. We had the lead.

I left Dirk in to pitch the eighth and he was perfect. Six up, six down since my public lesson. I had been worried that he'd play Reggie Jackson to my Billy Martin at some time tonight but he didn't. He just sat by himself at the end of the bench like normal. No teammates were particularly inclined to join him so he got the silent treatment. Too bad it wasn't for the right reasons, with a perfect game or no hitter on the line. I had never managed one, my closest being a guy for the Orioles getting to the eighth in '93.

We didn't score in our half either. As the scoreboard thermometer showed freezing, the game went to the top of the ninth and I called on Stu Grissom, the closer. He was an excellent one, a career minor leaguer who managed to convert 92% of save opportunities with average stuff. He had never gotten a shot at the majors and turned 30 in August. That would eat at a lot of guys but I never talked to him about it. Grissom was workmanlike. He came to the ballpark every day, said what he needed, and only what he needed, to do his job, then went to wherever it is Grissom goes. Grissom had a long black beard that wouldn't recognize a razor in a Gillette factory, strings of bright silver now mixing in. It stood out, much like his mannerisms from the normal ball player. Imagine a tattoo parlor owner or a mad scientist on a ball field. In fact, Stu stood out from anyone's norm. It wouldn't surprise me to learn Stu went home to a glass maze of rats like the old *CSI* character with the same last name.

Grissom had four pitches, a rarity among relievers, but his primary pitch was a split finger fastball that hitters couldn't lay off of. It started at the knees and ended in the dirt but, no matter how often Stu threw it, hitters swung anyway. That night, Stu didn't have it. His splitter was flat and it was up about waist high. At 90 miles an hour, it wobbled like a juicy slab of bacon. He let the first man on with a sharp single to left. The next batter hit a line drive but right at Alex who made the catch look like the most natural thing in the world.

Stu changed to his breaking stuff after the second batter. It was junk but you can get away with that at this level and Stu induced a weak ground ball with tired eyes for the hole between Trev and Alex. Trev cut in front of Alex which was the right play since his momentum was carrying him towards where the throw had to go. He fired to Chuck at second who relayed to Andre for a game ending double play. I saw the first base umpire go up with the closed fist signaling an out but no one was running off the field.

Chuck was in a heated argument at second base with the crew chief. Crew chiefs are not who you want to get in a fight with, especially in the first game of a series. I bolted, at least by AARP standards, out of the dugout to get between Chuck and the umpire. Especially after the display earlier, I needed to protect my player publically. The dugout TV with the in-stadium closed circuit feed had yet to show a replay so I didn't know what exactly I was running out to argue. That was a first professionally. Mrs. Munro, my high school debate teacher, would have said that was the norm back in my younger days. I didn't like debate class then and didn't expect to like this now.

The crew chief for this squad was Rex Stout and he was known to be quick with the hook. At 32, he was the youngest crew chief in the International League, and he viewed brooking any dissent as affirming that he wasn't up for the challenge. As I got closer, the conversation came into focus. "I dare you to tell me you've made that call once all year," Chuck barked.

"You dare me?" Rex replied.

I stepped in front of my player. "Yeah, I dare you," I said.

"I don't owe you nothing Freeman. He never touched the bag. You got the out at first. We've got two out with a guy on second," Rex said.

"I never touched the bag?" Chuck exclaimed.

I cut him off. "It looked like a good relay from there." I motioned with my head toward the home dugout. "Did you really choose the final play of the game to become a stickler on the Area Rule?" The Area Rule is an unspoken agreement between the middle infielders and the umpire that if they have possession of the ball and are near, which sometimes gets stretched to within a couple of steps, the bag then they'll get the out call. It has become a staple of how the game is played, to the point that even with TV and instant replay it goes unquestioned. "That's fucking bullshit Rex."

They were right, he is quick and his motion wastes no effort. I was ejected in a seamless flick of the hand. "Go put a T-Bone on that face of yours, it looks like it hurts."

I'd forgotten all about it to be honest. My face had frozen hours ago. The ejection had gotten me hot under the collar but I didn't push it like Wednesday. There was no reason to give the league more of a reason to throw a hefty fine my way. Two ejections in two games with a guest spot on all of the highlight shows would not be looked upon kindly, I might get a stern call from Detroit.

I didn't have to wait long to know how things unfolded. Not five minutes after finding my way next to a space heater the locker room was filled with celebration. Wampum had tracked a ball down against the high wall in right to rob Syracuse of the tying run. He really did rise to the occasion against the

92

Indian teams. It's funny that a mascot which was meant to highlight the noble warrior aspect of their culture drew his ire when he did nothing but poke fun at his heritage at all other times. Maybe it was similar to anyone but blacks using the n-word. I just wish I could find a way to channel that intensity every night.

CHAPTER TWELVE

We finished out the series with two more wins, our first sweep of the year. A good weekend made it easier to find reasons to spend more of the day at the ball park. I got to Fifth/Third Field by ten Saturday morning to find The Walrus halfway through another run. He was even slower than his first run, cardio and stamina still demons rather than angels at this point. The first two weeks you work out are awful, like quitting smoking. You're sore, tired, irritable, and nothing happens. You don't lose weight or gain definition and thoughts about how little it took to get you to such a pathetic state taunt you. The Walrus had a long way to go and my involvement could only hinder his motivation. I retired to my office where I was subject to a tongue lashing from the assistant GM of the Tigers. I was expecting it and the victory later in the day, Drake's first of the year, let it roll off of me.

The game on Sunday was kid's day, a light hearted affair that saw us get to the Chiefs bullpen by the third inning. Toby Mack didn't have his best stuff but we didn't need it. We won 17-8 and I had pulled almost all of my starters by the fifth. Wampum had six more RBI and every man in the lineup got a hit including Alex, his only hit of the series. The weather had returned towards normal, sunny and just shy of 80, and the families responded with a solid turnout, probably 75% capacity. After he was pulled, Wampum managed to take control of the grill in the Fowl Pole picnic section. To the delight of the kids he taught them how to do smoke signals.

With exuberance, they fanned billows of charcoal ash into a visual Morse code. I laughed when he told me later that he taught them to signal 'fuck you' to the Syracuse bench. I'm not sure that is true, I wasn't aware Northeastern Indians used smoke signals at all.

After twelve runs, I volunteered to take over for The Walrus at third. He had done another stadium session Sunday morning and his signals had carried more than a touch of gingerness all day. The offensive explosion had made sure he was signaling a lot and with a long bus ride to Rochester coming later in the day I knew he was going to be stiff. I hadn't coached third in over 25 years and my judgment at when to send a runner home was rusty. The only boos of the day came when I sent Brock Bisby, an utility player who had replaced Chuck earlier, and he was thrown out by a good fifteen feet. I took the jeers with relish and gave an insincere mea culpa that was accepted by the fans with equal insincerity. With the sweep we improved to 21-29, two games from getting out of the cellar in the four-team West Division.

"Driver, know any good places to eat around here?" The woody foothills of northwestern Pennsylvania were bathed in abundant orange evening sunshine but lacking in abundant humanity. I knew of some spots around Erie because of my travels as a roving instructor but the turnoff to Erie had come and gone already.

"We'll be in New York State soon, there's a great burger joint on the other side of the border," the driver said.

"That sounds good." I looked at The Walrus sitting next to me and turned back towards the driver. "They do anything but burgers?"

The driver looked at me in the rear view mirror, returned his eyes to the road and was silent for a beat. "They make a mean chocolate malt. Haven't tried anything but the burgers though for a meal. Once you have one, you'll know why."

I felt a hand on my shoulder. "It's ok Har. The guys got to eat and they earned it today," said The Walrus.

"I wouldn't be much of a friend if I blew your diet a couple of days in Wal. We'll just find a Mickey D's, they've got salads at least."

"Shit, those salads have more calories than a burger and fries. Same thing goes for most restaurants since they started trying to pretend that they're healthy," The Walrus said.

"Subway then, six incher?" I really was trying to be good. Living on the road isn't easy for coaches or umpires. It's a constant battle characterized by expanding waistlines, a tragic coronary that serves as a come to Jesus moment, tightening belts, and the cycle starts over.

"Harold Freeman, I said I had taken care of it." Full name. I must have touched a nerve.

I shrugged and said to the driver, "Lead the way then. I don't think I caught the name of this place?"

"The Grease Box."

I gave another look towards The Walrus, he just nodded his approval.

#

The driver wasn't wrong. The Grease Box was a slice of heaven that not even the scourge of arthrosclerosis could taint. There was another one of those adult words, the kind a three-game winning streak made the little boy in me stop caring about. Nestled on the western edge of a steep, narrow glen that must have been millions of years old, the team enjoyed the scenery bisected by fading light and darkening shadow. I had a quarter pounder with Swiss cheese that oozed juice from the bottom of the bun and the largest milk shake The Grease Box offered. The Walrus sat next to me with a small container of homemade salad he had tucked underneath his seat. I admired Wal's dedication and forethought but I did not envy him.

"Beautiful, isn't it?" The Walrus said, more than asked.

"Yeah, it is. The mountains back home may be grander but I've never been much for the desert. I'd give up the brown and red for green any day of the week," I replied.

Baseball players are creatures of habit, one of those habits being a universal appreciation for sleeping in late. Tomorrow was Memorial Day, an afternoon start, and team policy was to be at the field for batting practice by 10:30 in the morning. I demanded that they get some sort of breakfast but it wouldn't be much. Seeing as it was closing in on eight in the evening and we still had several hours to Rochester, plus check-in, we'd be bumping up against curfew less than two hours after settling in. This would be the last major meal before tomorrow's game, the interim a modern day equivalent of the fasts before battle that Wampum's ancestors were known for.

At least I'm assuming the Seneca Nation did that.

It was an orgiastic display of food consumption. Andre, in true form, had a larger than life diet of ground cow. The Grease Box's menu operated similar to a Wendy's, quarter pound patties up to a triple decker sandwich and after that additional patties were made to order. Andre devoured a 13 patty burger, two straining buns containing American cheese, lettuce, raw onion, pickles, ketchup, mustard, miracle whip, and over three pounds of meat that slid precariously like the bridge in The Temple of Doom. The buns broke into pieces under the pressure of Andre's vice-like grip but the sandwich held together. Three of my mouths would have failed to fit the monstrosity in the giant's hands, he suffered from no such problems and it disappeared with alarming quickness. Trev Fryer and Pigpen didn't slouch either.

Sitting in between the infielders was Alex. He had steadied our defense so far better than I could have hoped and already fit in as one of the guys. Despite his Cuban heritage and relatively recent arrival in the country, Alex spoke impeccable English. According to those newspaper articles I had clipped in my garage, he hadn't spoken a word when he first got here. The Dodgers had tried to hire an interpreter but he insisted on having an English speaking roommate to travel with and picked up the language, as well as our cultural mannerisms, in a hurry. In some ways he was too All-American to actually come off as American. His boyish good looks made him appear younger than he really was and his understated sense of humor was endearing. Several of the leaders on the team took to him like a mentor to a pupil. Alex's ability to instantly establish a relationship didn't appeal as much to LL but even he seemed to have developed a professional, if icy, camaraderie with the Cuban. I didn't want to test it by locking the two of them in the same room though.

The series with Syracuse had seen just one error in three games and that was committed by Toby Mack, today's pitcher. He had gotten a comebacker and had too much time to think about his throw to first. He held on too long and threw it into the ground a good eight feet on the outfield side of the bag. My defense wasn't just making the routine plays either. I counted a handful of plays that guys simply wouldn't have gotten to a couple of days ago. Trev had made a great catch on a pop up, leaning over the tarp and into the first row of seats. Alex made a sublime stab on a ball behind second base, flipping it to Chuck with just his glove. Andre wasn't just picking balls during practice, coming up with a short hop on a bang-bang play at first on Saturday.

The Walrus caught me looking at my new shortstop. "He's going to start thinking you've got a thing for him," Wal said.

"Huh?"

"You're ogling the poor kid."

I shook my head. "No. Just thinking."

"Yeah, he's good. Speaking of, he's got a single and a couple of walks in three games. He also has four strike outs. Rodney is dying to get a crack at him. That batting stance is driving him nuts."

"Always Mr. Fundamentals, isn't he?" I said with a grin.

"It works," said The Walrus.

"It does. Except in this case. I'll be personally overseeing Alex's hitting instruction."

"And why is that?"

"Just playing a hunch is all."

"You think Rodney is going to fuck him up? I can't see how he'd get much worse."

"You'd be surprised," I said absentmindedly, now staring back at the fading sunlight and what was left of the view.

"What are you going to do?"

"Me? Nothing."

The Walrus eyed me for a second, flicking his pupils towards the reflection of the inside of The Grease Box that was trying to dominate the pane of glass in front of us over the foothills outside. I could see him looking at Alex's reflection with a thought. "You really think he's overthought his way into this?"

"The kid was rock solid for a year and a half. That isn't a flash in the pan. We both know that sometimes this game seems set out to crush what's different. Just look at how it treated Bill James until Beane won with sabermetrics out in Oakland."

"That's because the numerical stuff is bullshit." The Walrus, ever the conservative. "That stance won't work. Maybe you do have a thing for him."

"His stance today won't work. I watched the tape on the kid, it was different once."

"How's that?"

"The coaches saw nothing but what was wrong without realizing that they weren't shitting on just a stance, they were shitting on the person. The problems in his swing, they're because Alex is trying to be what others want of him. He looks hesitant because he is. This non-stop tinkering has been as helpful as telling a lefty to bat right-handed. Not even Ted Williams would have made that work," I said.

"That's…interesting. I don't know I buy it but I'll give Rodney the bad news."

"Give Alex a month with no one trying to get inside his head. Then Rodney can do whatever he wants."

My gaze had also settled in the reflection of the diner window. Alex was laughing at one of Trev's jokes. That was unusual, Trev wasn't particularly funny. I wondered if he knew a joke that didn't start with a priest on a golf course. Andre roared too so it must have been good. I made it a point to ask Trev about it tomorrow. Some levity might not be a bad addition to the usual pre-game Our Father and Al Percy's intellectual rah-rah rhetorical bonanza. Andre was now asking Alex if he was through with his fries. After that Herculean sandwich it was amazing he still had room for more. No wonder why the guy had never met a case of wine that could get him drunk. How did that anesthesiologist ever keep the giant asleep? Nothing was small with Andre but a new thought now pushed its way to the front of my brain. I wondered what the cost was. He was a spectacle, seemingly immortal, but his father hadn't made it past 45. To hear him tell it, no man in Andre's family, except for an Uncle Jim with normal genes, had ever lived long enough to collect Social Security. Behind the large shell of charisma, I thought I could see a flicker of that doubt weighing on him.

CHAPTER THIRTEEN

The charter bus pulled up to the team hotel where things went smoothly, the norm for the best stop in the I-League. The Rochester Red Wings had been an affiliate of the St. Louis Cardinals for decades. The Cardinals are probably the most professional organization in the game and it filtered down to their farm teams, including their ex-affiliates, as well. Even now, the Red Wings were the still the winningest team in International League history. They just did things the right way. Rochester isn't too far from Cooperstown, the home of the Hall of Fame, mecca. Upstate New York reveres baseball, the appreciation permeating everyday life once summer takes the reins from Spring. Combine a model affiliate amid fervor for the game and in Rochester you've walked into a scene out of *Field of Dreams* without the corn. Our bus idled as the stowage compartments underneath were emptied by a contingent of bellhops and hotel staffers.

The travel secretary had faxed over room assignments to the hotel earlier in the week and, for one stop, someone besides the team would be taking up bags to the player's quarters. We had gotten a wing of the hotel, rather than just a floor. It just so happened to be the wing that contained the hotel suites. I got off to make sure that the equipment bags weren't hauled off. The players were supposed to tie neon green tags to their personal belongings with their name written on it but a couple had fallen off and I played traffic cop. A pretty female was making googly eyes at LL through the window. I tried to not pay it any attention.

I gave the signal when we were all clear and the team disembarked, spilling into the hotel lobby. I figured check-in would take a while as it did elsewhere but the staff was ready for us. The hotel manager stood behind the high countertop, lined with something that almost passed for real granite. He called us to attention and began ticking off players' names, two at a time. After every pair was named, a woman in a navy blue blazer and tan khakis passed out room keys. Four more assistants stood by to chaperone the players to their rooms, each assistant responsible for situating a floor apiece. What normally took a half hour was done in five minutes.

The Walrus and I got a suite together facing the front of the hotel. I agreed to take the room with the window so I could sit at curfew and watch to ensure all of my players had gotten back. I didn't expect many to go out tonight after the game and the long bus ride but as I pulled open the drapes I spied LL sneaking away to a strange car with the girl from the bus. I yelled out the window, "Hey, Rodrigo! I hope you don't forget curfew. Now that you are riding pine that would be an indiscretion that could not be overlooked."

He tried to pretend that he hadn't heard me but she did. She stopped and they got into a conversation that I couldn't hear from the fourth floor. LL began to gesticulate wildly which told me the talk wasn't going the way he had planned. She began to walk away while he stood there watching. She got in to her car, the tail lights red into the distance. He would be alone for the night. He glared up at me, saying nothing, before storming back into the lobby.

The Walrus knocked on my door and entered without waiting for my answer. "Did you just cock block The Latin Lover?"

"Yeah, I guess I did."

"Haven't you done enough to that kid this week?"

"It'll be worth it, trust me."

"You've said that twice in three hours. Just be careful, schemers usually live long enough to see their plans blow up. You aren't a master psychologist, Har. That isn't meant as a slight, it's just that we've been at this a long time. I know you and the friend I know isn't Tony LaRussa. Leave that shit to him or Bobby Cox."

"Harry we've got a problem."

I'm not a heavy sleeper and The Walrus boomed loud enough to wake the dead. The combination caused me to shoot up so fast I nearly hit the ceiling. Before I had come down I was alert and staring at the alarm clock which read 3:49 in red block numerics. "It's the middle of the night Wal."

"We've got a fight going on floor two between two guys. I don't have names but the night manager is threatening to call the police." We both stood in silence listening as unrest spilled upwards into the suite.

"Wal, you keep that from happening, I'm on the way down." I walked out of my suite in a tank top that didn't cover enough of my saggy chest. I had passed that age about five years ago that no matter how fit I was it stopped being

105

publically passable. I didn't have time to care about how I looked though. "Floor two, that's the infielders right?"

The Walrus didn't bother to put his hand over the receiver. "Yeah. I told you not to cock block the poor kid."

"Is LL involved?" I asked as I turned the handle to the door. Hallway light stormed in without asking permission, I squinted until my eyes adjusted.

"Just told you I don't know. The manager didn't say. I think someone has been trying to call the room, I'm hearing a lot of clicking as if someone's on the other line. Probably Trev, he's such a goody two shoes."

I grumbled at myself for asking a stupid question. I'm a light sleeper but that doesn't automatically mean I'm with it when I open my eyes. I barely heard the last of The Walrus's words, turning right toward the staircase. My knee wanted me to wait for the elevator but my adrenaline said I didn't have a second to lose. Six steps down my left knee popped, sending pain shooting up my thigh for a split second before pleasure settled in behind it. Between the third and second floors I was actually taking the steps two at a time. Maybe I could pull off bleachers. I tugged on the door to the second floor hallway but it didn't release. There was a monitor that required a key card to grant access which I had left in the room. I could see through the small window in the door, latticed with metal wire to keep someone from putting their hand through it, a melee in the hall. Andre had someone wrapped in a bear hug like restraint. Sure enough it was LL. Trev was in the middle playing peace keeper, guess The Walrus was wrong about him calling, and I couldn't see who the other party was. That didn't stop me from having a strong hunch. I pounded on the stairway door until someone finally looked my way. Trev pulled it open from the inside.

The other guy in the fight was Alex and he had definitely gotten the worst of it. His left eye was already developing a shiner. "Did you fight back?"

Alex seemed taken aback that I didn't care about the why or the fact that he had taken a couple good shots but he responded. "Yeah."

"What hand did you use?"

"My left."

"Good. Never use your primary hand for a brawl with anyone. Not even if you have to charge the mound. Pride means nothing if you have to walk around in a cast." I thought about *Crash Davis* for the second time this week.

"And you," I barked as I turned on The Latin Lover, "What. The. Fuck." He ignored me, continuing to yell at Alex in Spanish. I gave him an open hand slap designed to drive the red from behind his eyes. He was on the verge of losing control and now that I was standing close to him I could tell he had alcohol on his breath. The bartender in the lobby had a nice tip for the night. I made a note to talk to him tomorrow. "Look at me Rodrigo. Is your hand broke?"

My slap had sent the proper message. He examined his swollen knuckles. "I don't know. I got him pretty good. He hits like a girl."

"He doesn't hit like a girl, he'll be able to throw a ball this afternoon. Doubt we'll be saying the same about you. What the hell were you expecting to accomplish by this stunt? Give me a reason not to throw you out of this hotel, and off this team, immediately."

He said nothing, just stared red hot intensity. I liked what I saw but was in a bad spot. Maybe Alex would throw me a lifeline. I looked his way. "Did you do anything to cause this?"

"No! I was sleeping and he started pounding on the door. I pulled open the door just far enough to stretch the chain lock. He went crazy, yelling at me in Spanish about some blood grudge and put his shoulder into the door so hard he tore the lock off the frame." Andre let go of Alex and pointed at the door to give credence to his story. Shit. I was going to have to send LL on his way. An hour ago I would have been happy to do so but this newfound inevitability felt bittersweet now.

"Skip, can I see you for a minute?" Al Percy had come up from his first floor room and had poked his head out of the stairwell. Talking to Al was the last thing I needed right now, my head didn't have enough power to deal with a dissertation on a couple hours of sleep. What the hell could he possibly need to talk to me about?

"It was you trying to call up to the room."

"Yes." My statement hadn't been a question but Al answered it like it was.

"Al, if this is some trivia lesson on what kind of gun Alexander Hamilton fired when he was killed by Aaron Burr I'm really not in the mood right now," I warned.

Al was oblivious to my warning. The man had no people

skills until he got up on a soap box, then he could speak with the best of them . "Ha, good one Skip, didn't think you'd have a sense of humor right now. No Burr and Hamilton stuff although the subject is quite fascinating."

"Al."

"Sorry Skip, didn't me to ramble."

"Al, I don't want musings or apologies or hypothesizing. What do you need to tell me?"

"I think we should have this discussion in private, sir."

"Don't call me sir. I'm your manager, not a gentleman. Maybe you haven't noticed but now isn't a good time. Don't you think a talk between the two of us would be better when I'm not putting out a fire in the wee hours of the morning?"

"With all due respect, I don't think I'm making myself clear. Our talk is about this." He gestured with his hand to encompass the after effects of the melee.

I stared death at him, unsure whether he had truly pertinent information. With Al you could never tell. He had been the team's catcher for the past four seasons before his legs began to break down. They often call a catcher's equipment the 'tools of ignorance' because only a fool would suffer the abuse that a man takes behind the plate. While many catchers have good people skills, they have to handle pitchers who are notorious basket cases after all, no one would mistake them for Rhodes Scholars. Al was the opposite, obviously brilliant with a particular interest in English and history. His people skills were equally, and just as obviously, lacking. Al should be on a college campus, locked like John

Nash behind ivy covered walls where people will overlook his eccentricities for genius. However, Al demanding a conference with me in private wasn't a normal thing so I decided to trust that he wasn't being damn weird for the sake of it. We found privacy in the stairwell.

"What is it?"

"LL was quite boisterous with his exclamations during their scrum, sir."

"Don't call me sir."

"Sorry, sir."

I sighed. "Don't apologize or call me 'sir' Al. Please, please tell me you didn't request a meeting with me to tell me that LL was loud during a fight. Al, that isn't exactly rare."

"Sir, I didn't petition a conference to tell you that, no. It is cogent as it permitted me to surmise the source of The Latin Lover's agitations."

"That's a little better, what's his beef?" I asked.

"His beef can be found," Al chuckled, "as Mondale would've been want to express, with a distant geopolitical event that caused personal tragedy for the Montero family."

"You're sense of humor needs work. What does my new shortstop have to do with a family trauma of LL's?"

"Are you acquainted with the Mariel Boatlift of 1980?" Al asked.

"1980? I was playing ball and thinking about getting married Al. Why in the hell would I be familiar with Mariella's boat lock?"

Al laughed. "No sir, the Mariel Boatlift. Castro started

citizens on a mini Armada of rafts, sending them to Miami where we granted a hundred thousand Cubans citizenship. Jimmy Carter was naive enough to think Castro wasn't offloading his refuse on our shores. It turned out, many of those who were allowed over weren't being shown the pier because they were political refugees. Castro sent us his criminals, the worst of the worst, and con men. If you've ever read Solzhenitsyn, you'd know that it takes a lot for a Communist to decide you're unfit for paradise. To be considered too depraved to be a comrade... well you know what I mean."

"Al, honestly, thanks for giving me a history lesson I didn't know. When does this relate to a fight between my new shortstop and the jealous teammate he took a spot from?"

"Skip, it isn't as notorious but Cuba didn't send criminals from just Mariel at the time and they didn't all come here."

"Where's LL from, the Dominican right?"

"Correct, sir."

"Damn it, no sirs!"

"I'm sorry. That is correct."

"Cuba send any maximum security monsters to the Dominican, Al?"

"If I heard The Latin Lover correctly sir, it certainly appears so. LL didn't come from much, his whole family lived together in a small house in the barrio. It seems a Cubano murdered his Uncle in their family room. All of the children slept on blankets out there and he was protecting them when an incursion turned to senseless murder. LL wouldn't have even been born yet. He says his mother remembers his Uncle's blood splashing on her face," Al recited with a lecturer's flourish.

"The situation is a lot more complicated than I had taken it for," I said.

"It usually is, and I figured you'd want to know about the fact that Dominicans and Cubans aren't particularly predisposed to mutual hospitality."

"I've been pushing LL hard all week. I thought it was the only way I could get him to break from his nonchalance. Is that a fancy enough word for you Al?"

"I find it agreeable."

"I didn't know he was sitting on a powder keg of recriminations. The fire in his eyes tonight, that's exactly what I wanted. Now I have to figure out if every time that fire is lit it will blow up or if it can be directed for a good use."

"Indubitably, Skip. I'm afraid I have limited exposure to the current scientific findings of psychology that may be apt for this scenario. I have always found the field to suffer from the confirmation bias of the theorizers. It is easy to diagnose sickness in others when you see your own neuroses in your patients."

I didn't send LL into minor league exile but he wasn't allowed to leave the hotel for the entire series and was not to be paid for the games he would miss. There was some grumbling among the players but nothing that didn't dissolve the minute we took the field and the ump yelled, "Play ball." If anything it brought my starting infielders closer together. We went another three games without an error and Alex got International League player of the week for an unassisted triple play turned behind Three Way on Tuesday night. We didn't play well the first game with Gas Can Jones living up to his name. We were now two months into the season and my number three starter had one win (decent underlying stats) and my number five starter had a goose egg (terrible stats). Every fifth game I toyed with the idea of going to a four man rotation or moving Mendenhall to the starting rotation. He was now flourishing in the set up slot just as he had been solid as a middle relief guy. Both scenarios made me worry about inning count and what had happened to Three Way when we were together in the Rays system. Here I was using twelve pitchers and throwing an automatic loss in my rotation and getting shit for it on local radio. Of course if they weren't accusing me of being a moron for running a pitching staff the way my bosses told me, they were stoking juicy rumors about why Alex and I both had mashed up faces and another player had been locked in the hotel. You'd never know from the pre-game interviews that we managed to sneak out of Rochester with 2 out of 3 and were now tied for third in the division at 23-30.

CHAPTER FOURTEEN

"Apartment sweet apartment," Gail said, beaming, as she removed her hands from my eyes. "What do you think?"

"I see you've been busy while we were on the road." Gail surprised me by taking a plane ride out of Sky Harbor International Airport less than three hours after her last final let out. While we finished out the road trip on a high note with a sweep in Gwinnet who looked destined for the cellar again this year and taking two of three from our division rivals in Louisville, Gail had been packing up all of my stuff at her sister-in-law's to go to a high rise apartment that she had used her last paycheck to make the next two months' rent.

"You were out on a nine game trip and didn't hear from me once. You didn't think that was odd? By now I figured you'd know that if I go radio silent without a big fight that I'm up to something."

"Like having a child with the mail man."

Gail laughed, "Something like that, you silly goose."

"Mrs. Freeman, please don't mistake me for a goose again. I'm a Mud Hen. It could cost me my job."

"Say, what is a mud hen?"

"I have no idea."

I grabbed the building keys from her and headed for the service elevator. She had been waiting in the parking lot to Fifth/Third Field near the player's entrance this evening when the charter bus returned us to Toledo for the first time since the calendar read May. The success of the trip had held off road weariness for a while but somewhere north of Dayton on I-75 everyone had wilted. Conversations with The Walrus dried up. Good Hands Alston was in the next row, equally silent except for a moan that escaped his lips when he shifted in his seat. The ice had turned to water in the plastic bag that was leaking onto his hamstring with diminishing efficiency. We had gone from upstate New York to the Deep South and back while playing nine games in nine days. I had been looking forward to bed, probably on the undersized sofa in my office as I doubted I had the wherewithal to make it up towards Detroit tonight.

As we entered the parking lot, it was surprising to see two cars parked next to each other a couple of spaces away from where the players' vehicles were grouped together. It was shocking when I realized that both cars had women sitting on their respective hoods chatting as if they had been old friends and that one of those women was my wife. "Hey Wal, why is my wife in Toledo and talking to your new girlfriend?" I asked.

His response was classic Walrus, "She's not my girlfriend Har but we had agreed to do dinner tonight. Turns out she has some things she wants to talk about that I have been encouraging her in pursuing. The better question to ask might be, what exactly has she told Gail about the day you two first met?" Bastard.

"I think that's everything Hon," I called out as my sweaty, sore body tried to straighten out one more time without injury. Gail had moved to the bedroom where she was already busy unpacking some of her personal belongings.

"What's in that box, dear?" she asked. I tried to read the permanent marker scrawling from where I was standing but even bold strokes of black ink require reading glasses from this distance now so I stooped with caution to get a closer look. It hadn't been a heavy box nor was its shape warped by the weight of the contents inside like some of the other boxes I had brought up. The note on the side of the box simply said celebration.

"Don't know, it's light and says celebration on the side."

"That's perfect," she nearly squealed. "Just the box I hoped you had. Bring it in here."

I walked into the bedroom, fully furnished which was a plus, but it was traditional in nature much like the rest of the apartment and Gail had always gone for contemporary. It had always been a source of tension between Gail and my Mother, probably a small spat as far as most mother-in-law relationships go. "Is this going to work for you?" I asked.

"What?"

"You know exactly what."

She looked around the room. "The lease is only month to month, I'll survive through the season I think."

"This place was let month to month? It's pretty snazzy. How'd you manage that?"

"Oh, you know. Women can be very persuasive," she replied coyly. My wife was better than most at that, especially at her age. She's got the Rene Russo look going on from *The*

Thomas Crown Affair. I had no doubt that if she saw fit, she'd be able to leave me for a forty year old guy who had more money. Luckily, I'm all charm. "Dear, you're all sweaty."

"Well, that's what happens when a guy lugs boxes to an apartment. You should be happy I can still do that stuff at all."

"Aww…poor baby. I'm not letting you on the bed like that though. Towels are already up in the bathroom, go take a shower."

"What if I don't want to?"

"Then you'll never know what's in the celebration box."

"You sly minx," I said with a devilish grin.

"I love when you smile like that," she replied with a wink. That was all I needed to decide that the bathroom option was a sound one.

"You should join me," I teased from inside.

"Tempting, but I think I'll pass. Don't stay in there too long though."

She didn't have to tell me twice. Once I figured out how the damn thing worked (I'm ashamed to say how long that took) it was a quick scrub, no prunes. I toweled off and peeled back the shower curtain to find that she had hung a change of clothes from the hook on the inside of the bathroom door. It was just a pair of underwear and a cotton t-shirt but the note taped to the garments said, "Hopefully these won't be on too long."

I walked out to see Gail sitting on our new bed with a small checkered cloth with a spread of wine and finger food; cheese and crackers, some cold cuts of meat. "That looks

117

rather precarious," I said.

"I thought you might be hungry and I definitely needed some ambrosia after all of the hard work I've put in during the past week." She raised her wine glass filled with a deep red merlot.

I sat down gently at the edge of the bed. "You've certainly surprised me. I wasn't sure that was possible but tonight definitely did it. I picked the right girl."

"How do you always know the right thing to say?" she said with an undercurrent of huskiness to her voice.

I poured my own glass of wine, took a sip after I filled it too close to the brim, and looked at her receptively. "Probably the same way you knew I could use a snack," I joked.

She laughed softly, just enough for the sparkle to find its way to the corner of her eyes. There were a few more lines there than when I had met her but the beauty had never faded. "You know what they say about the way to a man's heart…" I moved my hand to the platter in front of me and lifted a cracker. My other hand moved towards the cheese and meat to make myself a bite sized sandwich but Gail placed her hand on mine. "Let me," she said.

"On one condition."

She cocked her head, trying to probe where I was going with this. "Sure."

"Why did you go with the picnic motif?"

"Don't think of it as just a picnic Har. Think of it as a meal in a wild forest, a great adventure. Tonight is the start of something new, our next adventure."

"I think I like the sound of that." I ate the crackers and spread directly from her hand, lingering with my teeth on her finger which I gave a playful nibble to. "There are worse ways to begin a journey."

Next I made her something to eat and Gail took it directly from my hand in an equally seductive manner. We clinked glasses and washed our food down with some more wine. After exchanging a handful of more bites I said, "there is just one problem with your plan."

"And what is that?" she nearly purred with lust.

"It is putting a crimp in my animal spirits."

"I've seen you work your magic in more restrictive places than this, Mr. Freeman."

"I was a younger man then." I took the two corners nearest me and nodded for her to do the same on her hand. We delicately moved the cloth and what was left of the food off of the bed and onto the dresser against the wall. I stepped to her and kissed her for the first time in what seemed like ages. We ended our embrace long enough for her to sit onto the bed and slowly scoot towards the pillow, her eyes locked on mine.

"You kiss better than the mailman."

"Is that so? I'm sure that isn't the only area you'll find me exceptional at." I moved in a graceful motion I didn't know I possessed anymore, fluidity until my chest was above hers. We kissed again, my mouth locking with her own until I moved to her neck and my hand pulled at the straps of her thin nightie. It fell to her waist, exposing her breasts to my hungry mouth. I reached for the nightstand, brought the bottle of merlot towards us and dripped its remnants onto the front of her.

"Oh, he doesn't do that either."

I moved to clean Gail of the sweet elixir I had created, a heady mix of fermented grape and the intoxicating taste of her skin. When I finished I began to make love to the best woman a fool like me could ever have been lucky enough to find. It was lustful, passionate, shallow, playful and, at all times, eloquent. It was the first time she had been mine in over three months. Absence had indeed made the heart fonder.

CHAPTER FIFTEEN

The warmth that had suddenly surged into the Midwest over the past week was still present the next morning. I eased out of my contented slumber, taking my time to enjoy the feel of Gail within my arms and the meditative thrum of the air conditioning which was already working hard. I felt her breathing speed up as she followed me from sleep to consciousness a half hour later. "Mmmm, are we cuddling this morning?" Gail asked.

"Love to but I have to go find The Walrus. He's been exercising every day in the morning at the ball park. AC is already on so I doubt he'll wait too long this morning," I said.

"Didn't you guys just have a four hour bus ride yesterday to talk shop?"

"Yeah but we were wore out. Today will be more productive. I've found The Walrus does some of his best thinking just after a workout. Too bad that he let himself go for so long."

"He'll make it work. I already noticed a change for the better when I saw him yesterday. He's handling the break up quite well but dating a 20 year old might be a bit much, don't you think?"

I got up from the bed reluctantly and walked to the curtains to take my first look at the view from up here. Haze settled over Farr Park, obscuring everything from the Maumee River east. I could just make out its murky waters, brown silt and fertilizer run off seeping at a snail's pace towards Lake

Erie. "Wal isn't dating Amber. I'm not sure exactly what their relationship is. She was kind of lost and I think he has been lending a supportive ear."

"I know they're not dating dear, just testing you. I am kind of curious why you never mentioned that you saw her naked though."

I spun around on my heel, "How did you find that out?"

"Well, you know, we had time to kill and it just kind of came out."

"That's the kind of stuff girls talk about when they are just chatting? I don't want you to give us guys grief over locker room talk ever again."

"Easy, babe," Gail said. "She's a nice girl and it doesn't sound like that was your intent. I want to know about it, is all. She's good looking and I can't compete with that anymore, hiding something like that can only lead to jealousy. I just don't want to see something come between us. We've had a good run and last night did nothing to make me worry it isn't going to get better."

I moved to the side of the bed, leaned down, and kissed Gail deeply. "Hon, you can compete with anyone. Don't ever think differently."

I was right. It was muggy, tropical really. The kind of oppressive stickiness that seems to bring out the bugs in hordes. The late Spring had at least kept the mosquitos at bay but everything else was out in abundance. Flys, gnats, you name it, stuck to your shirt to die in a miasma of human fluids

122

acting like nature's best bug trap. If you weren't doing bleachers, like me, it was worse. Without prejudice, they landed on my neck, arms, shirt, and face. The insects reveled in the attention they got from buzzing in my ear, drawing an instinctual swat attempt that failed at all times. "It's awful out here," I said.

"Not good. Not Georgia heat though," The Walrus replied.

"Ok, tough guy."

"Aren't you from Phoenix? This shouldn't even register."

I shrugged. "We always have our air on. Honestly I think the worst thing you could do to get used to the heat is live in a place that is 110 all summer long."

"It has been two weeks, I don't feel much more athletic," Wal said with reservation.

"I've noticed improvement. Gail said she'd noticed a difference too."

"Are you saying that the two of you wasted last night talking about me?" The Walrus said with a smirk.

I smirked back. "I didn't say that at all."

We transitioned after a while to the lineup, whether Andre's last five games were a flash in the pan or if he was going to end up challenging 40 home runs this year. Wal wasn't sure, I was the optimist. Too bad first base in the Tigers organization is locked for the foreseeable future. We talked about whether his power might end up being trade bait, especially if Andre continued to improve at first like he had since Alex solidified the infield. I said I hoped not, I liked the guy. The Walrus commiserated saying that everyone does. We talked about Alex's bat and whether the sharp singles against Louisville meant anything. Walrus was still sure that his stance could never lead to success but I pointed out how his hands were beginning to still before the pitch without anyone saying a thing. I said that he was going the other way like a guy should to bust a slump. The Walrus said that may be only because Alex can't get around on a fastball. I thought about how Al Kaline used to talk about it not being a bad thing getting jammed up and in but didn't bring it up.

We talked about the rotation and I brought up letting Mendenhall assume the fifth starter's spot. Walrus liked it, you can never have too much left-handed pitching he argued. I brought up the fact that Mendenhall had never done more than 74 innings in a year and being moved to starter, even here in June, would get him to around 150 by season's end assuming he pitched well. The Walrus talked about working in a system of skipping starts when an off day or the All-Star Break allowed us to keep everyone else on proper rest. I liked the idea and wondered why I didn't think of it. Neither of us knew who we could get to replace Mendenhall as the eighth inning guy and I eventually ruled that a set-up man was more important than the last spot of the rotation. The Walrus talked about how Drake was more comfortable on the mound. I joked that a first win will do that for you, especially when it was just bad luck that he wasn't getting much run support. The Walrus said that if he kept calm for too much longer we'd have to stop calling Drake 'Ducky.'

We talked about fielding, namely who would replace Good Hands in left. The Walrus and I both agreed that Marcus Woods wasn't a suitable replacement long term. He talked about putting Brock Bisby out there, Bisby hadn't been doing much playing since the infield shake up. I floated out a radically different idea. I said I wanted to put LL in left. Walrus didn't harrumph or protest but I could tell at first blush he wasn't a fan of the thought. He had lost weight, or at least mass, but it had been a long time since I saw him meditate for so long. He stared forward until his eyes crossed towards his nose, painted red from exertion like a clown with a splotchy brush. The Walrus asked if LL had ever played left. I said I didn't know, didn't think so, but he had something to prove and I liked his odds with a chip on his shoulder. The Walrus said go for it. I had already made up my mind to.

"I have a favor to ask, Har, since you're here."

"What's that?"

"Amber suffers from a lack of confidence so I suggested to her that she should do something that terrifies her, see that failing is just a step to success if you let it be."

"Sounds like good advice. What do you need me for then?" I asked.

"I told her to think of something that she thought she'd be terrible at while we were on the road trip. That's what dinner last night was for, to check on her progress. She surprised me, said that she had booked a slot for Open Mic Night at the comedy club tonight."

"Which club?"

"The only damn one around."

"Sorry, I don't know. Guess I haven't made a conscious effort to make Toledo home until recently."

"The one down in Perrysburg, The Funny Bone."

"Please tell me they didn't actually name it The Funny Bone," I pleaded.

"Oh, they did. It's a chain, there's a bunch all over the country. They are pretty big time actually."

"That name is so bad though. Do they serve ribs there?"

"I have no idea," The Walrus answered.

"I've got this picture of some overweight Ohio farm girls with their Daisy Dukes and a checkered shirt tied at the belly button coming around collecting barbeque splattered bones in metal pails," I rambled.

"I think it's a bit classier than a redneck club that *Maxim* would sponsor for fat chicks Har."

"So you want me to come for moral support then? When Amber's routine bombs?" I asked.

"If it bombs," The Walrus corrected.

"Why me? I didn't think Amber liked me much."

"She loves Gail."

"Oh...that could be dangerous."

The Walrus smiled. "Yeah, it could."

CHAPTER SIXTEEN

Turns out the Funny Bone Club is pretty easy to find. Just take I-75 past the Turnpike to 475 and it is right off the freeway. Gail had gotten my brother to agree to us borrowing a vehicle since it was only used when the kids found their way back home. The 2007 Ford Escape had plenty of room to pick up The Walrus on the way and we got there early. It was still another hour before the steaks were to come out so I made the club rich by ordering too many appetizers. The Walrus didn't seem to care about my rudeness, he just picked from his small Tupperware container of greens. While this raised some eyebrows, no one went so far as to call The Walrus on his malfeasance. I groused that I'd never get away with it and Gail gave me a sharp, obvious poke in the ribs saying aloud that I would if I was more of a gentleman.

Slowly the room filled around us to about three quarters of capacity, not bad for a weeknight. A few didn't seem to have any allegiances to tonight's acts but most did. A cluster of suits made me think a lawyer or banker might be on tap. A group of young white kids who dressed as if a couple of holes in their punk rock t-shirts would make them look tough were laughing childishly about how "bamf" it was that one of their friends actually took the dare. I was surprised they were let in at all. A group of moms looked like they had decided this week's book club would be postponed to fulfill someone's "dream" that probably had to do with a mid-life crisis. I was under the impression that running marathons was the vanity project du jour but a good parenting comedy routine might not be so bad.

I had three trays of appetizers which Gail helped out on by only eating a single cheese stick. I had the rest of those, buffalo wings, and some spicy dough balls that were referred to obliquely as 'poppers.' All of the pregaming made my steak seem just ok. Gail ordered lightly buttered perch, probably fresh from the lake, which she said was quite good. Gail and her fish, it's pretty hard to get fresh seafood when you live in a desert so she always gets it when she is out of town. Plus, she knows I won't try to steal a bite, can't stand the stuff. The lights dimmed as our plates cleared. The emcee rose from his seat to head to the microphone that stood naked and alone under the glare of harsh light.

"Is this seat taken?" I recognized the voice.

"Trev?"

"Small world, huh Skip?"

"Seat's all yours," The Walrus chimed in.

"Oh sorry Wal, didn't see who you were coming in. It gets pretty dark in here during shows," Trev Fryer said.

"Trev, I'd like you to meet my wife. Gail, say hello to my third baseman." They exchanged an awkward handshake, fumbling more than clasping hands because their eyes had yet to adjust, as the emcee tried to warm up the crowd and succeeded modestly.

"So you come here often then, Trev?" Gail asked.

Me and The Walrus were both staring at him now, surprised at this encounter. Our eyes had now compensated some, capable of reading vague facial expressions. "I like to get away from things a bit, when the stress of performing in front of people gets to me. Prayer helps but laughing is better. It's nice to sit in darkness and watch someone else for a change," Trev said.

"I'm surprised you are ok with the raunchiness of live comedy," I blurted out. Gail's elbow got another workout.

"Why's that?" Trev asked.

Gail glared at me to pick my words carefully. "I don't know, you just seem more…traditional in your values than the cussing and sex jokes we'll probably hear tonight."

"Yeah, it gets bad at times but if practicing Christians stopped watching anything that could be deemed inappropriate we'd never see anything. Culture would like you to think that makes us 'bible thumpers' weird, I'd argue it says a lot about the culture and probably not for the better. I've never watched the amateurs so I'll probably just laugh at how bad they are rather than care what they're actually saying," Trev responded.

"So you don't know anyone going on stage tonight?" The Walrus asked.

"Nope. How about you guys?"

"We're here for moral support for a girl named Amber. They haven't said when she'll be going on," Gail said.

"How do you know her?"

"I met her through one of the guys on the team," I said. "Wal's been helping her with some stuff."

"I wouldn't say help. More like mentoring. You know,

typical twenty year old girl stuff," The Walrus said.

Gail leaned into my ear and whispered, "I like him. He'd be good for Amber."

My eyebrows furrowed and I mouthed, "Trev?" at her wordlessly before exchanging a look at The Walrus. I got another elbow but it seems like Trev hadn't noticed our communications, looking at the emcee as he introduced a middle aged man wearing a sharp suit, navy blue with a heavy pinstripe.

The lights came up after an hour for intermission. We had filtered through seven acts in rapid fire succession. Several routines lasted maybe five minutes but a couple pushed up against the ten minute time limit. One guy, who wasn't any good, was so determined to get through his litany of unfunny one-liners that I thought they might go find a shepherd's hook to yank him off the stage. The guy didn't even have a theme to his work. It grated on the audience like tired knock-knock jokes until the emcee saved us by talking loudly over him until he got the hint.

"Well, that was interesting," I said trying to be diplomatic.

"Some weren't too bad," Trev chimed in.

"Yeah, who did you like?" I asked

"I thought the banker's dead pan act was hilarious," said The Walrus. Gail and Trev were quick to agree.

"It wasn't bad if you like stereotypical humor. Reminded me too much of *Office Space* though," I said.

"Oh, you and your encyclopedia of movie knowledge,"

Gail said.

"Hey, I married you when I was young. Trips out of town meant a lot of hotel TVs for me. I can't help it if HBO repeats a movie twelve times until it's stuck forever in a guy's head."

"It's just you honey."

"I bet if we get into a bunch of chick flicks and Katherine Hepburn stuff you know as much as I do."

"You two bicker like a married couple," said The Walrus. That ended it. We got another round of drinks before the lights went down again. Amber was up first in the second half of the night, I didn't envy her. The jokes of the emcee, a professional, were probably better than anything she could write, certainly they would be delivered better. Now that we were heading towards the end, the crowd was a bit restless. If Amber hadn't been the first act after the break they might tune her out but in this slot she had their attention and a short leash. All of a sudden, the room looked to be swimming with sharks.

Amber made her way from the front row, up the handful of steps to the stage. Her walk did not exude confidence and she wilted under the light, a dying violet with a microphone. She gripped the microphone as hard as death itself and leaned in to say her opening line. She got too close, feedback overwhelming her timid voice. A flush of red hit her cheeks as she jerked back sharply. She could not have asked for a worse start and she knew it, squeaking out a small laugh that was childishly endearing. I waited for the boo birds to start, Amber had given them enough chum for a whole set without getting a line out. They never came, instead her coquettish amateurism melted them until the crowd was putty in her hands. She couldn't have been able to see that, blinded by the light trained on her, but I could see she sensed it and confidence trickled into her demeanor.

"Let's try that one again. Anybody out there into nature documentaries?" I saw a couple of hands go up. "Four, that's it? It's ok, you can be honest." Another twelve were raised. "Me personally I love them. I don't think I'll ever forgive Discovery for shifting to pawn shops and garbage pickers." She paused to a laugh. Guy's easy to please. "They make me wonder if Adam ever asked God just what the hell he was thinking." A small smattering of laughter at the seemingly random observation.

"Hear me out," Amber said. "I had a whole host of unusual pets growing up. My parents ran a farm about twenty miles south of here. As a little girl I had a pet cow, a pet pig, a pet chicken but they had a habit of disappearing. When I got old enough to figure out what happened to them I cried an entire day screaming 'How could you?' So they got me a pet I would never lose to the slaughter, a skunk." Laughter.

"He really was the cutest thing. I called him Armani because of his stripes, his stink gland got pulled out and he was just the gentlest thing. When my cousins came from Pittsburgh, I loved to take advantage of all the things they didn't know. Once I led them into a patch of poison ivy, rubbing it all over myself and telling them to do the same, that it didn't do anything. I neglected to tell them that I was rare in that I was immune to it." Laughter. "I grossed them out once just by showing them where milk comes from. And the first time I showed them Armani… hoo, the scare of their lives." Laughter. "They stopped coming, I wonder why." More laughter.

"It was great growing up with an unusual pet until I began wanting Armani to cuddle and he wouldn't do it. My pig never cuddled either." Laughter. "I longed for a puppy, a cute Golden Retriever but my father wouldn't have it. To this day he has yet to give me an explanation." She gave the crowd her saddest expression and 'awww' filled the room. "Instead I got a boa constrictor that I got to feed dead mice, a rat, even a pet rock. I wasn't even born in the 80's." Laughter. "My life was like a nature documentary. Every time I see a great white jumping out of the water in slow motion to rip apart a seal, so majestic in a primal way, I shake my head and think poor Adam." Laughter.

"Can you imagine, God makes him and says 'I made you in my image and you will rule over all the creatures of the land and sea. Why don't you name them.' Adam's probably like 'cool!'" Laughter. "I wonder if he lost his voice?" Laughter. "I can just see God snickering as he brought Adam the hippo and the giraffe, the zebra and a beautiful array of hummingbirds knowing that the insects were saved for last." Laughter. "He tried with tsetse and mosquito but about ten minutes in I can just see him saying, 'God, really?' That's why we call them gnats." Laughter.

"Nothing was really pet material. When Adam asked God

for a companion because he was lonely I wonder if God had his fingers crossed behind his back when he said, 'of course I thought of that.'" Laughter. "I doubt Adam bought it when God pulled a snake from the tree and said, 'Here! He likes to squeeze, I mean cuddle.'" Laughter. "Adam, poor guy, he was just like me, wanting a puppy dog. A loyal, obedient friend whose only needs were to be fed and scratched in return for unconditional love. You'd think that God would have got that right. Instead Adam just got lonelier and demanded a companion that was truly evil, a girl." Hoots from the guys.

"I can just see God asking himself, 'what the bleep is a girl?'" Laughter. "Adam was like, 'you know, a partner like all of the other animals have.' I'm pretty sure God tried to warn him, 'outside of the penguins and the wolves the rest just hit it and quit it.'" Laughter. "Well you know how it went, God made us out of a rib in a garden and told us in the first chapter of his book that men were made of dirt." Laughter. "He didn't really think that one through. The girls who only ordered the cliff notes Bible got that far." More laughter. "We've been a thorn in His side ever since. It didn't take long for Eve to make Him mad. Samson had Delilah. Right on down the line. There are what, three billion of us now? Think of what He sees every day. All of that could have been avoided if He just thought to give Adam a dog. Thank you." The room filled with the loudest applause of the night.

"She's pretty good," I said. "Reminded me of Cosby's material a bit. Presentation could use some work though."

"I thought she was great," Gail said.

The Walrus yawned. "I'm about ready to fall asleep, do we have to stay for the rest or can we get going?"

"Your friend is very talented. I doubt you'll need to provide much moral support tonight," Trev said with a grin. I detected a touch of smitten wistfulness in his voice.

We all made our way outside to the parking lot, waiting for Amber to join us. She came out at a sprint, hopping up and down when she reached us with far too much bubbliness. "How was I? Did it go as well as I thought it did?"

Everyone paid her compliments, Trev's was the longest and most profuse. "I'm sorry, I don't think I know who you are?" Amber said.

"I'm sorry," said The Walrus. "Meet Trev Fryer, one of the players."

"Nice to meet you Trev Fryer," Amber squeaked. She wrapped an enthusiastic hug around all of us before speeding out of the parking lot on Cloud Nine. I pulled out the Escape in a more reserved manner.

"He likes her," I said to Gail.

"You doubted me?" Gail responded.

"Actually yeah."

"You'd think after thirty years of marriage…"

"Has it really been that long?"

Gail rolled her eyes. "Most days, it feels a lot longer than that."

CHAPTER SEVENTEEN

With Gail around, I was happy to spend the next day procrastinating about getting to the ball park. The euphoria that comes with reunion was still in full bloom. It was a six game home set, three against Norfolk who led the South and three against Lehigh. Starting around four o'clock my cell phone started buzzing but I didn't bother picking up for The Walrus. I trusted my staff to get pre-game going smoothly without me. Wal was probably freaking out about our conversation yesterday, putting LL in left without any instruction. I left the apartment at a little after five, Gail giving me a deep kiss at the door to wish me luck. Toledo traffic doesn't have much of a rush hour but an accident slowed me up so I didn't get to Fifth/Third Field until about half past the hour.

I was the last one to the stadium by a long shot and my casual entrance into the full locker room drew a lot of curious glances. Tucked in front of the white board was an easel that hadn't been there yesterday morning. A large rectangle sat on the easel and was covered by a white sheet, Al Percy crouched by its side to ensure the confidentiality of what lay underneath. "Lord Al, today's lecture requires a visual aid?" He hated when I called him Lord Al, like Tennyson. I braced for a rebuke stating that Percy's prowess with the English language paled in comparison to the great poet. I didn't get it.

"I've been trying my hand at statistics the past couple weeks Skip. By my calculations, we have a 98% probability of attaining a playoff spot if we can ambit 86 wins on the season. After our road excursion we're at 28-31, or a 58 win deficit."

"Ok, what's that have to do with a mysterious easel?"

"All shall be illuminated." Al pulled the sheet down revealing a large picture of a hideous beast. It was tall, far larger than an adult male, with jet black, coarse hair. Grey horns spiraled and curled backwards above its animal face. The wild eyes were blood red matching the blood matting hair around the mouth. The creature stood gleefully on two feet, one hooved and the other humanoid. His fingered hands held onto a large spoon to stir the contents of a pot sitting over a fire. The creature stood in a cave that had stacks of bags piled in the background. One sack was in the foreground, opened with a small child's head exposed, his tiny eyes looking out in terror.

"What the fuck is that?"

"The Krampus," Al replied as if I had just asked the dumbest question.

"Is it eating stolen children?"

"He only takes the naughty ones. He comes for them at Christmas according to lore in the Alpine countries."

"That sounds terrifying."

"Yeah, Christmas is a time for celebration. This is even worse than commercializing it," Trev said.

"The Krampus dates to well before the time of the Christ. His current interpretation is a modernized version of an ancient pagan God. He has been clashing with Father Christmas since around the time that decorating pine trees became attached to Jesus. Before that their dressing up was for marking the Winter Solstice and reveling the fact that longer days were coming," said Al.

"Well, Christmas trees were a lot better idea. Those can't cause any nightmares," I said.

"You've obviously never decorated a blue spruce," said The Walrus. I stared at him as if to say he wasn't helping at all. "What? Those things prick and it hurts."

"So, Al, why is a nearly life-size Krampus now terrifying everyone in this locker room?" I asked.

"It is elementary. The Krampus is the fate of the naughty. At this moment, we are not qualified for the playoffs which means we are failing here just like impish German children."

"That's a bit of a stretch, isn't it?"

"We need 58 wins." Al walked to his locker and pulled out a bag. "Inside this bag are an identical number of blocks which provide a far more uplifting picture. For each victory, the hideous Krampus is partially covered until we make our objective. They stick to the board using magnets."

"How did you connect baseball to German Christmases exactly?"

"The Germanic people have a storied tradition of giving to this sport."

"They do?"

"Honus Wagner's sepia portrait wouldn't be a prized possession otherwise," Al said.

I looked at The Walrus for clarification. "He's talking about Honus's baseball card, the most expensive in the world."

"Oh." I turned to look back at the ghastly Krampus. "What the hell, I'll allow it." Al preened with vanity while some others complained. Alex talked about how El Chupacabra was child's play compared to the Krampus. Jermaine Willis broke into laughter. "And you guys want to make jokes about blacks?" I smiled at that as I walked into my office. I had a lineup card to fill out.

Larry Rother, the Norfolk Tide manager, and I shook hands behind the plate as we handed our lineups to the umpire. Larry was one of the good guys in the game and it was nice to see him off to a hot start this season. I made a note to wish him all the best come Thursday when we were done with them. "It has been a couple of crazy weeks for you, huh Har? Seems you're popping up in the news every time I catch wind of what's going on around the league."

"Hopefully they're talking about the fact we've won ten of twelve," I said.

Larry smiled, "Something like that."

I laughed and started to walk back to my dugout. Two familiar faces were looking at me with zeal and waving frantically. I yelled to Gail, "I think this is the first time you've been to a game of mine." Both her and Amber yelled something that was washed away by the pop song coursing from the speakers. "I'll have to be on my best behavior." With a wink I took the steps down to sit next to my buddy The Walrus. He was looking dourly at me.

"You didn't pick up your phone earlier."

"You called?" He was going to see right through that.

"Yeah." Terse but it conveyed the wanted message. "LL has never fielded a single ball in left in his life, never played a ball off the wall or had to hit the cutoff man. I can't believe you're sending him out there," The Walrus said.

"Left is the easiest position on the field."

"Har, you played left."

I smiled, "Yeah, what does that tell you?"

Our side took the field for the top of the first. "LL wasn't a great fielder at his natural position. I can't see why he would take to a position he has no experience at like a duck to water," said Wal.

"What's more important, talent or passion?" I asked.

"Passion. Talent," The Walrus paused for emphasis, "and experience, don't hurt though."

"Good or bad, it should be entertaining."

It wasn't pretty but LL made all of the plays he had to. Unfortunately, there were more balls hit to left, and more runs, than I'd have liked. Toby Mack was scrapping his way to a five inning start with four earned. Mud Hen fans had a lot to cheer about as well. Andre had a two-run homer and Trev, probably trying to impress Amber in the first row, added a home run of his own. As he trotted around third I could picture Amber and Gail whispering about how good Trev's backside looked in uniform.

The Tide had their leadoff hitter up for the fourth time to start the sixth inning. He was a switch hitter but hit for better average and more power from the left side of the plate. Playing the percentages I brought in a left-handed specialist to turn him around. The Tide's number three hitter was also left-handed so I was hoping to get a full inning out of Robert Charmin today. Charmin's stuff doesn't get above eighty-five but his long arms allow the ball to start behind a left-handed batter which makes it nearly impossible for them to pick up what Charmin is throwing. To lefties he features a fastball on occasion, mostly a get-me-over pitch to keep them honest, and a lazy slider that floats off the plate outside like a roll of toilet paper being launched over a tree during a high school prank. Robert Charmin never seemed to mind being called 'TP,' his stuff was soft after all. To righties, Robert lived away with a plus changeup that was rarely a strike and tried to freeze a batter with two strikes every once in a while by painting the inside corner with his fastball. Robert rarely saw right-handers.

Trev moved in until he was standing just inside of the bag at third looking for a bunt. The leadoff hitter took strike one, laid off a changeup down and away, then fouled a bunt back behind the plate to get two strikes. Trev had charged the ball hard as he was taught to do and caught Amber and Gail yelling from the first row. I could see him smile at them, not breaking his stare as he settled back into his position in front of third base. I tried to yell at Trev for him to move back, with two strikes there wouldn't be another bunt attempt, but he was entranced with who was sitting behind the dugout more than he was with the game. Trev didn't notice that Robert

Charmin had gone into his motion and delivered at the inside corner. The pitch didn't fool the hitter and he turned on it, driving it square in two hops at my distracted third baseman. Trev heard the crack of the bat, trying to return his attention to where it should have been all along. He wasn't fast enough to locate the groundball to make a play with his glove. Trev was left with the awful choice of resorting to sticking out his chest and flexing to absorb the impact. The ball caught him flush in the diaphragm, dropping to the grass in front of him. Trev staggered backwards like *Paul Bunyan* withstanding a charge from *Babe the Blue Ox*. On adrenaline, Trev reached down and fired across the diamond to get the speedy runner by a couple of steps. Without waiting for the team doctor he began ambling towards the dugout like a drunk. Trev made it down the steps but passed out from the pain before he got to the bench. Luckily, Amber and Gail couldn't see that.

"He didn't use his jaw to knock it down like George Kell, at least," I said to The Walrus.

The Walrus was more concerned about Trev's health than my joke. "He'll make it," I said, "but he won't do that again." I turned down the bench towards Brock Bisby, "You're in for Trev."

I mixed and matched out of my bullpen through three scoreless, but nerve racking, innings. It helped keep thoughts about Trev from dominating the evening. I had come across as callous towards his injury but the mask was skin deep. TP gave way to Claudio Vega who struck out two before walking two on eight straight balls. Claudio has never learned to repeat his delivery and his command has always lacked because of it. In any relief appearance you may get something great or something cringe worthy. Tonight, he showed a lot of both. Claudio being used in a late inning situation is not my preferred option, enough to give a guy an ulcer to be honest, but the specter of extra innings made me hold Mendenhall in reserve. I called to Pigpen to have a long conversation on the mound after the second walk. I had twelve pitchers on my staff and none I wanted to see in such a situation. Two righties were warming up in the pen but I didn't know who to go to so I was now hiding my indecision between the conceit that neither was loose yet. I figuratively held my nose and went with Marquise Winston. The first pitch exploded up the gap and all the way to the wall. Two runs came in, we lost 6-4.

I sat up in the apartment's living room with my cell phone next to me until I got the call with the all clear on Trev. He had a bruised sternum and it hurt to breathe but nothing broke. He was officially listed as day-to-day. A sigh of relief found its way from my chest as I hung up. Tomorrow when I got to the field it would be back to business but, alone, I got to show to no one in particular I was a human being.

There was no way that I was going to eat a series opening loss and then throw Gas Can Jones against one of the best teams in all of the International League the next night. Given the off day the past Monday, I decided to skip my number five starter for my ace. Three Way continued to live up to his word in game two of the series, going seven and two-thirds scoreless for another win. Dirk Bobbsey followed suit making it six scoreless innings, his pitch count driving him out of the game early with Mendenhall and Grissom picking him up.

Without the clean-up hitter, the offense scratched out enough. On Wednesday, Jermaine Willis had his best night of the year with a walk and three singles. In the first inning he stole second with one out but was stranded. In the third inning he ignited a rally with two outs. His previous steal caused him to be the center of attention for the pitcher who threw over several times. The Tide first baseman was on the bag and the second baseman was cheating to cover if Jermaine tried to steal again. I missed Good Hands in the two spot in my lineup but Chuck was able to send a grounder the other way and through the giant hole on the right side of the Norfolk infield to put two on. Andre didn't waste the opportunity, hitting a home run.

Wednesday's game saw Lord Al Percy shine, driving in a run on three hits. He scored twice, once driven in by LL and the other time by Alex, their rivalry starting to spark production at the bottom of the order. Alex's double was off the wall on the fly, his average now at .275 with power coming on since the call up. I looked at The Walrus as Alex gave the sign of the cross at second base. "Don't say anything," The Walrus warned.

"It'll be short, four words," I teased.

"Don't."

The hideous Krampus now had two more tiles

obstructing his cave of Christmas horrors.

CHAPTER EIGHTEEN

The Lehigh Iron Pigs were living up to their name this year, looking content to go wire to wire in the sty of the East. The first two games we won easily, Drake didn't have a single ball hit back up the middle against him, and cruised comfortably. They say good pitching is contagious and the starting staff was finally showing that, four quality starts in a row. It's funny, the quality start is one of those stats that baseball guys scoff at and there's good reasons for it, but string those puppies together and managing becomes the easiest thing in the world. I was about to gloat about how at this rate there wasn't going to be enough work for my seven man bullpen then Gas Can took the hill.

Strong southwesterly winds that crashed into the stands behind the plate and raced out of Fifth/Third to left. It was an offensive bonanza, eight home runs and twenty-two runs in a game that went eleven innings. Alex drove in the winning run with a home run to left that was estimated at 400 feet.

Clenched fists and cheers exploded over the dugout railing with the mayhem spilling out towards home plate, waiting for Alex to finish his trot around the bases. About halfway between third and home, Alex slowed until he was nearly running in place. Andre roared at home, his meat hook of a hand waving him in with such vigor that I think Alex was actually scared. From my location, a step onto the grass in front of where the dugout opened to the field, Alex's fear didn't look unjustified. Without warning Alex sprinted towards home, trying to touch the plate and get to the safety of the club house, before his teammates had time to properly celebrate. Andre reached out with one arm and pulled the Cuban off his feet. Andre delicately placed Alex's foot onto home plate before presenting his catch to the rest of the mob. I could hear Alex screaming don't as he disappeared into the sea of humanity.

"Is that rape?" The Walrus asked.

"I'm pretty sure it can only be construed as rape if the victim has a whistle," I joked back.

"Some of those 'atta boy' pats have a bit of zip to them."

"They're having fun, we're having fun," I said. "I missed this."

"So did I, Har."

We went to Indianapolis next. I was confident in my team, good rolls never seem like they are going to end and we were definitely riding a hot streak. Placing the .500 mark in our rear view mirror we now had second place in the division in our sights as summer officially began. Standing in our way were the Indians (original, huh?). The Indianapolis ace, Griff Vernier, was doing his best to get a call up. He started the season hot and was getting better as we neared the All Star Break. If he made it a full season down here it looked like he was a Triple Crown pitching contender as he had a comfortable lead in strike outs and ERA and was a win better than John Targas of the Columbus Clippers. The West only has four teams but it had plenty of pitching.

Three Way had put together four straight wins but his stuff didn't compare to Vernier's. If Three Way was going to match him he'd have to out pitch him. Both pitchers faced early threats, we had men on first and third with one out in the first but a strike out from Trev in his first at-bat since the injury, and a weak ground ball from Lord Al ended the scoring chance. Indianapolis got a two-out double to right but LL chased a ball down at the guard rail which separates the field of play from the lower level of seating. He hit it at mid-thigh causing him to flip so that the back of the head wound up in a lap in the front row with his feet making it to the second. LL's *Sonic the Hedge Hog* rotation didn't collide with a person, the fans had leaned defensively into the seats next to them, so his tail bone had no cushion from the hard plastic backing. LL raised his glove in triumph to show the third base umpire the ball. Once he had awkwardly made it to his feet, still in the stands, he struck up a conversation with a female a couple seats over and stole some roasted almonds from another.

"He definitely has his swagger back. That'll hurt in the morning though," said The Walrus.

I watched him climb back over the railing, in a controlled manner this time, too controlled. "He's smarting all right. Do you think this rivalry with Alex has gone too far? Both are hitting well, in LL's case better than ever, and LL has survived out in left as a novice. That's good but his drive to prove himself has him making up for getting a bad read on the ball or taking a bad route by playing reckless. He's called off both

Jermaine and Alex pretty aggressively on balls that were easier plays if he had just backed them up in the past couple weeks."

"I'll talk to him about it," said The Walrus.

"My position, my lecture," I said. "I put him through a lot the past month so a fuel check is probably needed. Good Hands is unable to even do short sprints still, so LL is my left fielder and is very important to this team. I need to find out where exactly his head is at, channel the good and try and diffuse whatever is still lingering from Rochester."

Kevin Costner starred in three baseball movies and *For Love Of The Game* is easily the worst. Given the other two are both classics perhaps that isn't as bad as it sounds. My problems with the movie stem from the idea that a ball player is at his best when he blocks out everything else. It is unrealistic to think that. Imagine a football team that claimed it didn't care about home field advantage and didn't feed off the energy of the crowd. In football, the media lionizes the "twelfth man" as not just a quirk of the NFL or college experience but a game changing asset.

To watch a pitcher at the top, or near the top, of his game is to see someone who is in tune with everything, not nothing at all. On the road, he hears the heckling from each individual fan. He grips the ball and can feel how the mud that was applied by the umpire before the game interacts with the ridges of his finger tips. He can count each seam as he changes grip from pitch to pitch, delivering all of the weapons in his repertoire with accuracy. His foot finds the same groove in front of the plate, aware of the loose sediment that has rolled into the hollow since the last pitch. He can sense the thoughts of the catcher before he puts down the sign and knows when to break from the game plan. He hears the calls of the men behind him. He hears more, the heart beats that arc across the infield. Before he enters his wind-up he knows their potential range, where the ball can be hit that will result in an out. To see a pitcher at the top of his game is to watch a human being reach a realm of understanding of the universe around him that most people associate with drug use.

Pitcher's duels invoke involuntary admissions from those watching that any pitch could be the deciding factor. Perhaps because of this, every pitch becomes the deciding factor. As Three Way and Vernier settled in, a memorable night unfolded. Neither team had a hit after the first inning with Vernier walking Wampum in the fifth, his moral crusade driven energy only inspiring a lone base on balls. Even with enthusiasm, batters tonight were hopelessly outmatched, like the dissenter in Tiananmen Square against a convoy of Chinese tanks. The bottom of the eighth finally saw a hard hit ball, a high drive down the line in left. The ball ran out of steam and began to curl towards the stands. As the guard rail continued from home plate it broke its parallel track with the foul line. As the rail moved closer to fair territory it grew in height to ten feet. The wall took a ninety degree turn when it was equal with the foul pole. The intersection of unforgiving concrete barely ten feet out of fair territory provided a trap for left fielders. With experience you learned to slide and try to backhand the ball slicing away from you, safely grinding to a stop before you made contact. LL didn't have experience. LL took off after the ball and didn't slow down as he disappeared from my view. An image flashed before me of his wrist absorbing the impact of a collision, shattering as hand and glove bent backwards at an unnatural angle. A fly ball was enough to energize the crowd but their roar couldn't drown out the sickening thud that traveled most of 330 feet back to my ears. That wasn't a wrist.

I didn't need word from Jermaine in center or Trev at third to know something awful had happened. I didn't listen to my knee and broke for the crumpled heap in front of the foul pole as fast as I could. The heap didn't move but it was still alive, a low moan painfully escaping from a face I couldn't see, tucked at an unnatural angle towards LL's chest. I didn't try to roll him over since it was impossible to know how bad he was hurt. A wave of relief that I hadn't discovered *Bump Bailey* broke apart as I leaned over LL. His lower jaw was hanging at a 45 degree angle from where it should have been.

He didn't move his head when a foreign object floated into the corner of his vision. I could see his pupils roll toward me, the pupils dilating as they recognized me. Another soft moan escaped his broken jaw, almost as if by mistake. The soft utterance sent a tremble through the rest of his body, a tear rolled down his cheek to be enveloped by blood. I knelt next to him, "Rodrigo, don't say a thing. You're hurt bad. Doc's on his way." He cried out again, louder this time with a greater

151

tremble and a larger tear. His eyes moved from me to the glove on his left hand. It opened and revealed the ball. "You did good, LL," I whispered.

I looked back to see where the help was, it had felt like an hour since I had gotten out there. The rest of the world returned and a hush sat over the stadium. It had been just a couple of seconds. The doctor was within 50 feet now, his pace quickening. My worry must have been apparent. I thought about how that was a bad precedent, leaders must be calm in the face of a crisis. I desperately wanted to be sitting in my apartment waiting to hear about my player's condition so my concern was kept between me and God. The Indians' medical staff was now rushing out of the home dugout.

Sometime after forever, they were joined by an ambulance through the groundskeeper's entrance and a host of EMTs. I had long since retreated from LL's immediate vicinity, trying to bring calm back to my demeanor. The ball in his glove played in front of my eyes. Tomorrow we would begin again in the bottom of the eighth, at least the catch counted. The pain, the hours of rehab and determination, that was ahead for him. It may be small solace but I imagined that it would prove invaluable. My mind thought back to that day in Minneapolis, my foot catching a seam in the AstroTurf. My knee pivoted and moved to get back to third base to avoid the pickoff throw but everything below it stayed in place until I felt that first pop. The tag on my shoulder that ended the inning I only remember because of film. Fixing knees then was a crap shoot and mine didn't turn out well. I had to rehab knowing all of this was because of an embarrassment, knowing that my knee could never get back to the way it was. I was glad that LL didn't have to think about the same.

I walked back to the dugout and told The Walrus to pull the team off the field and get everyone back to the hotel. I had a long night ahead of me in the waiting lounge at the local hospital.

CHAPTER NINETEEN

"Sir, visiting hours have ended for the evening." The nurse couldn't have been five feet tall and her words came out smaller still. I sighed, I guess that they had to pay lip service to the rules but it was obvious that this girl was not in any mood to enforce them. Somewhere else I would have probably laughed but hospitals have a funny way of reducing a man's threshold for games. My expression was severe enough to make her gulp hard before adding, "Only family is allowed to be in the emergency wing overnight."

"I'm his manager. He is family." I paused to force a smile to try and ease the nurse's apprehension, "In a dysfunctional kind of way."

"I see," she squeaked, returning without issue to her work station. If Trev was here I'd needle him about how a girl like that could possibly inherit the world. He wasn't though, instead I was sure he was talking to Amber back home. She had taken an interest in his recovery, it seems that his interest in her was mutual. Not that I was complaining, I had figured his bruised ribs would keep him out for this whole trip and, given the injuries to Good Hands and now LL, my lineup didn't need to be missing its clean-up hitter as well.

Thoughts of baseball were short lived, as it should have been. For a major city, Indianapolis was quiet tonight. The large campus of St. Vincent's on 86th had only two arrivals after 10 PM. Sitting in the lounge with *CNN's* replay of their primetime shows as my only company caused the night to drag on. I found a chair that backed against the wall and tried to curl into a position that would let me catch some shut eye. My eyes closed but my brain never stopped, the haunting image of LL's jaw unfolding on the back of my eyelids. I heard shuffling as the nurses changed shifts. The new crew didn't give me the spiel about how I was here past visitor's hours and I was glad for it. My eyes closed again. I heard more shuffling but I kept my eyes closed. I figured that I had probably fallen asleep without realizing it so I didn't bother to check out another changing of the guard.

The steps got closer, maybe the janitor? It could be a security guard. My eyes opened now to see a short man in a doctor's white coat. His head was bald, reflecting the harsh glare of the fluorescent lights above. As my eyes adjusted to being used again, his features came into focus. He looked like so many older doctors. The little bit of hair left on his head was unkempt and crawling over his ears. His forehead was heavy with wrinkles, the sign of a serious man who had spent his life dealing with serious things. "I believe you are here on behalf of the young ball player," he said in the smarmy way that doctor's talk, as if everything is meant rhetorically.

"Mr. Rodrigo Montero, yes. He's my left fielder."

"Don't tell anyone I am talking to you, Mr. Montero's condition is protected information according to HIPAA. Since you are not family nor Mr. Montero's general practitioner I am legally forbidden from sharing the details with you."

I held my hand up, reached into my pocket and produced a release form that all players are required to sign once rosters are finalized. "That's already taken care of. Mr. Montero is single and has no family in the country. I have permission to act as his legal representative, as does the team doctor and trainer."

"That's good, his recovery will be a long one. In this day and age, when guys return in a couple of months from a blown knee, I won't rule out Mr. Montero playing again this season." He paused, "Did I touch a nerve?"

"What? Oh, no. Go on," I said.

"But I wouldn't count on it. The damage to Mr. Montero's jaw was extensive. It fractured in multiple locations and dislocated to such a degree that we actually had to reconstruct the hinge…the pivot point that allows a man to open and close his mouth. The ligaments tore, and the muscle there stretched to a degree that I have rarely seen in my days as a surgeon." The man ticked it off as if he was discussing a culture on a petri dish. That's how I need to learn to let players go.

"When do you think Rodrigo is going to be ready to go home?" I asked.

"Oh, it will be several days yet. The damage was quite traumatic."

"We are out of here in a couple of days so let me get back to you on contact information for his transport back to Toledo. When will he be available to visitors?"

The sun was crawling over the eastern horizon when I made my first call of the day. The calendar switches over in the middle of the night, others consider it a new day at dawn or when they wake up. For a man who never slept, it felt like a continuation of what everyone else called yesterday. The lack of orientation was matched by fatigue but if Herby noticed it in my voice I knew he'd say nothing. I hadn't talked to anyone in the organization so I didn't know how much people knew about the situation. When baseball is your job, selling advertising space or corporate suites or school group packages, it can be the worst fucking thing on the planet. I doubt that any person that has been involved with the operations aspect of a team hasn't come to hate the sport for a period of time. Except for Herbert Penniford the Third that is, and no he isn't a butler, although he sounds like he should be.

The guy doesn't wink at you when you meet him but you can't help but notice a twinkle in his eye. It positively shines when he says with a smile, "Nice to meet you. Please, call me Herby. Before you ask, I never wanted to be a dentist." He doesn't make much but I think he'd probably be the groundskeeper for free. Happiness is a funny thing, sometimes you don't know if you've found it. If you ask, people will say that the question itself is a pretty good indicator that you aren't but I think that's Freudian bullshit. Life's complicated. I'd tell you to watch Herby for a day and see how you compare. The phone didn't get to the second ring before he answered, voice like noon even though it was just past six. I asked Herby to watch for my wife later in the morning and said he needed to let her into my office so she could pull something out of the second drawer on the right side of my desk. He said, "You can count on me," just like he always did. I wondered if Herby actually did maintenance this early or if he just sat in the outfield, coffee cup in hand, and enjoyed the smell of morning grass as it was unlocked by the energy of the coming day.

I toyed with the idea of calling Gail but I knew I'd be waking her up. Gail had never been a morning person although a long career as a teacher had broken her of some of her worst excesses. I decided nothing could be hurt by letting her sleep another hour or two. My own eyes were trying to close even as I stood upright outside the emergency entrance. Activity was picking up at St. Vincent's and Rodrigo still hadn't come out of his post op slumber. Given how doped up he must be, that might not happen for a while yet. It was a choice between sleep that might not come, and would surely be interrupted by The Walrus, or food. It wasn't much of a choice at all.

My walk from the hospital made me desperately wish that Indianapolis was an older city with a downtown that was clustered in a tight geographic area. I thought for sure that the hospital would have a street level café, one with metal patio chairs arranged on the sidewalk that hummed with commuters going to work, located nearby. I didn't see it, walking until I thought it might have been better to grab a bite from the hospital cafeteria. That is a thought only the clinically insane, or the truly desperate, could conjure. From two blocks away a Dunkin' Donuts sign came into view. I dragged my feet through the urban desert, hoping that my destination wasn't a mirage. I'm not a huge Dunkin' fan, their coffee is always a tad burnt, but I was in no state to be choosy. Every muscle from my lower back on down groaned as I took my seat with a chocolate crème donut and black java. Both were gone in a minute which burned my throat some but the relief that washed through me as my body worked to frantically break down the breakfast into energy made it a fleeting memory.

I loitered for a while then began the trek back to the hospital. On the way I phoned Gail, hoping that 8:45 was late enough. It wasn't, she was groggy when she picked up, "Har, what gives?"

"Did you listen to the game last night?"

"No. It's kind of early for chit chat don't you think?" I often wondered why she married a morning person.

"We had a serious injury. I spent the night in the emergency lobby at the hospital here. I need you to do me a favor. Hopefully it's not too early for that." I get testy when I don't get enough sleep. I'd have to apologize for that later.

"Oh God, sure I can help. What happened?"

"My left fielder, Rodrigo Montero, broke his jaw after he went face first into the wall. He's going to be here for a while, well after we have to get to Scranton. I have emergency contact information to get ahold of his mother down in the Dominican and have her brought up here. No kid deserves to lay in a hospital bed alone recovering from something like this."

"Will do, I'll have her on a flight to Indianapolis tonight if she has a visa and proper documentation."

"I have no idea. I doubt it. She doesn't know English so I don't know if you can talk to her. I just need the number, you going down there to look it up will be faster than going through team channels."

"I taught high school in Phoenix for decades, you don't think I know a little Spanish? I'll get her up here if it's possible."

"She doesn't have much and I don't want her to blow her savings on this Gail. Pay for the flight out of our bank account."

"Will do. If she can't get here, then what?"

"I always thought you were a pretty good nurse, how does a trip to Indianapolis sound?"

"I could think of better ways to spend the week," Gail quipped. "Is he good looking?"

I laughed then I laughed some more once I figured out how much I needed it. "Ask Amber."

"Oh, Mr. One Night Stand, huh? I don't think you've ever called him by his first name. God, it's too early to think hard. It sounds like he might be out of commission for a bit so I think I'm probably safe. When's the game tonight? I'll get back to you on everything before then," Gail said.

"We have to finish last night's game. Yeah, the injury was that bad. I have to check with Wal but I'm guessing resumption is probably around six, an hour before the other game is scheduled to start."

"Got it. I didn't realize I was signing up to work at a

triage clinic by moving up here. First Trev and now The Latin Lover." She paused, hoping I would laugh again but I didn't. "Babe...this wasn't your fault." Gail hung up. I was just reaching the hospital campus. Staring at St. Vincent's I didn't know if she was right or not.

CHAPTER TWENTY

We won the restarted game. I don't think any other result could have been possible. Alex hit the game winning home run in the ninth inning. Our depleted lineup caught up to us in the final two games as we only scored three runs, all driven in by Gary Wampum, and lost the series. LL's mother had never left the city of San Juan in her life and that wasn't going to change now. Gail had sent me a text just before game time telling me she was at the hospital. I was sure she had already developed a relationship with the nurses in charge of overseeing LL's recovery.

After the series finale, I brought the team to St. Vincent's so that they could show support for their teammate. I walked into the room to see Gail sitting by the window, hair pulled into a tight bun like a school marm. She was reading *Great Expectations*, already a third of the way through Dickens' tome. She had always read fast and with LL's jaw wired shut there wasn't much to do besides dive into a book.

She hadn't noticed me walk in. "I hope you brought a mobile library with you, speeding through books like that," I said.

She jumped, saw it was me, smiled, and pointed to a book bag sitting in the corner all in one motion. It's amazing how you can communicate so much so quickly when you have developed a bond with someone. "I'll be fine."

"You should have let me buy you a Kindle a couple of years ago."

"What, and reward Amazon for destroying book stores? I'll pass."

"How about a Nook then?"

Gail gave me a dismissive look. "Do they even make those anymore?" She had never been one for having a conversation twice. "I'll stick with paperbacks until they pry them from my cold, dead hands."

"Ok Charlton Heston, I don't think that'll happen. Besides, it's rather obvious by now that they won't pry them from your hands, they'll burn them. I've got a whole team standing out in the hallway here to see their teammate, you don't mind if the two of us grab a bite to eat while they stop on in, do you?"

She smiled, "Not at all."

I came back up to the room to say my piece, expecting everyone to have cleared out. Gail waited in the hallway, pretending to be engrossed in a conversation with the day nurse at the desk. As I entered the room, a narrow circle had been carved out immediately surrounding the bed with hospital gift store items crammed everywhere else. There was still one Mud Hen at bedside, saying something in Spanish to LL. A heavy amount of gauze and bandages covered the lower half of his face with a small hole cut out where his mouth was. At some point he'd graduate to using a straw to eat, right now I think it was more for breathing purposes. LL was a mouth breather when he slept, even with his jaw wired shut that was a hard habit to break. I had no idea what Alex was saying to him but I could tell in LL's eyes that he was comforted by it. The haze of medication had dissipated from his corneas, like the lifting of a thin sheet of skin. LL's lower body shook but his mouth stayed still, the laugh squeezed out of his face through a succession of rapid blinks.

Alex got up, shot me a timid look then exited the room. I made a note to ask him about that at a later time. For the first time since the injury two days ago I talked to LL while he was lucid. My words rang hollow and I made it worse by fumbling through awkward small talk. I stopped midsentence, taking time to chastise myself for blubbering like an idiot. There was no reason to say anything other than the truth. "Rodrigo, take all the time you need to get healthy. This team, myself, my family, we'll all be here to make sure you have a proper support network to ensure a complete recovery. Just look around, if you think we've forgotten about you." I gestured to the room around us, trying to ignore the stuffed tamale gag gift (where in the hell did they find that at) and the teddy bear dressed as a Casanova with a truly lecherous look on his face. Other things were much more heartfelt but I had to admit, if it were me in that bed the bear would be my favorite. Maybe I could find a female companion with a slutty bodice on the verge of falling off to send back from Scranton. "I may not have always shown it but I respect you as a ball player. You will always have a place on my roster."

LL directed me with his eyes towards the stack of gifts to his left, asking implicitly for me to grab something from the pile. I began to lift things up slowly, one at a time. LL answered by giving a thumbs-down until I saw what he wanted. The damn things still look almost exactly the same as when I was a kid. The hard plastic red border fit in my hand like an old friend. I handed the toy to him with a smile on my face and waited. He focused intently, spinning the knobs, the left one far more often than the right. After two minutes he groaned, regretting it instantly, and weakly shook the toy to start over. It took him five minutes to complete the simple message but it was worth the wait. LL handed the etch-a-sketch to me, the board read "thank you." I squeezed his hand, held it for longer than I planned, and headed past Gail without saying a word to rejoin the team. I think she saw the tear in my eye anyway.

The next three weeks saw the team win about as many as we lost. The makeup game against the Clippers was shoehorned in on a mutual off day and we ended up losing. National embarrassment for nothing. We had been unable to beat Columbus in the first half. The schedule was set so that we played them much more often in the second half, if we were going to make a run at the division the team was going to need to figure them out. We entered the All-Star Break at four games over .500, a game back of Indianapolis and ten games back of Columbus in the West. Good Hands' hamstring finally healed and he took the field in left the last series of the first half. Trev didn't hit a lick in Indy or Scranton/Wilkes-Barre but had returned to form by the Break. Three Way was voted onto the All Star staff but the rotation fell wrong so he was scratched from appearing. He hadn't lost a game since May. Dirk Bobbsey continued to be strong as well. Andre had 25 home runs and Lord Al Percy was sixth in the league in RBI. Clyde Mendenhall joined them on the International League team, the only Mud Hen to get into the game. The Pacific Coast League won 8-4, probably because my guys rode pine. Or at least that's what I told myself.

Gail made sure my vacation was anything but. Alex agreed to watch LL for us who was allowed to go back to Toledo five days after the team had left Indianapolis. He was doing a lot better, the swelling now almost nonexistent. His jaw had another couple of weeks before it got the all clear and was still wired shut. He was pretty easy to care for though. He was back walking around and off painkillers so he was cogent. Everyone was now used to communicating with him via his note pad. His English had actually improved quite a bit. On top of that, he discovered Campbell's tomato soup and asked for it nearly every night. I could do that.

I got dragged to the Toledo art museum and the Detroit Institute of Art in the same day which was really more than I could take. I enjoyed the trip to Greenfield Village a lot more. Gail was never going to get me to care about art but history had taken, except for the Boat Lift that is. I could not tell Lord Al or he'd never shut up. Besides, he had an insane board to add squares to. He didn't attach the squares in any particular order so the picture remained a mystery. In the upper right quadrant a creepy eye seemed to follow you wherever you went, Santa's I presumed. A model railroad had mercifully covered most of the terrified child peering from the Krampus's sack. One time, someone had shuffled the pieces to the wrong spots drawing a long, sustained denunciation from Lord Al that I found out later borrowed heavily from Blake.

THE SECOND HALF

CHAPTER TWENTY-ONE

"We need to get Wampum going Har," said The Walrus.

"Damn Wal. Is that the way to greet a guy you haven't seen for four days?" I said.

"Oh, pardon me," Wal said sardonically. "Mr. Freeman, how was your break, sir? Good? Good. Mine was wonderful as well. You may be interested to know that our right fielder has hit .220 since we played in Indianapolis and we don't play anybody that will draw his ire for another four weeks."

"You were happier when you were fat," I said with a mischievous grin on my face.

The Walrus grinned back. "I've got a long way to go before you have to worry about me not being fat."

"In all seriousness Walter, just a couple of days without seeing you and I can tell you've lost weight. You've got to be down about thirty pounds since May. If you keep losing like this the diet Nazis are going to be on you for losing weight too fast."

"Maybe I'll beat *The Biggest Loser*, without all the prize money of course."

"I'm sure *Baseball America* will do a puff piece on you. What were we talking about again?" I asked.

"How to get an Indian to hit a baseball," Walter said.

"When's the bus leave for Columbus tomorrow?"

"1:30, why?"

"Can you corral everyone here? If so, I'll meet you guys down there."

The Walrus sighed, "I don't want to know what you're thinking."

"No, you don't. Oh, LL was at the doctor's earlier today and they were impressed by his progress. Wires are out and everything already, two weeks before they were supposed to be."

"That's great."

"He is still on soft foods, jaw's still fragile, and he can't do any activities that would cause exertion so we aren't out of the woods yet."

"It's a start," said The Walrus.

"He wants to travel with the squad. Make sure he is on the bus, will you?"

"I think it can be managed. I know a lot of the guys are anxious to see him."

"Wal, I never saw anything like that...hope I never do again. I'm telling you, kid's going to be back out on the field by September. I can feel it in my gut."

"Hey Har," said The Walrus as I turned to leave, "LL wasn't your fault."

"I don't believe that."

My growing fondness for history did not carry over to Union clothing. The wool was itchy and clung too tightly to my athletic frame. I was constantly scratching, failing to reach an irritated spot just below my shoulder blades. Every stroke of my nails pressed the material against my skin, fueling another, more urgent, itch in its place. The navy blue wool was heavy, made heavier by the mock general's regalia that decorated the shoulders and left breast of my uniform. The weight combined with the summer heat to create a steady perspiration that made the itching worse still.

Union life wasn't my cup of tea either. The food was terrible. I had tried to argue that a man as important as William Henry Harrison must have dined pretty well, even in the field, but that hadn't been received well. At the camp I was fed a cup of what could only be described as gruel heated over an open fire. I'd take gruel over what I was being fed on the march to the stadium. The loaves of hard tack, mold at the edges for authenticity, that I had been rationed were disgusting. Imagine rotted Pop Tarts without the filling or the icing. I was beginning to wonder why I had agreed to such indignities, even the white mottled stallion I was saddled atop couldn't compensate for how I felt at the moment.

Columbus is home to one of the largest volunteer Civil War reenactment groups in the country. Calling on men from as far away as New York and coal country in western Pennsylvania, they could raise an entire battalion on a summer weekend. Even with a last minute inquiry for a Friday afternoon march my request had been accepted. I was blending time periods some but Harrison's army of 1811 looked pretty close to the regiment that now paraded towards the home of the Clippers.

In the Spring of 1811 residents of Indiana became concerned with the presence of a training camp for Indian warriors located just north of Lafayette. The warriors came from a confederation of different nations, setting aside ancient divisions to face the new threat of whites in the Midwest. The new American nation was no longer hemmed in by Appalachia, moving into territory in large numbers that had previously only been of interest to a small number of French traders. This newfound bond among the tribes had been orchestrated by two brothers, Tecumseh and The Prophet. Their base of operations was known as Prophetstown and could no longer be ignored. The Governor of Indiana, the General Harrison, led a force north to destroy Prophetstown in November of '11 when it was known that Tecumseh, the true strategist of the group, was away.

Meetings between Harrison and The Prophet led to an agreement that no battle would take place until more talks had been engaged in the next day. That night, the Indians of Prophetstown attacked the American forces. They came in two waves, first attacking the southern end where they met officers such as Spencer and Rodd. From the north they ran into Gieger and Funk. All of these men would play a role in the War of 1812. The attacks were repelled, resulting in The Prophet being kicked out of the confederacy he had so much hand in creating, left to struggle to survive as an outcast for the rest of his life. Tecumseh would be a valuable asset to the English in the war and was killed in action in a battle near Detroit. William Henry Harrison embraced the nickname Tippecanoe, riding it to a wave of popularity that lasted his entire lifetime, a wave that brought him all the way to the White House defeating Martin Van Buren in the election of

1840. It was the most widely known Indian defeat until stories of Comanches and Apaches filtered in from the West toward the end of the century. I was a poor Harrison in my borrowed, and ill-fitting, Civil War uniform but I had done my best on short notice.

I rode into the Huntington Park lot on my horse, staying in the back of the regiment until the two cannons that had begun to drag behind caught up to us. A small procession from the front carried the flag of the United States and authentic nineteenth century rifles forward at the order of their unit commander. They marched with perfect rhythm forty paces, spinning on their heel to face away from my horse. The commander gave orders for them to pack the guns with powder which the men followed, ramrods entering the barrels just below where bayonets gleamed with potentially deadly intentions. Another command brought the guns to position, butts resting in the crook between chest and right shoulder. "Fire!" followed by the emphatic pop of fifteen blank shells echoed through the Columbus Arena District.

I was shocked that my horse handled the noise with such aplomb (a word I know only because I've been told I lack it many times). With a gentle kick of my heels and a couple of clicks of my tongue, the horse clomped slowly forward on the asphalt. A crowd had gathered across the street wondering why the ghosts of Grant had descended on a minor league baseball stadium. The door to the visitor's clubhouse cracked open, the glare of afternoon sun keeping me from seeing who had peeked out. It shut and I brought my horse to a stop in front of the riflemen. I could hear the cannon crews prepping the guns. The clubhouse entrance opened again, this time all the way, and The Walrus's still ample frame filled most of it. "Har, is that you?" Wal asked, squinting at me. "I said I didn't want to know but maybe I should have asked. What the hell?"

I grabbed my saber at the hilt, pulling it from its cover and extending its polished blue-silver steel towards the sky. I dropped the blade until it was pointing directly at The Walrus and the cannons boomed behind me. The force from the artillery powder was enough to send the wheels rolling backwards on the pavement. The blocks that were placed to stopped the movement skittered backwards until they finally dug in and wedged the wheels to a stop ten feet later. The boom made the rifle unit sound like child's play. The residual from the firing didn't just echo back, the sound roared off the surrounding buildings and washed backwards causing small rocks and clumps of dirt and litter to rattle on the ground.

The Walrus held his hands to his ears, "God damn it, I'm going to be deaf from that."

"Do I have your attention Walter? I am here for Mr. Gary Wampum," I said.

"Well, he knows you're here. Hell, the whole fucking world does. When the cops arrest you I'm not bailing you out of jail and I'll make sure Gail doesn't either." The Walrus looked behind him at the crowd of Mud Hens that had now followed him outside the Park. "Wampum, you out here?" Wal bellowed with unfiltered amplitude.

"He's coming," Andre bellowed back in his sonorous

tones.

Gary pushed himself through his teammates and passed The Walrus, coming to a stop fifteen feet from me. He wasn't sure what to make of the scene but the sight of my regiment had him on guard. "Yes, Skip?" Gary asked with strained politeness.

I cleared my throat, reaching to a pouch made out of hide on my left hip. Slipping my hand inside I pulled out a folded piece of weathered paper that looked like it could contain a message from a spy, or orders. "I am not aware of any Skip in my force. My name is William Henry Harrison, general in the United States Army and Governor of the newly formed State of Indiana. It seems that your conduct Mr. Wampum has been egregious of late."

"Yeah, how do you figure...General?" Gary gritted out through clenched teeth.

"Since my victory at Tippecanoe it appears that tribes have sided with the British in the current war. Tales of scalpings and raids are floating in from across the region." I paused because Gary looked like he legitimately wanted to kill me. "Your own conduct Mr. Wampum, by comparison, has been exemplary. President Madison has informed me directly to convey the following message, 'continue your recent habits of not hitting the fucking baseball. Your efforts are greatly appreciated in ensuring that the white man wins.'"

The team erupted into laughter while Gary's cheeks just got redder. I'm surprised no one made a Redskin joke, Andre probably would have if he could have seen the face I was looking at. As it was, he was laughing so hard he had been reduced to doubling over on one knee. Even Wal was laughing and he was usually sensitive to this kind of stuff.

Eventually the guffaws died down, but Gary had yet to move. We stared each other down. I blinked first offsetting most of the power I had from my position on horseback. Gary moved closer, putting his head next to that of my mount, never removing me from being the object of his gaze.

"You're not even dressed in the right time period," Gary said.

"There aren't many 1812 enthusiasts."

"No, people need to celebrate the freeing of the blacks so they can supposedly atone for this country's sins. Hell they celebrate that fool Custer. Funny, they don't talk about, or feel particular remorse, for the atrocities committed against my ancestors. There are no men roaming the country side with pregnant Injuns being forced to march at gunpoint. I wonder why? Too bad it's not raining out. I'd wish pneumonia for you too." He turned his gaze to the horse, whispering in its ear something in Senecan. The horse rose onto just two feet, fore quarters pointing at a similar angle to my saber from earlier. I had no chance, tumbling backwards and landing hard on the dusty lot. Gary laughed now as he headed back inside.

No police got called, cannon attacks must be common in Columbus. The regiment cleared out quickly, open trailers being hauled by heavy duty pickup trucks carried away men and artillery within minutes of my fall from the saddle. Those guys had done that a time or two. I kept the uniform though, rented through the weekend. Standing at the bottom of the dugout steps I tried to exude serenity, my hand tucked inside the front of my pants, just behind the belt buckle, like Napoleon or another great general. I tried to avoid the stares from Gary at the end of the bench while we hit and from the crew chief who would have thrown me out just for walking on the field in the costume if he could have gotten away with it.

"Tippecanoe, huh?" The Walrus asked with a wry snide to his comments.

"It's all I could come up with for this area."

"Western Indiana isn't exactly next door, there was no Indian skirmishes in Ohio?"

"Plenty, most of the French and Indian War in fact. Some of those get pretty gruesome though. Not exactly the tone I was going for."

"You look ridiculous."

"If Gary hits tonight it is worth it. You said it yourself, he has to get going and he needs a chip on his shoulder to do that," I said.

"This isn't what I had in mind. Are you going to wear that thing all weekend?" The Walrus asked.

"Maybe, why?"

"Because you are fidgeting like a worm on a hot griddle. Bet that wool itches. Especially for a guy who doesn't wear underwear."

"You have no idea."

"And I bet it's hot too." The Walrus was enjoying this.

"Yeah."

"Maybe you should sit down, resting will cool you off and you can scratch against the bench back." I turned and gave him a stern look, half joking. "What, can't you sit down?"

"It's a little tender." The bastard laughed at me.

Gary Wampum had four hits that night and we won. Three Way went seven, giving up just two, another quality start. I wore the General's uniform again on Saturday and Sunday as well. The heavy wool trapping the sweat until it was saturated to the point that hanging it up in the hotel bathroom at night couldn't air it out. It hadn't been a superstition of mine before the weekend but I figured it couldn't hurt to make sure I wore exactly the same attire the whole weekend. The crew chief threatened to throw me out because of the smell again the second night and wouldn't let me out of the dugout to deliver the lineup card prior to the finale. The rest of the team used only half of the dugout, trying desperately to create a buffer zone from the noxious aroma coming off of me. Every couple of innings I walked to the other end of the dugout just to see them scatter. Gary Wampum had eight hits in the series and we swept Columbus to pull within seven. Road sweeps against playoff teams are rare so it was a weekend to savor. We still had a lot of work to do but we had sent a message that the division title would come down to the wire. With the sweep, the team leapfrogged Indianapolis to get to second place. We would never be behind the Indians for the rest of the year.

When I got onto the team bus everyone gave me a Bronx

cheer because I had changed and the uniform was back with the civil war reenactors where it belonged. I got the last laugh however. My bag got stuffed near the back of the luggage compartment where the vent for the air conditioning pulls from. Every time someone wanted to cool off, the smell of three day old undershirt blasted into the bus. We were back in Toledo after just the one road series. I never let that chip get off of Gary's shoulder, his new introduction music, played every time he came to bat, was 'Tippecanoe and Tyler Too' for the rest of the year.

CHAPTER TWENTY-TWO

"Har, you're going to want to get down to the park. The guys up in Detroit called and it is definitely a conversation you need to take," said The Walrus.

I had already been up, just waiting for an excuse to get to work. Gail was probably going to throw me out soon, she had known me long enough to recognize that look in my eye (not that one) and had long ago given up on trying to rein me in. Funny thing about guys when they are keyed up, we get annoying. There was a good tickle or bear hug or rib poke coming that Gail, for some reason, had never been fond of.

Rusty Chevrolet puttered into the player's garage at the stadium with its characteristic exhaustion. It wasn't more than a couple of miles but the car had gotten to the point that it was tired before it had a chance to warm up. The Escape was needed this weekend too, back in Michigan. I called Gail and asked her to go buy a car. That got her excited, a gentle suggestion that it shouldn't be too chickish was received with less enthusiasm. I knew she was smart enough to find one that could handle a lot of miles, you never know when I'll be back to roving instructor, but I had a sneaking suspicion my new car was going to be used and pink.

I walked into the club house to see Trev waiting for me and Andre sitting at his locker, liberally swigging from a new keg. "What do we got this time, the usual?" I asked.

"No," Andred bellowed, "not even wine."

"When did you decide to join the rest of us heathens and

imbibe with the traditional stuff?" Imbibe? Where the hell did that come from? Maybe Lord Al was rubbing off on me after all.

"My brother recommended it. He's logging somewhere in Michigan, Norway I want to say. Says this microbrewery up there puts out some top notch stuff. I went with the porter, hearty for a man of such refined tastes like myself," Andre said.

"That sounds right up my alley," I said. I walked into the office and checked the mug sitting on the corner of my cluttered desk to make sure nothing was growing inside. I was ok with the stain of dried coffee that ringed the bottom. "Do I get to give an opinion?" I asked as I held my glass out.

"I am the little brother of the family," Andre warned. My mind really did picture *Paul Bunyan* at that image. Andre filled my cup and I took a gulp. There was no need to worry about delivering a bad review to Andre's brother. The dark beer was nearly perfect, smooth and flavorful with a nice body.

"Give my complements. Who makes it?" I asked cheerfully.

Andre picked up the nearly full keg without effort, positioning the small sticker close enough to his eyes to read. "Says here it is the Keweenaw Brewing Company."

"Keweenaw? Never heard of the place. How about we go with the KBC, that's a bit easier to say. You didn't come in here nine hours before game time just to drink beer though, right? It's good but I'd recommend catching some rest before fielding practice."

"Got a new bat to start on," Andre said. "Had a dream that Missy is going to break soon."

"A dream?" I asked.

"Yeah. You know bats Skip. If you treat them right they treat you right. She's had a good run but I got the vision, same one I always get before one goes to heaven. Faithful until the very end."

"Alright, I'll be in the office if you need anything." Trev had been standing patiently at the end of the locker row, waiting for me to give him the time of day. Ever the gentleman, that one. "Looks like you need to see me Trev, why don't we go inside."

"I'd appreciate that," Trev said. I led him into the office, gestured at a chair for Trev to sit but he said he'd prefer to stand instead so I closed the door and eased into my chair, my feet immediately propping themselves up on the small patch of surface area that was still bare. "What can I do for you?"

"I don't know how much you've been paying attention to me and Amber," Trev started.

"You're dating. Congratulations, Gail is super excited about it so unfortunately I have to do some gossiping."

"Yeah," Trev said with hesitation. "The comedy routine that we went to that she did so well on was essentially a confidence building exercise. Amber has the voice of an angel, used to sing in the choir at her church as well as a gig here or there. She stopped after a bad break up, guess it hit her hard and got pretty ugly. She wants to do the national anthem before a game."

182

"Wow, not exactly the conversation I was expecting. I bet she'll do great at it," I said.

"The gig is booked for the rest of the year," Trev said with dejection. "I don't know if there is anything that can be done but I was hoping that maybe you could pull some strings."

I sat tapping my index finger on the edge of the desk for a moment, thinking. "I don't know that I have enough pull to bump someone but I can ask. It probably wouldn't be fair to have Amber jump ahead of someone so I will take a look and see if any of the anthem performers are purely musical acts. Maybe we can combine Amber and an instrumental gig." Trev gave me an uncomfortable look. "Is my solution not what you were looking for?"

"No, it's a great idea. It is just that...don't girls dig musicians?"

I laughed which seemed to make Trev realize the silliness of his insecurity. "I won't pair her with a guitar player Trev. Maybe an accordion? Polish-American night hasn't happened yet so a nice anthem polka with vocals can be her gig."

"I'm being stupid, aren't I?"

"You two have been into each other since you met, I doubt that she's going to leave you for the minor league circuit version of Jimi Hendrix. You've got a lot to offer girls Trev, just believe in yourself."

"Thanks for the vote of confidence, Skip. It's just sometimes girls find me a bit dull, is all." Trev pulled himself off the wall and moved to open the door. I asked him a question before he got the handle turned.

"Do you really think that Andre's bats warn him through dreams that they are going to break soon?"

Now Trev laughed. "I have no idea, my bats must be mute. This whole 'love the bat' thing the two of you have going on, I don't get it. It wouldn't be the craziest dream story I have heard though. The Good Book uses dreams, the angel Gabriel coming to shepherds in the field to warn that Herod intends to kill the Baby Jesus being one. Some would dismiss that stuff as mumbo jumbo but I'm not one."

"So it's not crazy?"

"I'm saying I can't tell you. Believing in Bigfoot is crazy, dreams having some semblance of the future seems pretty tame by comparison." With that, he left. I stared at the door for a minute, thinking about ten things at once so they all cancelled out. I drew out a slow blink that refocused my vision on the door handle. The Walrus didn't say what Detroit had called about but I knew implicitly that it had to do with sending back some of my players. It had taken over half the season but it seemed that the Tigers were finally getting healthy and considering they had managed to stay in second place with their depleted roster many were still convinced that the team was the favorite for another American League pennant. If you had asked me six weeks ago if I was excited about restocking my roster with first stringers I wouldn't have been able to nod fast enough. I would have been the eager dork asking out the best looking girl in school. Now though, the dynamics on the field and the mix of personalities had changed, gelled into a quality minor league team. Dialing that familiar 313 area code, I was about to say 'no thanks' to the advances of the homecoming queen. It was going to be an ugly conversation.

"Abe, this is the third time in an hour you've told me to do something that is anatomically impossible after I answered your question," I said as patiently as possible. The assistant GM was even angrier than I had anticipated. "This team was last place a year ago with the guys you are sending back down. They weren't the problem but they weren't the solution either. This team, come down here for a game, is playing better than any other club in the entire league. We're twenty games over since the middle of May and just seven back of Columbus. I need a fifth starter and will be happy to use Swansey but I want to play my guys. They've earned this."

"And I told you that your job is to serve the big league club. We're the ones that matter and if we need to utilize the farm team differently from what you think is best, it doesn't fucking matter," Abe said.

"We've got a shot at the title! We have both been at this game for a long time, you know that few guys on any Triple-A roster are going to make it in the Bigs except for emergency patch jobs. This may be the highlight of these kids' careers, that magical accomplishment that they'll be able to tell their children about. This is their shot to earn the best Christmas morning you could ask for." Lord Al was rubbing off on me. The half complete Santa Claus grid floated in my mind.

"Then where exactly do you want me to send four minor

league players?"

"I just said I'd take one. I could bump the other three to my bench and send three of my guys down to Erie but that's complicated. Why don't you send the guys I don't want there directly? That won't change their availability to you should you need to call them up again and Erie's got the split season thing going. It might be the boost those guys need to get them to the playoffs. Double-A playoffs have a slew of top-notch prospects to challenge Alvarez, Bourgoin, and Trawley."

"If I do this you better win a title. This amount of insubordination won't be looked on kindly unless it leads to results."

"I accept full responsibility for doing your job for you, Abe," I said icily.

"Har, you've been around a long time and have left your mark on this organization but that doesn't mean you aren't a fucking prick at times." I wondered if Abe had chewed the eraser off his pencil yet. He was the consummate bureaucrat, probably how he had nearly squeaked his way to GM each of the last three off seasons. I hear his pay gets bumped every time someone tries to raid him. Dave must swear by the guy but I respected those who write down their orders with permanent marker myself. Leaders take responsibility, one of my favorite history stories from Lord Al is about Eisenhower on D-Day. The fucker wrote out a letter the night before the invasion to give to Washington announcing his resignation should Operation Overlord fail. Dwight, the quiet order follower from Kansas, turned into quite the gambler. History is written by the winners though and someday people will take for granted the guts that took. They probably do already.

It was finally time to get out of the office, when I opened the door two players had bloomed into eighteen with another three out doing early BP. I was more than happy for The Walrus and Rodney Young to oversee that. My interest was in Andre's project. The new bat was starting to take shape.

Andre didn't use the branch of a tree struck by lightning for his bats like the movies. He always started with a heavy slab of Oak found in the back room of the Furniture Palace. You'd be surprised how often legs were broken in transit from the manufacturers. Andre had peeled off the laminate and cut the stool leg so that it was at 41 inches, just below the maximum length allowed by MLB Rule 1.10. The wood was still squared, except for the top which had been rounded nicely. A small trash can sat at the giant's feet with sawdust and a half dozen pieces of sand paper, the rough grit worn away. For any other man the project would be months of work but Andre's large meat hooks were pretty comparable in efficiency to a small wood lathe.

Force and power weren't the only qualities of Andre's wood working abilities. He was now focusing his attention on the center of the rounded top, nimbly carving out a shallow cup maybe an inch in depth. "I never noticed you were a cup guy," I said.

"I've never tried one before but Trev and Lord Al swear by it. They're having pretty good seasons so I thought it might be a good time to experiment."

"Andre, you're going to reach 40 home runs this year. Are you sure you want to mess with what's working?" I asked.

"I'm not real superstitious."

"Yeah, so you are creating a bat by hand just for the hell of it, huh? Get that weak shit out of here, we're all freaks when it comes to superstitions in this game."

Andre shrugged. "I'm not superstitious about that."

CHAPTER TWENTY-THREE

I must have been in a good mood because the normal pre-game jitters were nowhere to be found. I felt them more as a manager than I had as a player, the game being out of my control. I had no interest in pacing and the earlier conversation with Abe wasn't weighing on me. My butt was comfortably sunk into the bench pad and I had no intention of moving until Garret Drake needed to be pulled. My mind roamed to an unusual subject, with Brandon Swansey coming back to be my number five starter I now had two guys in my rotation that had to do with birds. Funny coincidence on a team named after a bird. Maybe. I had never figured out what a Mud Hen actually was and here we were nearing the dog days of August.

Drake even had a bird inspired nickname, 'Ducky." Unfortunately it was purely coincidence, not related to his last name at all. Garret had a habit of getting hit with drives back up the middle. He doesn't have bad stuff but even when he scatters a couple of hits, one seems to be a line drive that catches him or comes close. Last year, in Pawtucket, Garret took a ball to the head. It actually fractured his skull and I am glad I was not there, especially after dealing with LL's jaw. A shattered jaw and a broken humerus were the worst things I had seen and that was more than enough for me. Needless to say, Garret has become twitchy when another ball comes close to him. No, twitchy is too nice of a term. Garret suffers something akin to a nervous breakdown, flinching and jumping at ghosts for the rest of the game like a chronically abused spouse.

Teammates and the rest of the staff have tried everything to quiet his mental discomfort but nothing has worked. The Walrus even took him to a shrink, Garret spent the next start whispering before every pitch that the he needed to be one with the ball. A looping pop up over the mound elicited a girlish shriek along with a drop to the fetal position, Garret's hands covering from his temples to the vulnerable spots above the ears. Garret never went back to that quack but he was never going to live down the incident and Ducky stuck, I can't remember who first coined it. Everyone knows it is cruel so no one is keen on taking credit. Most pitchers who have suffered what Garret went through never make it back on the mound. His resilience should be celebrated but instead he's mocked. Now, when a comebacker occurs, Ducky is rendered useless for the rest of the start. It had been six weeks since the last episode, and in the interim Ducky had become a true number three starter making our rotation as formidable as Columbus. In the series opener against the Charlotte Knights, that changed before the end of the first batter.

Lloyd Reynolds, a wiry black guy who was famous for tripping on the last jump of the four hundred hurdles in the US Olympic trials in 2008, hit a screamer that found the gap between Ducky's ribs and elbow. Lloyd was a cocky son of a bitch who had been the focus of NBC's pre-Olympics hype for weeks before he choked and missed the Games completely. One of those guys who clearly had talent but couldn't handle letting it speak for itself. The blunder must have shook his ego pretty good though, he never ran track again. Lloyd had enticed NFL scouts with his speed at the Combine and got a couple of signings over a three year span but never made it off the practice squad. *ESPN*, and the Reynolds machine, always had an excuse when it didn't work. Now he was onto baseball and equally mediocre, if not more grating with his showboating and self-promotion. I watched him call for time as he rounded first base before starting the Reynolds trademark celebration, a flamboyant, arrogant strut. Next time up I was going to be sure to have Ducky put one between his shoulder blades. If I could get Ducky to settle down.

I saw my pitching coach get up to go have a conversation with Ducky. I cut him off at the pass, "Jimbo, I've got this one." I didn't give Jim a chance to argue with me, making my way up the steps and onto the field.

Ducky had done this act before, walking in a circle behind the mound to collect himself. Poor guy was actually trembling, and tonight was a sellout, he was falling apart in front of ten thousand people and substantially more listening on the radio. As I got closer I could see that his eyes were closed. Ducky was navigating pretty well considering but up close you could see that a step or two had been different than he was expecting. His lungs were heaving, slowing down as his zen routine began to work, only to speed up again when a misstep occurred. "Hey," I said in an understated way as I gently put my hand on his shoulder.

"What are you doing out here Skip?" Ducky asked.

"Oh, you know, it looked like you might be a bit shook up is all, Garret."

His trembling got worse. "That noticeable, huh?"

"Don't fret about it, I just want to get you back to yourself so you can pitch the rest of this start. How do we get you to put the fear of getting hit by the ball out of your mind?"

"If I knew that I'd have done it a long time ago."

"Help me understand it then, let me see if I can help. Most guys walk away when they went through what you did but you're here and not landscaping somewhere so I know you have the toughness to get through this."

"I'm not that strong," he nearly whispered. "After Pawtucket I started having post-concussion symptoms. Fancy way of saying I was scared shitless Skip. Sure I had headaches, months after my skull healed they were still coming on strong like a migraine that lasted for a week. The headaches I could handle, it was the nightmares that scared me."

"Nightmares? I've talked to the team doctors and they didn't say anything about nightmares."

"I didn't tell them. Thought people would think I'm crazy, guess it's too late for that now considering they all call me Ducky," Garret said.

"What did you dream about that scares you so bad?" I asked.

Ducky had returned to walking in circles with his eyes closed but my question caused him to stop one more time. His stare showed too much white above and below his pupil. "The worst things. When it actually happened I blacked out before the pain could be comprehended. I'd have dreams though where the pain that I had passed out from seeped into my subconscious. It was different than the headaches, I was sleeping but could tell that my head was actually cracked. Even now I will spend a night feeling those old fractures like fault lines of lava. Sometimes there are images too, I can see myself laying on the field but I'm dead and my brain trickles out of my ears before the side of my head blows out from the inside with grayish pink muscle falling out. It's horrible."

"It sounds like it but you know it isn't real. The real trauma you suffered was bad enough Garret and you've made it through that. You're past the true challenge," I said.

He took a deep breath. "I know that. I can control it until…this happens."

"I'm about to get yelled at by the umpire. If you can't go, no one will fault you but I need the ball because this game is too important to not have my best option on the mound."

"Are you taking me out?"

"That's up to you. Are you taking you out?" Out of the corner of my eye, I could see blue coming this way, a dark object being peeled away to reveal pink. "We don't have any time to hesitate."

"Hey Har! I've dusted home three times already, can't do it again. We got to get this show on the road," Tim Ietta, the youngest member of the crew but tasked with calling balls and strikes tonight, yelled. He didn't wait for a response to continue making his way to the mound.

"I'll do it," Ducky said with sudden resolution.

"Fortune favors the bold," I said with a smile. Tim reached the mound just as I began to turn to head back to the dugout.

"They always leave just when I get to the party," Tim joked to Garret. Tim was one of the good guys in the league. Rex Stout could learn a thing or two.

"Hey Drake," that dipshit at first was yelling at my pitcher now. I turned to give him a stern look, vacillating between Lloyd Reynolds and the Charlotte first base coach, warning both of them to keep Lloyd from saying what he was about to say. "Quit being a pussy man, I've got to get down to second base. Nike needs a good photo op for their new gloves." Lloyd did that thing where you join your hands together so they overlap into a single logo on the palm of the glove. He actually had his face, mugging like a fool, sitting above a large swoosh on his hands.

I was surprised that Andre showed restraint but he did. I took a look at Chuck at second and Alex at short, they were not as understanding. Andre had been conditioned to be a gentle giant over the years. My first year as a roving instructor the talk of the minors was Andre's choke slam of a Dunedin player when he was playing for Lakeland in the Florida State League. Andre gave a growl Lloyd's way as a warning. I was more direct, looking back to Tim now. "Next time that fucking prick is up to bat, I'm going to have my pitcher hit him with the best fastball he's got."

Tim didn't bother to give me a warning. He yelled out to first now, "I hope you guys heard that." Lloyd and the first

194

base coach yelled back asking what Tim meant. "That was a really stupid thing to do," Tim yelled before returning to his place behind Pigpen. Dude was pretty cool.

The long delay had fans restless but they kept their tongue as Ducky threw a couple of warm-up pitches, another courtesy from Tim. His delivery was perfect, the shakiness nonexistent. His fastball had a couple extra mph, popping the glove with purpose. Jimbo looked down at me with eyebrows raised and I just nodded back.

"What the hell did you say to fire Ducky up like that?" asked The Walrus.

"I just gave him the option to hand over the ball, let him decide," I said.

"That's it?"

"And you thought I couldn't pull off Tony LaRussa," I said with mock indignation, hoping that a joke would lighten my mood.

"I am impressed."

"Two other things: Ducky's having nightmares, that's why he's freaking out and that douche bag at first base called him a pussy. There's going to be a fight. Be prepared to take the lineup card from me because I doubt I'm going to be sitting on this bench come the ninth inning."

"He did what?" The Walrus asked, stunned.

"You heard me," I growled. The joke earlier had already disappeared.

The Walrus left my side, walking down the bench to tell everyone what had occurred. It was unusual for me to need to keep guys who weren't in the game focused but as word spread down the line the antics that were a normal part of the dugout scene died out. The Walrus called out to the bullpen using the phone to let them know too. As Ducky got out of the first unharmed and the players came off the field I looked into every eye. Never had I seen the team unified to such a degree with a common purpose. I climbed up to lean over the dugout railing to look down to the bullpen. The body language of my pitchers told the same story.

Alex walked up to Ducky as he sat down and said simply, "We've got your back." The Cuban really did speak like an American.

It was not a fun night to be Lloyd Reynolds in the field. Jermaine Willis started things in the bottom of the first pointing with his bat, a la Babe Ruth, straight at the Charlotte centerfielder. The first pitch from Chad Warford, Charlotte's starter, was down and away in the extreme. Warford had held on to the ball too long causing his fastball to bounce five feet in front of home plate, skittering towards the left-hand batter's box just above ankle height. Jermaine swung anyways, stepping across the plate and connecting flush as if he had been an ace cricket player sometime in his past. The pitch may have been a ground ball but the hit was not. The ball seemed to seek out Lloyd on a line. Line drives are often the hardest balls for a good outfielder to judge, Lloyd wasn't particularly good and Jermaine's hit froze him. The liner landed five feet in front of him and careened into his shin without losing an ounce of steam. That was going to leave a welt. Lloyd had yet to unfreeze, stunned by the read and then the pain, finally hobbling after the ball and throwing it back in to the cutoff man. Jermaine's speed had him into second base without a slide and Charlotte had an error on the board. Every player on the team stood at the railing in the dugout and bullpen cheering, Andre bellowing out whoops that Gary Wampum soon matched.

Good Hands pointed to center, calling his shot as well. The line drive didn't reach Lloyd Reynolds on one hop like Jermaine's but it was hit accurately and blistered across the centerfield grass until it took a high hop and collided with Lloyd's wrist, another bruise in the making. The ball trickled away from Lloyd, allowing Jermaine to score uncontested but Good Hands, not the fastest player on the team, was held to a single.

Andre pointed Missy towards center, drawing a roar from the crowd. He too hit the first pitch, a ball out of the strike zone but nothing was safe from the lineup that night. The giant's amazing power was square behind the drive, the ball ripping through the heavy summer night's air. It picked up speed the further it flew, the whine that trailed after it rising into a scream. Lloyd back pedaled furiously, trying to get far enough away that the ball's trajectory might change to avoid heading straight for his forehead. He had been playing back, given Andre's power, and now found himself onto the warning track without slowing down. Andre's drive went into Lloyd's mitt, pushing it into his chest with enough force to push the air from his lungs at the same time Lloyd collided with the centerfield wall. He hit, and stuck, as if he had been pinned there by a stake. Slowly Lloyd sank until he was in a sitting position, back against the wall and legs splayed like an exhausted pin-up girl. Andre was out but I was sure it must have been the most satisfying out of his life. Lloyd didn't recover allowing Good Hands to take second base on a tag up. Lloyd still didn't move to get the ball back in, the right fielder now rushing to his side to take the ball and get it back in as Good Hands took third. The Walrus waved him home and he scored without a relay throw.

Trev followed with another hit to center, over the wall for a home run. Every batter for the entire game recorded an out or a hit to centerfield and, to their credit, Charlotte forced Lloyd to remain out there playing the proverbial ball retriever on the driving range. The offense sent an appropriate message and I called off my earlier plans to have Ducky get even. Lloyd could barely swing the bat because of the punishment he had taken by the time he got up for his second plate appearance. Like an American League pitcher during Interleague play, Lloyd stood with his bat on his shoulder watching three pitches go right down the middle. It was the same story for each subsequent at-bat. We won easily, the team vaulting into first place in the league in batting average and runs scored. Production was now coming from up and down the lineup with Chuck, Wampum, Alex, and Pigpen all delivering consistently. We won the next two easily, Brandon Swansey delivering the first win from the fifth starter's spot all year in his Mud Hen debut for 2014. We were now six games back of the Clippers.

CHAPTER TWENTY-FOUR

August brought with it some zip to an already scorching summer. If Toledo had any cacti, they too would have been struggling under the potent combination of heat and tropical humidity being drawn from the Gulf of Mexico across the nation's heartland. Coming off an empty day on the calendar, we were set to depart for eastern Pennsylvania around 10 AM to get to Lehigh for a game later that night. I made it to the field about 7 expecting to be the first one to the stadium, instead finding two cars already in the parking garage. In the quiet of the light summer morning, the city seemingly empty as families took off for a last hurrah vacation before school started up, I could hear the ping of an aluminum bat. Wood bats have to be used at any level in the professionals and there are plenty of teenage leagues, loaded with potential prospects, which mandate the same. Was The Walrus hitting? It was possible, the pings were hollow, indicating a soft swing. To hit lazy flys for shagging with an aluminum bat would take little effort, the kind that would look attractive to an old man who had just gotten through a hard morning workout. I wondered who he was hitting to.

It was The Latin Lover, a true surprise. LL had moved back to his studio apartment after he had the wires removed and had been a part of the daily routine around the clubhouse ever since. He did more chores now than in the past, asking to help out with more than I was comfortable allowing. His jaw was obviously still fragile and my guilt made sure I took extra precaution. He had made a couple of lispy comments about starting back towards a spot on the team but I had brushed off the requests. The team doctors had agreed with me, laughing at the notion of LL being anything short of four weeks away from beginning his rehab in earnest. LL must have gone to The Walrus behind my back.

"So how long has this been going on?" I chided.

"What?" The Walrus was trying to play it cool, taking a loopy swing that led to one of the laziest fly balls I had ever seen.

"Doctors told me last week that LL taking FP was a terrible idea."

"Yeah, and when did doctor's orders ever mean something to you Harry?"

"Since he," I pointed out toward LL, "was able to smile at me laying sideways."

"Your Mee-maw could hit a fly ball with more spunk than this. We've been doing fifty a day in the morning. You should know of all people how helpless it feels to be in a dugout and unable to contribute to the team. I seem to remember getting a collect call or two in the first half of '88 when you were trying to play baseball on one knee."

"That was different."

The Walrus didn't bother to look at me, sending another can of corn towards LL. "No. It's not. Besides, there are rumblings that the Tigers are considering calling up Alex soon. He's made quite the impression with the scouts."

"So that's who Chad's boys have been down here looking

at," I mused. "How'd you glean that information?"

"Easy, I'm not the manager. You guys are always the last to know."

"Well, officially I don't approve of this. I don't even know about it."

After the shellacking we put on Lehigh back home, I was expecting them to have their dander up. As we entered the final twenty-five games of the season, jobs for next year were now on the line and I figured that, plus revenge, would be a powerful combination to end our recent hot streak. The first night's game did not play out that way with Andre hitting his 38th, a grand slam, which broke the game open in the 3rd. We ended up winning 12-3 and Three Way got his fourteenth win, tying his career high. Columbus lost at Indianapolis and we were within five games of first place.

Dirk Bobbsey did not fare so well the next day. He had set off a minor panic, his whereabouts unknown until a half hour before first pitch. I didn't have time to yell at him or get answers as his pre-game bullpen session required his immediate attention. Dirk was still folding his uniform into his pants as he walked through the outfield, drawing the female equivalent of wolf whistles from a party of girls in the first row. One of the girls had a cheap tiara that must have been taped or pinned somewhere in her unkempt black curls. She had a pink sash that carried the message "Available: One More Week" diagonally across a tight white tank top. I thanked God that bachelorette parties were a lot tamer when

Gail and I got married. She was already half in the bag and it didn't take a genius to figure out that a trip to one of eastern Pennsylvania's finest adult clubs was still to come. Call it a double standard if you wish but it just doesn't seem proper. Good thing LL was still recovering or I was sure it would have been an awkward morning for someone in the group, blushing bride indeed.

I personally oversaw Dirk's throwing session, looking for clues as to whether his mysterious absence was going to have an effect on his performance. Dirk skipped long toss, whirled his right arm three times in quick succession that apparently was going to pass for a stretch, and kicked at the dirt in front of the practice mound with a clipped motion. His brevity drew a howl from Jimbo but Dirk ignored it like he had the drunken bridal party. The first pitch from the wind-up was a strike at 97, the bullpen catcher didn't have to move his mitt. Jimbo let out a whistle that stood in stark contrast to the utterances of a minute ago and I left the session without a word. Mr. Bobbsey and I would be having a conversation but it wasn't going to be now. It's bad mojo to mess with a starter who is having a good warm-up.

Lehigh's starter set us down in order in the first, three strikeouts on nine pitches. I had only seen that happen once before, it is amazing how this game can still surprise you. The rest of the start wasn't as successful, he was taken out in the sixth with four earned. The Iron Pig bullpen stranded Good Hands at third when Andre popped out softly to the second baseman. John Turrell could have caught the ball without a glove under normal conditions but this catch may have been the scariest of his career. Missy had broken, fulfilling Andre's premonition in grand fashion. The ball had cut in on Andre's hands, connecting below the barrel where the bat tapers to the handle. By the time Andre had finished his swing, all that remained in his hands was a thick stub of oak, mostly encased in tape. The crack ran upwards, branching out into a spider web pattern that allowed shards to spray in every direction. The force of Andre's mighty rip was like fertilizer to a bomb, the jagged pieces nails seeking targets. The catcher and the home plate umpire both let out cuss words as splinters tore into their skin. The guts of the bat, no longer trapped by the casing, made a line towards Turrell. The sharp point where the handle originally cracked, arced across the infield, a dangerous javelin coming to rest deep in Turrell's shin. To his credit, with nearly two feet of wood sticking out of his lower leg, Turrell still took three steps to his left to make the catch. With ball in hand and the sparse crowd gasping, all Turrell could do was stand there, looking down. The Lehigh medical staff rushed out to check on Turrell while our doctor did a rush job, pulling splinters from Nathan Habler, the Iron Pig catcher, and everyone's best friend Rex Stout. The delay was considerable.

Andre used the time to carefully comb through the grass and dirt surrounded home plate, collecting as many pieces of Missy as he could manage. He came back to the dugout, pulling a small lunch box from his hole in the bat rack. Opening the case Andre emptied his left hand, the contents sprinkling with a soft patter against the metal. Lastly, Andre put the handle in and closed the box, snapping the latches that ran across the side shut. It had been only one handful of debris but Andre's hands are larger than other men's. I'd be willing to wager that eighty percent of the bat that wasn't stuck in Turrell's leg had been picked up. That left a lot of bat out there though, more than Andre had ever lost before. Andre walked up to me with his hand out and I slipped a patch into his palm without a word. He carefully peeled the non-stick backing off, applying the patch with care to keep it from rolling. The POW-MIA symbol managed to speak somberly without a word as Andre returned the box to his allotted space with a tender kiss on the box's lid.

The Lehigh staff had Turrell in a supine position on the infield dirt now. The first baseman and shortstop crouched, coerced into duty holding Turrell's shoulders still. The team doctor ripped the wood from Turrell's shin without giving a warning. Turrell howled in pain and he spasmed involuntarily against his teammates hands. The hole that was now unplugged let loose a blob of thick, dark blood and sediment. "Shouldn't they get him off the field?" I asked uncomfortably.

"Maybe they're worried about an infection," said The Walrus.

Faint sirens could now be heard but it would still be thirty minutes before Turrell was put on a stretcher and lifted by gurney into the back of an ambulance. The uncomfortable nature of the situation was making me antsy, I couldn't stop thinking that EMTs should have been on hand like they would be at a major league stadium. Suddenly, I came to the realization that I was cold, real cold. The night came in earlier and with more bite now that fall was nearly here. I looked down the dugout to Dirk who was sitting by himself, as usual. He had a jacket slung over his right arm but the heavy layer of sweat had long ago moved from cooling him down to chilling him to the bone. He was trying to pass it off as nothing, and his characteristic indifference almost fooled me. I walked down to him and leaned in saying, "Why don't you grab Pigpen and take some tosses down in the bullpen to keep your arm fresh?"

"Yeah," he replied gruffly. One word. Dirk was never going to win a personality contest. He did have ten strikeouts tonight though and with only two earned runs on his line I could live with the rest. I walked back to the other end of the dugout, avoiding the scene on the field while I came up with busy work for myself, grabbing for the phone. It was picked up on the first ring, a record I think, and I asked for 'TP,' Gus Charmin to get up and begin loosening. I was asked if I thought they might call the game and I replied no. Unlike LL in Indy, John Turrell had no chance of dying tonight. I hung up the phone, turning around to find Dirk's face just inches from mine.

"This is my start, I'll finish it."

"I can't afford to risk this delay blowing your arm. TP is just a precaution, in case things don't fire up properly or you aren't as sharp once this game gets going again."

"You can't take me out."

206

"When did your authority supersede my own?" I asked with a strong hint that Dirk had used up today's allotment of goodwill.

"Supersede, great choice," piped in Lord Al. He shut up quickly when Dirk and I both shot him a look.

"This isn't a question of authority. This is my game and that's final," Dirk barked. I waited for him to leave for the bullpen but instead he stood and glowered at me, daring me to leave my order out to the pen as is. The confrontation had now become the focus of attention of everyone in the dugout and I couldn't emasculate myself or I'd risk a larger mutiny later on. The worst thing that can happen to a leader is to be exposed for having no clothes, authority is really your only tool. We continued to lock eyes until the roar of applause echoed downward, marking Turrell's placement into the ambulance.

"You better get some warm-up tosses in. I don't think it would be a good idea to skip stretching twice in one night." Dirk left without saying anything.

"What the hell was that?" I asked The Walrus.

"Who knows."

The delay totaled fifty minutes when it was all said and done. Under any other situation I would have pulled Dirk for a reliever. I could feel an ulcer coming on. John Fogerty's *Centerfield* tried in vain to return the contest to idyllic, all-American innocence. Dirk's fastball was still a steady 95 and he struck out the first batter with his patented changeup, the batter swinging so early that he could have done the old *Bugs Bunny* routine before the ball made it to the plate. Dirk had really mastered that pitch. A good changeup is only possible when the arm motion mimics that of a fastball. Rather than grabbing the ball with the pads of the fingers, it is gripped by the palm which causes it to be about ten miles per hour slower than a fastball. Hitters have to read the arm motion, swinging early to keep the fastball from being by them. Really good hitters can adjust mid-swing to a changeup but Dirk's was in a class by itself. I'm pretty sure the only way to hit Dirk's changeup is to sit on it and doing that with two strikes leaves you with a long walk back to the dugout if you guess wrong.

After the leadoff hitter, Dirk stepped off, uncharacteristic for him when things were going well. He lifted the rosin bag, manipulating it for an inordinate length of time until a large cloud of white powder trailed in his wake. I half expected Alex or Chuck to complain but they remained stoic, pulling up the front of their uniforms to keep their mouth and nose covered. Rex Stout moved to the front of the plate, yelling out to Dirk to quit stalling.

"What the hell was that?" I asked The Walrus.

"That's the second time you've asked that Har. I don't know."

"That's the second time you've been of no help," I shot back.

"Why don't you go out and get a fuel check? TP is ready and I'll make the call to get Claudio up as well," The Walrus said.

"He's not tired. It almost looks as if he is nervous. Besides, Rex is a prick and he'll be on my case to get off the field before I get to the mound." The Walrus made the call to get the right-hander loose as I scanned the crowd for anything suspicious but I didn't notice a central casting archetype for a button from the Philly mob. I didn't see anyone who looked too much like a wire-rimmed weasel, the kind whose idea of getting free from the family involves administrating a featherbedding scheme, either.

Back on the mound, Dirk's composure did not return. His normally perfect posture was replaced with a slouch, shoulders sagging under an imaginary weight. "What the hell is that?" The Walrus asked.

"I thought you didn't like it when I asked you that," I said.

"That's different, I'm not a pain in the ass," said The Walrus, smiling.

Dirk was wild to the next batter, walking him on five pitches with the only strike crossing the inside corner after Pigpen had set up outside. He walked the next batter as well, this time on 13 pitches. The hitter fouled off seven while working the count out of an 0-2 hole. Dirk made a trip to the rosin bag one more time. "You should go get him," The Walrus fretted.

I didn't go get Dirk and got lucky when the number nine hitter scorched a ground ball straight at Alex for a double play. We went to the seventh inning with the Mud Hens still up 4-2. "You're in charge until I get back," I told The Walrus before stalking my way down the bench to Dirk.

"Hey, where are you going?"

I didn't look back, let alone respond. Grabbing Dirk by his pitching arm I pulled him into the tunnel to the visiting clubhouse without a fight. "Are you throwing this game?" I tried to talk quietly but the anger in my voice caused the accusation to come out louder than intended. We both looked back to where the tunnel opens up to the dugout to see if anyone had heard. When there was no stir I turned my attention back to Dirk, silently demanding an answer.

"No."

"Don't lie to me, Bobbsey."

"I'm not throwing the game for the other team. Why would I do that during a pennant race?"

"Shaving runs then? Cashing in if we win by a run?" I accused.

"No. I have no money on the outcome of the game," Dirk insisted.

"So you do have money riding on something?"

"I didn't say that."

"You didn't say you didn't."

Dirk tried to recompose himself. His body language improved but the cocky, arrogant swagger only flickered across him before dying out again. "I bet on me."

"Damn it Dirk, you just told me that you didn't have any money on the outcome. You getting a win requires us to get a win you idiot."

"I didn't bet on me getting a win. You've got this all

wrong. I trust my bullpen to hold the lead, if that was the case I'd have turned the game over to them," Dirk said.

"You're too self-centered for that."

"We're playing .700 ball the last three months. I'd be a fool not to trust my teammates!" Dirk actually looked hurt.

"Then why didn't you let me warm someone up to bail you out?"

"I need another strikeout."

"Who the hell did you find to take the other side of that deal? Even Atlantic City is shy about messing with minor league games, not enough money in the pot. Baseball is hard enough to bet on when people know who is who. The pool of people who know our rosters inside and out to lay down serious money is too small."

"AC? Hell no, I wouldn't risk getting in debt to the mob. And you're right about them not needing to risk money on a sideshow. There are a lot of new casinos this way that aren't as picky. I was late today because I had to get back from Delaware, little place run by Indians and connected to a horse track. They aren't allowed to do anything other than football but they take bets on the side, hoping it will build up their sportsbook clientele. They gave me 8-1 odds with the over/under at 11½."

"That doesn't sound so great, you've only done that once this year and you didn't fan more than ten all last year," I said.

"Lehigh is awful and I'm pitching better than I have in my life. Hell, if Three Way hadn't caught fire I'd be the focus of attention around here. I just need one more," Dirk said imploringly.

"I can't risk that, Dirk. You buckled out there last inning. We were lucky to get out of it unscathed. This team, your teammates, deserve me putting them in the best position to win. So far today you have gone AWOL to break one of the fundamental taboos of the game. Gambling on baseball is the equivalent of a cardinal sin. They excommunicate players for that. If they shit on Pete Rose for life, what do you think will happen to you? Look at the position you've put me in now. I can't cover this up and this team is going to lose it's number two starter. Could you be any more selfish?"

"I fucked up. I wasn't thinking. I was greedy. I'll take the heat for it but you can't pull me."

"I'll pay you back whatever you've lost."

"No you won't," Dirk said with resignation. "I put down 75 grand." The air hung thick between us, I turned to look back to the dugout and saw a host of ears. It seems that our conversation had generated a lot of interest but no one was brave enough to make it obvious they were trying to listen.

One of the ears turned until The Walrus was looking back towards Dirk and I. "Bottom of the seventh, we need our pitcher Har."

CHAPTER TWENTY-FIVE

Miguel Ramirez, the Lehigh leadoff hitter, singled sharply back up the middle. Michael Clark was up next and he walked to put the tying runs on base with no one out. "What are you doing leaving him out there?" asked The Walrus.

"I guess you didn't hear our conversation, then?" I replied tersely.

"No, not for lack of trying though. Harold, we need this game. What is going on?"

"Yeah, we do. It's not that simple though. Just trust me when I say that Dirk has put us in a real bad situation here." I didn't give The Walrus a chance to respond, resuming my frantic pacing from one end of the dugout to the other. The Walrus began pacing as well, with all of the players hanging from the railing we had the floor to ourselves. Every time we passed each other, Wal gave me a look of increasing seriousness. There was no way I could tell him what was happening, if this blew up into a scandal I had to protect others. Wal had been more than loyal, through everything, for so long. I owed him that.

Jimmy Pines took a pitch and scorched a line drive just foul to go 0-2. "Har, we've got a righty and lefty ready in the pen. You've got to go get him." I ignored The Walrus which just riled him up more. The next pitch was a changeup that Pines swung and missed on. I was already onto the dirt when I realized that Rex Stout had his arms extended and was sliding his right hand across his left, signaling a foul tip. Damn it, if he hadn't made contact it wouldn't matter if the ball wasn't caught on the fly by Pigpen. With first base occupied, it would have been a strike out automatically. I hadn't heard the bat come in contact with the ball and Pigpen was out of his crouch like a bullet to argue. Considering my chilly relationship with Stout I held back. My involvement wouldn't protect Pigpen, more likely it would exacerbate the argument until Rex tossed both of us. Pigpen asked for an appeal to the first base umpire, he refused to overrule Rex.

Everything settled and Dirk delivered another 0-2 pitch. Pines grounded out to Trev who went around the horn for a double play. Ramirez scampered to third but there were now two outs. Cam Weir, the Iron Pig cleanup hitter, dug in. Dirk poured in two fastballs that tied him up inside at the belt which Weir chopped weakly in foul territory. Pigpen called for another fastball but Dirk shook him off. The changeup was outside but Weir was looking for it and he served it softly over Chuck's head the opposite way. It was now 4-3 with the tying run on first and a lefty coming up. "You've got to go get him," The Walrus pleaded. "TP can get us out of this."

I grunted and shook my head. "Dirk is on his own, there's no help for him."

"He's thrown 45 pitches the last one and two-thirds, Har. He's up to 125 pitches, more than he has thrown all year. We've got people ready and he doesn't have it."

"Someday, when we are old, I'll explain everything Wal. Just trust me, right now Dirk is on an island."

Leo Derringer stepped to the plate, sitting on a changeup

214

and he got one. Not many righties throw a changeup to left-handers but Dirk does. Usually when Dirk gets in the most trouble is when he throws the fastball too often. That night was different, with the previous batter being the tell. Just as Weir had hit the change, Derringer connected as well. It wasn't a single though, instead a no doubt home run to right that Wampum didn't have to move on. The Iron Pigs led 5-4.

For the third time in two innings, Dirk found the rosin bag. Pigpen made to go out to the mound but Dirk shook him off. Pigpen froze, looking to me for guidance, and I shook him off as well. He returned behind the plate, slowly easing into his crouch buying time for a pitching change that wasn't coming. "Har, if you don't go get Dirk then I will." The Walrus was forceful in my ear, joined by Jimbo. Dirk looked at me, fearful that I was coming for him but I stayed put. The crowd had quieted after the exuberance from the home run. There was no taunting, as would be expected. Instead, the crowd seemed to view Dirk with something approaching pity. The uncomfortable empathy evoked the climactic scene from *Tin Cup*. Every hit slammed into Dirk's ego like the ball rolling off the false front of the eighteenth green until there was no pressure left. The image gave me an idea. "Dirk," I yelled to get his attention. "This is your last batter." Hey, it worked for Cheech.

You could see the pressure lift from Dirk, evaporating as he transformed back to his normal unpleasant self. He kicked at the dirt in front of the mound like a ranch horse at sunset, almost free to graze at pasture for the night. Dirk's lips moved, what they said would make a sailor blanch. The following leg kick was unencumbered, pulling his torso towards home. Pitch 127 of his start split the plate at 99 mph. Now it was the batter's turn to step out, trying to break Dirk's newfound rhythm. It didn't work, a 98 mph fastball at the knees on the black was waved at meekly. Dirk didn't make the mistake of going to his changeup this time. Strike three finally ended the ordeal.

As Dirk sulked down the steps I said tersely, "Shower. Now. After, wait for me in my office."

Neither team had a scoring chance in the eighth and it was now my turn to be isolated, ostracized for pulling a Grady Little. We were down to our last chance and, even if we were successful, I was the goat. In this case, I didn't have much choice but I also had no way to defend myself. To start the inning we turned the lineup over with Jermaine Willis up first. Things looked pretty good for a comeback. As Jermaine tended to his bat with a new coat of pine tar I saw Alex go to him and whisper something in his ear. Jermaine stole a quick look at me before nodding to Alex and jumping sprightly out of the dugout to the field without touching a stair. I motioned for Alex and he made his way over. "What did you say to Jermaine?"

"That it wasn't your fault."

"You know?" Alex didn't give a response, as if talking about it would bring the wrath of the baseball gods. "Fuck. No one was supposed to know."

"No one else heard." Alex gave his characteristic shrug. "I have good ears."

"My office after the game."

"Yes, sir."

Jermaine stepped into the box to face the Iron Pig closer, Dale Macea. Macea had few opportunities this season and made the least of them. He was in the top three in the league in blown saves. His conversion rate was a paltry 69%. I couldn't imagine continuing to go to Macea if I was managing the other side. Then my mind flashed back to May and the black hole I had in the set-up role before Mendenhall stepped up. A manager is only as good as the players he has at his disposal. Macea's repertoire consisted of a fastball with little movement and a slider that was either great or hung like a slab of raw meat. Macea had been leery of throwing the slider lately, which Jermaine knew. True to form, the first pitch was a fastball that Jermaine laced down the third base line for a double. He took a wide turn around second, staring down the left fielder, forcing a well-executed throw to third. I wasn't a real aggressive manager but in situations like this it was good to put pressure on the opposing defense. That is doubly true for a team that is as bad as Lehigh.

The Walrus asked for me to let Jermaine try to steal third but I decided against it. Baseball 101 says to never make the first or last out of the inning at third. Pressure is different from gambling. The Walrus wanted to flick me off, I could feel it, but he played the loyal soldier and went into the signs to Good Hands at the plate. Good Hands laid down a sacrifice bunt, placed perfectly to force the third baseman to field it. Jermaine was now ninety feet away with one out and Andre, a fly ball hitter, at the plate.

Macea decided to try and fool Andre, who was looking fastball, with a get me over slider. Andre likes to take a strike but he swung this time. Macea's slider spun without breaking, gently crossing the middle of the plate at 83 mph. The pitch never made it to the catcher's glove, Andre had number 39 and we were back in the lead. The team had never given up, it was rewarding to look at the line of backs spread out before me jumping with excitement. The thundering shot had quieted the few still left in attendance but where I was standing it might as well have been the last game of the World Series.

The Walrus pumped his fist, pointed at Andre as he rounded second base, and gave him a high five as Andre trotted past. This wasn't enough to sate his excitement, for the first time since the 80's I saw Wal leap into the air. It was the epitome of boyish joy in an old man, a microcosm of why this game is so special. The Walrus had lost 45 pounds in a little under three months, he wasn't a walrus anymore. Maybe a husky. Still, accounting for his slimmed down figure, the height on his jump was surprising. It isn't often that a man in his sixties gets a foot and a half off the ground. I made a note to tell Gail the next time she asks why I can't walk away from the game to describe the scene in front of me. Perhaps the guys would even forgive me for leaving Dirk in soon and let me join in. The separation, as it was, gave me the perfect perspective.

#

"Yer out," yelled Rex Stout.

Oh my God, Andre was going to kill him, he was going to finish what George Brett would not with Tim McClellan. If Andre restrained himself, The Walrus was already making a beeline towards home plate to make sure the deed was done. I was alone near the steps to the dugout, waiting to hear the results of a mysterious conference among the crew. After Andre touched home plate, the Lehigh manager had made his way out to ask for an appeal. Rex Stout had motioned to the ball boy to bring him back for a discussion and had asked for the bat. He held it up, one hand at the cup I had watched Andre craft a couple weeks ago and the other around the knob of the handle, slowly spinning it. Rex's crude inspection lasted two rotations of the bat before he called down Walt Hibaca, the oldest ump of the crew, from first base. The crew chief consulted with a man who had nearly 20 years' experience, Walt too holding the bat up and giving it a spin. The other umpires tediously joined the huddle with the same routine before Rex pulled out tailor's tape, one side bright white, so vibrant I could see it from where I was standing. The other side was the traditional yellow, little black marks every quarter inch, a bold tally at the half inch, and a thick black number every inch. Taking the tape and stretching it up the side of the bat had resulted in an out call and Andre's ejection.

My knee howled but I had no choice. Sprinting to where the umpires were conferenced ten feet in front of the plate, I stopped on a dime and dug in to hold my player and my coach back. "You had better get your team back to the dugout, Freeman," Rex barked smugly.

"Is that a threat?" I huffed out with strain.

"The bat is too long. You know rule 1.10. There is no room for debate."

"Was that measurement verified by another member of your crew?"

"I'm the chief and I took proper precaution to ensure the accuracy of the measurement. Are you accusing me of something untoward? That would be a very serious allegation."

Rex's bullshit just served to enrage Andre further. I knew Andre could push past me without effort but he had so far kept himself in check. I felt his weight ease from my back as he let out a howl. The animal frustration caused Rex to swallow hard, losing color from his red cheeks. "I would like the bat to be measured by another member of the crew," I said.

"My ruling is final and is supported by my colleagues."

I looked to each crew member, seeking signs of unease or regret and finding none. "Your problems are with me Rex. I get it, the last time you worked a series for us I showed you up. Don't do this though, don't take it out on my players in the middle of a pennant race. We both know that's a legal bat."

"Did you see what happened the last time he was up? I would have taken the bat to be drilled, if there was enough left of it to perform a proper inspection that is. I've never seen a bat explode like that, he swings a heavy bat so he can't be corking but I'm sure we'd find something fishy if we looked hard enough."

"There's nothing fishy about Andre's bat," I spit out. "I've never had the pleasure of watching someone put so much care into crafting a bat in my 35 years in this game." It was true, I'd have a guy from Louisville Slugger come up to learn a thing or two from Andre but he swung a heavier bat than was in vogue. Science upset conventional wisdom decades ago, determining that bat speed was more important than the weight in generating power. Ever since, weights had been dropping as bat companies switch to lighter woods. The average was now down to about 32 ounces. Andre being an exception, he liked his at 50 ounces. He was so strong the difference went unnoticed. I had asked him about it one time and he laughed saying Babe Ruth swung hickory during '27, Murderer's Row, a whopping 54 ounces. Rex throwing out the accusation that Andre corked, or worse, made me want to punch him in the mouth. "I want the bat so I can file an appeal with the league."

"And if I disagree?" Rex spat.

"I'll get out of the way. I hear Andre choke slammed a guy once down in Florida." Rex handed me the bat without hesitation. Now I held it in front of me, eyeballing it. "How long did you say the bat was?"

"44 inches. Now if you don't get off my field I'll be happy to send you to the showers with your ogre."

Thoughts of that long conversation with the assistant GM floated through my mind. His message had been unambiguous, if I got thrown out again I was going to be fired. After our conversation last month where I told him I didn't want his personnel back I had scraped away another layer from already thin ice. It was the only thing that kept me from going for Rex's throat. I had never experienced such a profoundly unprofessional action in my career. The worst part was Rex seemed to know I wasn't going to lose it. Andre was now gone with rage but Wal, who might have thrown a punch if I wasn't there a minute ago, had come to his senses and turned his energy to corralling the big first baseman. Alex, always in the middle, was assisting.

Rex kept quiet but he didn't turn away either. The bandages on his forearm were now dotted red, he hadn't stopped bleeding from the splinters that had been pulled from deep beneath the skin. I wondered if Gary Wampum gave a mean Indian rug burn. Rex could use one right about now.

I turned and put my shoulder into Andre's large torso. The three of us were enough to get him back into the dugout. When he finally acknowledged that we weren't going to allow him to tear Rex limb from limb, Andre made his way into the clubhouse without protest. Several small tremors emanated out to the bench and I didn't want to think about the destruction that awaited us post-game. I cradled Missy's replacement across my knees as Trev stepped in with two outs after the second lengthy delay of the night. The clock now inched towards eleven at night.

Macea threw a first pitch ball, trying to take advantage of the aggressiveness that our hitters had shown against him so far. Trev laid off a fastball up and away. The next two pitches were balls as well and the count sat at 3-0. Macea stepped off the mound and Trev was granted time, taking a minute to step out of the box. Trev looked to The Walrus for the signs, Wal in turn looking to me. I wasn't in the mood to flash signs to The Walrus so I just nodded. Trev had the green light. There was no way that Macea was going to put the go-ahead run on base with Lord Al waiting for his shot at the vulnerable closer. Trev was going to get a fastball he could hit whether he was swinging or not, he might as well take a hack. Macea looked an extra beat at Jermaine before entering his motion towards the plate. The catcher set up inside and the pitch was accurate. Trev pulled in his hands nicely, cleared his hips, and drove the ball a mile. If the ball stayed fair it was gone. It was a towering shot, it seemed to hang in the air forever. From the dugout I couldn't get a good read on it so I turned to gauge Trev's reaction. He dropped the bat and began trotting, it was gone.

Trev rounded first as the third base umpire, having moved into left to get a better look, threw his hands up to signal foul ball. Trev stopped with a stunned look on his face, looking around for another opinion, sure that the proper call would be made by someone. The Walrus didn't show such deference. He began a furious charge down the line, a one-man Light Brigade. Lord Al was too distracted or I may have made the joke to him. I had no chance to cut Wal off and he was tossed in seconds. The assistant GM couldn't get mad at that. I was slow to get The Walrus, content to enjoy watching his freedom to say, rather demonstratively, what I wanted to. The rest of the crew rushed to put a barrier between Wal and the third base ump, Rex sneering, begging for Wal to make it physical. The Walrus handled this by enunciating clearly a string of fucks that made Linda Blair, at her most possessed in *The Exorcist*, seem well behaved. Before Wal's head began to spin around I went to get him.

When I put my arms around his waist and whispered, "easy old friend," the f-bombs slowed into a string of stammering whats and hows. "We're getting off the field."

"I have to. Or I will kill someone."

"No. We all are."

I watched The Walrus, with his wits somewhat about him, begin to head for the clubhouse. Maybe he'd start cleaning up Andre's mess without me asking. I walked over to Jermaine at third base and waved Trev and my first base coach over. When they reached us, I told them to hit the showers and enjoy the impromptu day off tomorrow. I pointed to the bullpen and signaled for them to gather their gear. The players in the dugout had caught on and were already collecting their equipment. With two outs in the bottom of the ninth and the tying run ninety feet away, the Toledo Mud Hens, who had already taken the lead twice legitimately, were forfeiting. No one on the team argued and when I told them in the disaster zone, Andre had sure done a number on our clubhouse, that they had tomorrow off as well they understood. I guess my mistakes were forgiven.

It was 1:30 in the morning before The Walrus, Alex and I had gotten the locker room tidied up enough to feel comfortable with the cleaning crew seeing it. The door to my cramped visitor's office had remained closed the entire time. I wondered if Dirk was sleeping in there. For his sake, I hoped not. "So, you heard everything?" I asked Alex, giving him one last out.

"Everything what?" The Walrus asked.

Alex nodded somberly. "Yeah," he answered in conversational English. I might actually feel better if he acted like a Cuban once in a while.

Alex and I stood waiting for The Walrus to get the hint that he wasn't needed here anymore. Wal wasn't interested in taking it. "Wal," I said, "you've had a long night. Lot of stress. Why don't you take a cab to the hotel and get a good night's sleep?"

"Are you really kicking me out, Har?"

"Yeah." He tried to give me the puppy dog eyes, a first in our friendship. "That isn't going to work on me. Besides, you have an important task of your own tomorrow."

"I do?"

"I want you to get the team checked out and back to Toledo. No sense in us staying here any longer than necessary. When you get home, I want you to start the paperwork on registering a complaint against Rex and his crew. It won't get tonight or tomorrow annulled but it's a start."

"Where are you going to be?"

"We've got something to work out. The band will be back together in time for extended BP early Monday." I watched Walrus walk out the door to the parking lot, mad at myself that I was forcing him to stand out in the crisp night waiting for a cab. Shaking my guilt from my head, I led Alex to the office door. I still didn't know how I was going to resolve this situation. For the first time in years, I appreciated the fact I suffered from the partial insomnia of old age. It was going to be a long night.

CHAPTER TWENTY-SIX

Two rings before he picked up. I'm surprised Gary Wampum didn't screen me entirely, I'll take it. "Hau." Smartass. I got quite the ass chewing for using that greeting on Gary during Spring Training. From what I remember the word was mistakenly adopted by evil Anglo popular culture to mean a greeting. Its origins are murky, possibly traced to some French missionary that sounds like the dog. I'd be willing to bet that a bouvier is probably cuter than the missionary. Another possible origin was traced to the Lakota Sioux of the Great Plains. Either way, according to Gary it was quite offensive to address a Senecan in such a way. I guess Indians have different rules.

"Hey, it is your manager. Don't make a scene."

There was a shuffling and a pause. I really hoped he hadn't put me on speaker phone but I don't know phones well enough to tell. "What's up?"

"Delaware, what do you know?"

"Delaware? The state or the tribe?"

"Gary, what do you think? Would I be calling you to get information on the state? Have you been to Delaware once in your entire life?"

"Not by choice. And Delawares are a tough crowd. I'd avoid dealing with them if at all possible. Their men are short and have small dicks, they've developed quite the Napoleon complex about it," Gary said.

"Got it. Thanks."

Before I could hang up Gary asked, "What business do the three of you have with the Delawares?" I didn't answer. Who knows what stories they'll have come up with for our absence by the time we got back.

"What did Gary have to say?" Alex asked. Dirk was in the back seat of the rented sedan, sleeping. Our conversations last night hadn't yielded an answer yet on what punishment he deserved. In fact, he'd been rather blasé about the whole thing. We had just three weeks left in the season, every game within the division including ten against Columbus. Say what you will about the unbalanced schedule but, this year being just five games back for the division meant that every game would matter. Wait, blasé? Lord Al had me using too many adult words lately and I wasn't sure I liked it.

"It doesn't sound good."

"So you don't think we're going to get the bet back, let alone the winnings?"

"I'm thinking that if Dirk wants to walk back out of this place, he's going to need back up."

"Oh." Alex's voice was meek but I remembered him the night of Ducky and Lloyd Reynolds. He'd be ready, perhaps reticent, but ready. If it came to that.

Lehigh County is located in northeastern Pennsylvania, not too far west of Staten Island and New York City. Philadelphia sits south, a mostly straight shot once you connect to I-476. If you curl around the city and follow I-95 you end up in Wilmington. Wilmington was pretty big time for Delaware but that is like saying Providence is a big deal in

Rhode Island. If you weren't born here there wasn't a lot of reason to make a trip of it. In fact, the only thing I knew about the state was that a lot of companies are incorporated here. The old stock certificates for Disney that I had found in Mom's attic after she passed away made it a point to announce the fact. It seems that lax corporate law had made it attractive for casinos to settle here once the state legislature convinced itself that they were interested in spending the additional tax revenue. Gary's warning, mixed with the anything goes nature of a fledgling industry, settled wrong in my stomach. There weren't too many people who managed to get shot in the bright lights of Vegas or Atlantic City anymore. It'd be ironic if the gentle suburbia here hid something far worse.

We pulled up to Delaware Park Casino, muggy haze lying heavy just above the green tiled roof. The new white exterior still gleamed in the strong light of the summer sun, not yet faded with age. Dirk rousted himself from his sleep without any coaxing as the car came to a stop. "Got your ticket?" I asked.

"Right here." Dirk pulled out a green slip, piss poor handwriting was nearly illegible on carbon paper. I sincerely hoped the top slip was kept safely inside because it would amaze me if a pharmacist was able to make heads or tails of Dirk's copy.

"Let's go then. Who are we asking for again?"

"Braden Ravencroft."

I let Dirk lead the way. The place was small, a couple thousand slots ringed the outside with aisles leading to the table games in the center. Dirk said we had to go to the bar located in the back corner. I was hoping he'd weave us through the old women blowing their social security check on the machines but he followed the walkway past the enticing green felt. The clientele was younger here, mostly women who looked easy in tight dresses that Dirk was oblivious to. Smiles turned to pouts in a hurry. The guys were younger than the women. If they had ties on and traded their sport coats for suit jackets they'd be able to pass themselves off as young hot shots on Wall Street. Blackjack was busy, so was five card stud. A sign posted on a flimsy weighted stand reminded people to inquire at the cage about the poker room. Polished roulette wheels spun, coaxing a small white ball to land in the house's favor amidst the groans of an intoxicated man. Apparently Sunday wasn't a deterrent to early drinking for him. Lastly we passed two craps tables, my weakness whenever I went to Mohegan Sun back home. Compared to the reserved behavior of the dealers elsewhere, here the casino workers were clad in bright red vests and distinctive straw hats with a band of red, white, and blue hugging tightly just above the brim. They called out with the vigor of auctioneers and wielded their hooks with style. I had the urge to drop a couple twenties mixed with the desire to leave quickly. Dirk led us deeper into the casino satisfying nothing. That feeling in my stomach got worse.

The bartender was the first employee who I could be sure was an Indian. His dark hair, broad nose, and tan skin stood out compared to the dealers we had just passed. Gary was right, the Delaware were short, or he was at least. And he didn't have a smile on his face. Dirk didn't acknowledge him either, scanning the collection of TVs, glowing unevenly beneath the bright neon of the imitation stadium scoreboard above. Harsh reds and yellows rolled horizontally filled with today's major league games as well as latest odds for the races on the track outside. I smiled at horse number 5 in the 12:30 trotter. It seems that Foal of P 'n V was currently at 22-1.

Dirk hadn't been scanning the monitors, he was looking for a stocky woman, also Indian. As we got closer she got older, thick mascara and red eye shadow caked on to hide crow's feet. I didn't have to see the buried lines at the corners of her eyes to find the deep crevices between her mouth and cheeks. She didn't look like the type who smiled a lot so I guessed it had been a rough life. "Hello again Lydia," Dirk said. He actually smiled. The bastard was a prick on purpose. I made my mind up that if we ever got out of here I'd be happy to let the International League throw the book at him. "I'm here to see Braden again." She flinched, clearly afraid that Mr. Ravencroft wasn't familiar with not shooting the messenger. Lydia didn't say anything but took her time in turning around and heading for an unseen room. Dirk's smile had disappeared as soon as it came and he was once again oblivious to the wants of others. Lydia gave him every chance to change his mind but it was useless. Her arm was actually shaking when she lifted it to push open the door to the kitchen.

#

Braden Ravencroft was quiet as he looked studiously at Dirk's betting slip. Braden was a Delaware, short like the bartender but less fit. A scar cut jaggedly across his right eyebrow. It stood out, red even against his Indian skin. It looked fresh but I sensed it wasn't. Braden was self-conscious about it, his hand constantly going up to feel it hoping that this check would prove that the scar had always been a figment of his imagination. His hair wasn't pulled back into a ponytail, instead frozen by a copious amount of gel. His part was immaculate, Braden clearly paid attention to his appearance. I couldn't tell if there was gray speckling throughout or if the gel caused the light from the fluorescent overhead to make it look that way. Braden wore a sharp looking three piece suit, gray with incredibly thin lapels, maybe that was in style now. I'm not a fashion expert, I'd made a note to ask Gail but I was sure I wouldn't remember. The suit was unbuttoned and sat in a way so I got a good look at the vest, stretched against a large waist. It was a big vest too. Braden's left eye sported a monocle, I kid you not. He looked like an Indian Penguin.

"So you are looking to cash out, Mr. Bobbsey?" Braden asked in a quiet, unassuming voice which matched the airs of his attire. The scar above his eye sat in stark contrast to the reserved demeanor. Braden's tone was that of a complete stranger, it seemed odd considering Dirk was here yesterday and he was cashing out $675,000. Maybe Braden cleared this amount of money? He wasn't sweating.

"Yes." God, Dirk needed a personality. He threw a duffle bag onto the desk that we had borrowed from the team last night. I wondered if this is how it felt to pull off a heist. The movies never had it go so easy.

"I'm sure you can understand that it will take time to track down that much money, several hours. If it would be convenient perhaps I could persuade you to convert some of your winnings into credit here at the Delaware Park Casino."

"While the offer is made in good faith, I'm sure, I must insist on cash settlement. We have to be leaving tonight, busy schedule," Dirk said.

Braden slowly strummed his thumb on the edge of the desk, lost in a faraway thought. "Alright, let me get started on raising the cash. Because it is a Sunday, locating such a large sum of money will be somewhat challenging. Can I provide you with comps, perhaps some drinks at our fine establishment or a room?"

Dirk opened his mouth to answer but I was sure he would accept such an offer. The fool didn't understand how much trouble it would be if we were tied to this casino in any way. "No, thank you," I said. It would be impossible to blackmail us now, the only connection we had to Delaware Park was our involvement with an illegal bookie. If Braden burned us publically, he sealed his own fate in a cell in at least a state penitentiary, perhaps a Federal slammer.

Braden's monocled eye squinted at me, its movement exaggerated by the thick lens. What was most likely intended as a menacing gesture came off as quite comical. It was the first sign I had seen that Braden probably had earned the scar over his eye, this wasn't going to be so easy. With a labored waddle, Braden made his way through the room's only door. It was just the three of us with hours to kill. Dirk didn't seem to care, he might have actually been happy isolated from the rest of the world. It was killing Alex though. I could tell that he was dying to break the silence, itching to strike up a conversation. In the corner of the room, a small black globe hid a surveillance camera. It was possible that we were bugged as long as we were here as well. I talked to Alex with my eyes, imploring him to be quiet. With reluctance, he listened.

The air conditioning to the room had been cut a long time ago and it was stifling. Braden wasn't making this easy on us. Without the fan circulating air within the room, the heavy cloud of smoke which sat near the ceiling of the gambling hall pushed its way in. It had been over a decade since I lit up my last cigarette, the increasing potency of the fumes was too much for my adjusted body to handle. Burning eyes begged for closure and I didn't resist the notion. The heat made me lethargic. I had just about fallen asleep when Braden came walking back into the room, flanked by a well-built black man. He looked like he should be starting on a defensive line somewhere. The man carried an expensive looking brief case of cherry red leather. Near the handle was a five-digit numerical lock awaiting the right combination. A sturdy metal ring had a chain looped through it, the other end was a cuff that was locked around the black man's wrist. Even with the cuff's hinge extended as wide as it could go, the cuff was pinching skin to get closed. Braden opened a drawer to his desk, I couldn't see which one, and removed a key to unlock the cuff. With the case facing him Braden spun the dials of the lock, waited for a second until he heard the pop, and undid the latches.

Braden turned the open briefcase around to face us. "If you would please inspect the bills to make sure they are to your satisfaction."

Dirk grabbed a stack, hundreds bound by a ring of white paper in the center. The paper was blank except for a tidy 10,000 printed on it denoting the amount of the bundle. Dirk flipped through the stack in a hurry, I finally saw him passionate about something. A flash of anger coursed through me, Dirk had cost us the game because of this stupidity. He may have cost us the playoffs and he couldn't pretend to care but now he beamed like *Mr. Gutman* after locating the Maltese Falcon. One of my favorite Bogie films, that one.

Alex was equally enthralled, his tongue nearly tripping over itself as he breathily gushed about how $600,000 could do so much good for Andre, Three Way, Trev, the others, and of course his family if he could find a way to get some to them. I knew that I had to keep my cool, figure out Braden's angle because I was sure it existed. I realized then that I was in over my head. Anxiety tried to assert itself again in the form of returning nausea but I fought to play it cool. I had managed to have a successful major league career, a long managerial career herding young men (the current situation just reinforces how difficult that is), reared kids who it was impossible not to be proud of, found Gail...all of a sudden I was *Sam Spade,* ice running through my veins.

What would he look for? I grabbed a stack, counting just to make sure Dirk hadn't messed up in haste. There was indeed ten grand in the first one. Randomly I grabbed ten other stacks from each side of the case and from different rows (the stacks were set three deep). I felt satisfied that this was an appropriately random sample to ferret out any foul play. With a stack still in my hand I slowly tore the band and split the stack in half looking for a banker's button. No booby trap went off, I was relieved to avoid being inked. Slowly I pulled all of the cash out of the case, looking for some sort of weighted trap and finding none. I sifted through the unbundled stack pleased to see that the bills were nonconsecutive.

"Fill up the duffel bag," I said to Dirk and Alex, pocketing a couple bills from the stack in my hand. I was pleased with myself though I knew I hadn't thought of a thousand possible surprises. You know what they say about ignorance.

A yawn escaped my lips before I could catch it. The contagion spread to Dirk and Alex. The thrill of the payout had receded behind the lethargy that permeated the room before Braden had returned. "Are you sure that you don't want to stay here for the night?" Braden asked. "I hear the suite that is available right now is quite nice and it would, of course, be comped."

"No," Dirk pushed out through another yawn. "We really do need to get going." I zipped up the filled duffel bag in a hurry, trying to leave the room before Braden could do any more sweet talking. I ran smack dab into a muscular chest. Taking a step to my right, I tried again to get to the door. The same chest had moved to block my path a second time.

"Mr. Bobbsey, it seems that luck favors you. I have found that it can be advantageous for you to strike when the iron is hot. I have been an accommodative and generous host, it would only be fair if you allowed me the chance to continue to build a working relationship with you. We have an excellent *Sunday Night Baseball* matchup on *ESPN* tonight. Adam Wainwright is on the mound for the Cardinals against Clayton Kershaw and the Dodgers." Braden's voice was calm but it didn't soothe, instead adding to the sinister undercurrent of his request.

I took a step back from the black man. We really were going to have to fight our way out of here. He hadn't said a word, I didn't know his name even, but his presence dominated the room. We had numbers, three against one, but I still didn't like our chances. "I appreciate," Dirk said the word slowly, haltingly as if he didn't understand the emotion, "your offer Mr. Ravencroft." Mister? I never got that courtesy. He smiled earlier and now he was mistering. Fucking asshole. "However, I was being sincere earlier. We really do need to get going."

"Bernard," Braden said in a clipped manner. The black man stepped aside, I tiptoed past him waiting for a giant foot to extend out to trip me. Oh, who am I kidding? Michael Strahan here wouldn't bother tripping me, he'd put me through the damn wall.

We reached the rental car but I was still unhappy. We were about to travel across state lines in a car we didn't own with over half a mil in cash in the trunk. How could that go wrong? If I developed acid reflux I was blaming *Spade*.

CHAPTER TWENTY-SEVEN

Turning the key in the ignition had brought the sedan to life at exactly 6:47 pm. By the time we made it west on I-76 past Harrisburg the sun had disappeared behind the rolling hills that marked the eastern edge of the Appalachians. Traffic had been light from the outset, it being a Sunday evening, but was now dwindling further to only a vehicle on occasion. There was no major city from here until the turnpike, Pittsburgh still hours away. Dirk had gone back to sleep but Alex talked enough for both of them. The silence of the afternoon had served as fuel for an avalanche of words directed at me, and me alone. I wondered if the kid would survive solitary confinement as he gave me a detailed accounting of how much Fidel Castro had stolen from his people. Quite a bit it turns out, luckily I'm not a jealous guy because I hadn't come close to a couple billion in my life.

"Rumor has it you're going to be called up within the week," I blurted out to Alex. He stopped his motor mouth to digest the information.

"Really?" It was a nice reprieve to have him at a loss for words. The silence lasted for too long though, I had expected the shock to turn to excitement but it didn't. Mile markers passed by, now below 150. Traffic picked up momentarily as we passed a junction, south to Maryland didn't seem that enticing.

"You're awfully quiet over there," I said.

"What were you expecting?" Alex said.

"I was expecting you'd be over the moon."

"Over the moon?"

"Oh, don't play games Alex. You speak English more comfortably than I do. You know exactly what that means."

"If you had told me at the start of this season I would make it to The Show I would have said you're nuts," Alex said.

Dirk shifted in the back seat giving what sounded like a snort before he settled back into sleep. Alex and I stifled a laugh then waited to make sure the conversation remained between just the two of us. The slow breaths continued with a steady pace long enough to satisfy our wariness. "You earned it. Defensively I've never seen anyone better and you have been performing well at the plate. Your swing has really come along since you were called up," I said.

"I'm comfortable here. You made me comfortable."

"I didn't do anything. It was all you. Before you begin to worry about the team, we'll be fine."

I turned on the radio to catch what I hoped was the post-game show for the Wilkes-Barre game. Alex and I tuned in to find the leadoff hitter coming to the plate for Columbus in the top of the ninth. Columbus had had a rough weekend so far, losing the first two on the road and trailing in tonight's game 6-3. They were able to get two men on but the tying run flew out to the warning track in centerfield to end the game. Even with our wild two forfeit weekend in Lehigh we remained just five games back of first. Five back with ten games head-to-head. The Clippers had lost the wind from their sails when

240

Targas went on the DL three weeks ago with a strained oblique. Last time we played them we swept them in Columbus. The deficit was surmountable. I knew I wouldn't be wearing a Union Army General's uniform this time around. My back burst with a flare of itchiness at the thought of it.

"Really, who do you plan on replacing me with at shortstop?" Alex asked.

"It'll all work out."

"So you are perfectly happy with losing me, possibly losing the pennant, to let me play garbage minutes in The Show for a team that isn't my own?"

"Isn't your own? You're a member of the Tigers organization, they are your team. Besides, I think they have big plans for you, and even if all this is only about getting a look at you it isn't meaningless. It only becomes meaningless when you decide to waste an opportunity that others would kill for. Hell, do you think Dirk would care about us peons down here in the I-League if his ticket was punched? I know I didn't," I said.

My eyes had found the rearview mirror to look at Dirk, head slumped peacefully, as I mentioned him. They stayed because of the headlights that were closing fast. I tried to tell myself that it was just some dumbass kids joyriding or a guy who thought too much bass and some nox made him a man. The headlights switched to brights blinding me as they got within a hundred feet. My eyes went back to the road in front of me, hoping that we'd get a horn and the rev of an engine as they passed by on the left. Given our unusual cargo I hadn't dared to go more than a couple miles over the speed limit and the vehicle behind us had to be doing near 100. "But I was-" The brights got closer, drawing Alex's attention and ending our conversation. I was squinting now, the headlights of the car behind us filled the interior with the power of a spotlight. Even Dirk started out of his sleep.

I lost control of the rear end of the sedan as the vehicle behind us got into the bumper. I didn't dare slam on the brakes, allowing us to be pushed involuntarily to over 80 mph. "What the hell?" Dirk said, no grogginess to be heard. Luckily we were on a long straight stretch, slightly uphill so I didn't have to worry about us being pushed off a curve.

"Do you think Braden sent someone?" Alex asked.

"I'd be willing to bet," I said, trying to project calm. The vehicle behind us backed off and the brights were reduced to normal settings. With my eyes still adjusting, it was impossible to tell the model of the vehicle but I was pretty sure it was a pickup truck. The truck leeched forward again, aiming for our bumper just behind the right rear tire. We fish tailed at contact, the car's nose lurched right before whipping left. I was barely able to keep it from rolling over. We came to a rest in the median, damaged but still drivable. I turned the ignition off, pocketing the keys. The truck had overshot us, reversing to close in on our position. "Let me do the talking," I ordered as I got out. I hoped he didn't have a gun because there hadn't been another car now for at least fifteen minutes. He really might be able to get away with murder.

The driver's door on the truck opened, lighting up the cab

to reveal Bernard. He smiled a giant smile, talking with a voice that was higher than you'd expect, "You have something I need. Hand it over and this will be over without any problems."

"Of course Braden would send his lackey to fight his battles for him. Considering there are three of us I think he was too confident," I said defiantly.

Bernard wasn't comfortable with verbal repartee (damn it Lord Al), deciding instead to march straight for me with malice in his intentions. Alex stepped in front of me for protection. Bernard towered over Alex but the spunky Cuban showed no fear. I knew he had a good brawl in him, so hot headed those Latinos. Alex threw the first punch, a weak left-handed shot that Bernard didn't feel. Maybe I was wrong! Bernard laughed, "You threw the first punch. Anything going forward is fair. I'll try not to enjoy it."

"Alex, what was that? No wonder LL whooped your ass in Rochester, you punch like a girl."

"I thought the rule was to punch with my off hand," Alex said.

"That applies to teammates and ornery fans, not a bookie's enforcer whose day job is winning Mr. Universe," I said. "By all means, swing away."

Alex let loose a right that packed a lot more oomph. Bernard didn't grin after being on the receiving end of that one. With a growl he swung back, missing because of the Cuban's speed. Alex floated deftly like a boxer, keeping his feet moving with a grace that matched his footwork on the diamond. Alex didn't get another flush blow but he frustrated Bernard with jabs before hopping back out of the range of Bernard's powerful hooks. Dirk and I lost our senses for a bit, just watching rather than helping. Bernard switched from a boxing approach to a football charge that he was much more comfortable with. With deceptive quickness, he managed to drop into a three point stance and corral Alex like he was tackling an undersized slot receiver.

Belly to belly, Bernard lifted Alex off the ground completely before bringing Alex down hard. Bernard's weight crashed down on top of him. Bernard hadn't taken off his suit jacket before engaging us, expecting this to be easier. The seam at the top of the sleeve ripped when Bernard lifted his right arm up to land a TKO. He paused to growl in frustration, an opening that I exploited with a punch to Bernard's exposed rib cage. The punch caused Bernard to lose his breath and his arm came down in instinct to protect where my blow had landed. Bernard didn't abandon his goal of pummeling Alex and my subsequent hits had little to no effect on Bernard's muscular upper back, shoulder, and arm. Bernard's clipped punch wasn't enough to knock Alex out but I heard the sound of flesh on flesh and a pained grunt.

"Dirk, where are you? We need some help over here," I said.

"Skip, I'm trying to help but you need to get the hell out of my way."

"And what, stand by like you while he pummels Alex to a pulp?" It was an unfair charge considering that I couldn't see where Dirk was at the moment. All I knew was that only two of us were taking on this man that we didn't stand a chance against and my resentments toward Dirk from earlier had not yet abated.

"I'm not standing by, you're in my way." I looked over to see Dirk with the duffel bag unzipped by his feet, the rental's trunk popped open behind him. His hand was not in the large, central pocket but one of the side pockets. I could see the muscles tensed through his forearms and knew what he was grabbing. Dirk and Alex must have missed some when they were clearing the bag last night. I rolled to my left, world spinning out of focus until I stopped ten feet from the scrum. My eyes readjusted just in time to see Dirk deliver a fastball from forty-five feet that cracked with a sickening thud against the back of Bernard's skull. He didn't collapse, somehow rising unsteadily to his feet. How much more was in Bernard's tank? He had already had the wind knocked out of him and was suffering from the onset of a concussion. Disorientation caused Bernard to halt half way through his turn towards Dirk. Dirk let rip another fastball, this one connecting with Bernard just above the ear. Bernard fell, still alive, but out of it. I was glad Ducky wasn't here to see this.

Alex got to his feet looking dusty, bruised, and scared but not any worse off. I was going to have to answer to the assistant GM for the shiner, and assorted other bruises, that were sure to form if they did call him up. I had a feeling he would be discolored for a while.

"I'd love to see the look on Burgess Meredith's face when

he hears the news. I'd be willing to bet he might actually yell 'waa waa waah.'"

"Skip, what the hell are you talking about?" Dirk said annoyed.

"Burgess Meredith...you know, the guy who played the Penguin on the old Batman TV show." They continued to look at me like I was crazy.

"He did kind of look like the Penguin," Alex said after the fact, more in moral support than actual agreement.

Our rental car puttered into the first turnpike station, smoke billowing white from under the hood. I guessed a coolant tube had been severed when the undercarriage scraped hard on the crown of the median. The rear bumper sagged from the frame, coated with the black paint chips that scratched off of Bernard's F-150.

It had been a harrowing experience, approaching Bernard's limp body after Dirk knocked him out. I prayed he wasn't dead and with relief I had heard a raspy, yet peaceful, breathing coming from his prone, hulking frame. I thought of just about every horror film I had ever seen as I felt through the pockets on Bernard's suit jacket for his keys. This was reality though and he didn't spring to life in a supernatural way. It couldn't hurt to have his keys, just in case he did develop the ability to come after us again. I deemed his condition to be serious but not critical, a leap considering how little medical knowledge I have. We had called the police anonymously from a payphone ten miles down the road anyways out of guilt. Ever since, I was waiting for a cop to pull us over, blue and red strobes heralding the end to the most bizarre day of my life. It had been quiet however, perhaps they were all resting up for the next three weeks. With college kids going back to school and Labor Day, state troopers would be putting a lot of overtime in soon. Perhaps they were just avoiding answering our case. It would be a lot of paperwork.

Pennsylvania's turnpike is not a ticket system the same way as Ohio. You pass through several stations, paying small amounts every ten, twenty, maybe forty miles. The condition of our car brought with it a lot of suspicious looks and questions that I thought were the sole provenance of customs and border patrol. The two hundred dollars burning a hole in my pocket was spread liberally between our inquisitors to ensure their silence.

We pulled into the quiet lot of Fifth/Third Field around 1:30. Given her tender condition, I didn't push it to Toledo, staying around 55 mph. The car was in my name and I had been smart enough to pay the insurance. Thirty seven bucks had turned into a pretty good deal considering the damages incurred. Getting out of the car and stretching, I realized for the first time that I was as sore as the rental was. From my neck to my left ankle (what the hell happened there?), pain oozed out of every joint, tendon, ligament, and pore. It slowed me down, to Dirk's consternation. He was already at the trunk waiting for me to grant him access to the duffel bag and the hefty sum of money inside.

I popped the trunk, Dirk pawing for the braided straps that served as grips for the bag. He located both of them, pulling them together to lift the bag from the trunk. I laid my hand on his saying, "What do you think you're doing?"

"Taking my payout and getting out of here. It's late, I'm tired, and practice is in ten hours," Dirk answered.

"I have a different idea," I said. I kept my hand on Dirk's until he slowly loosened his grip on the bag, and even more slowly moved his hands away. I pulled the bag out, opening it just far enough to pull out some stacks. I threw seven to Dirk.

"This doesn't even cover my original bet," he said disbelieving.

"It's 70 grand more than you should have, 70 grand more than what you would have if Alex and I hadn't been there tonight. You lost us a game and put your teammates in jeopardy, I think I'm being generous charging you just $5,000 for that. You accept that and we're all square. If you have a problem with it, I am sure an arbitrator will view your actions with particular interest. To me, protesting this isn't worth destroying your career, and probably mine as well. You know who to contact if you decide differently."

I threw a stack to Alex, "Keep this secret between us. Use it for a couple month's rent and a sharp looking suit when you get to Detroit."

"Detroit? He's getting called up before me?" Dirk asked with exasperation. I think he was angrier about that then me shorting him.

Rusty Chevrolet took three tries to turn over, barely finding life. The trip back to the apartment caused it to labor nearly as badly as the rental after the accident. I was excited to see what Gail had found while I was gone. Turning into the garage, I broke up. Parked in my spot was a behemoth of a car, top pulled off. My new car was a pink Cadillac, crushed velvet seats. At least I liked that Bruce Springsteen song. If I wasn't so sore I'd go upstairs, wake her up, and make love to her like we were still kids. That would have to wait though, I needed sleep and the Avis branch opened in six hours.

CHAPTER TWENTY-EIGHT

Gail was remarkably calm when I entered the apartment in the dead of the night. She didn't ask me any questions about why I was so late. I had been smart and left the duffel bag in my locker in the manager's office at the field. Gail might have been curious about me trying to stuff that into the bottom of our closet. Just in case, I wasted little time hopping into the shower to try and wipe the dirt and blood off of me. My stiffness didn't wash away so easily. I got a raised eyebrow when I said I needed her help the next morning so that I could return a rental car.

I had wanted to return it as soon as they opened but she would have none of that. She drove me to the ballpark where I had left the car overnight. It was a little after ten o'clock when we began our convoy to Avis, her following behind me slowly in the absurd pink Cadillac. I had hoped a good story might worm its way into my brain overnight but I was still at a loss as to how I would satisfy Gail's impending curiosity today. I wasn't a particularly good liar and if I said nothing that would make her unbearably nosy. I was just going to have to tell her the truth.

The white smoke coming from under the hood turned to black as we snaked north. Traffic was light given the time of day, stoplights being the only hindrance to an uninterrupted drive. I prayed for green, worrying every time I had to idle that I might not get going again. An overpowering stench consisting of oil and burning rubber mixed with the black smoke to offend my senses. It became so thick that I had to stretch awkwardly, keeping my foot on the pedal while I stuck my head out the driver side window to see.

I coaxed the sedan to limp into the rental lot where it died not quite in a spot in front of the glass lobby. There was no one else here, the business class having already come to pick up their vehicles for the day. If I had a smartphone I would have snapped a picture of the girl at the front desk. The look on her face was priceless, mouth agog distorting comely features. As I got out of the car, still moving slowly, she moved to make a call on the phone at her station. By the time I had limped inside, four others were at the desk gawking.

"I'm here to return my car."

They all looked at me but no one said anything until the girl snapped out of her daze and remembered to ask, "Your name please?"

"Should be under Harold Freeman. I can't imagine they spelled that wrong."

She typed with impressive proficiency, scanning through a couple of pages on her terminal. "Sir, can I see your license please?" she asked. I slid it across the desk. "And this car was picked up yesterday in Allentown, Pennsylvania, is that correct?"

"Yes."

"Sir," she swallowed hard, "is the car going to catch on fire?"

I laughed, "No I don't think so. Sorry for the condition, I guess what they say about the quality of rental fleets is true.

Look what happens after just a little wear and tear."

"Yeah, wear and tear," she absently mumbled, her gaze fixed on a new geyser of yellowish fluid shooting through the grill and onto the front door. "It appears you're all set sir." No questions asked, maybe it wasn't so hard to be a criminal. The geyser steamed against August air, probably scalding to the touch. "Um, is there a side entrance I could use?"

Back to the ballpark I told Gail the whole truth. She didn't believe a word of it. As I got out, I barely had enough time to shut the heavy door before she sped off in a huff. Normally I would be happy to let her burn through her anger but this was a particularly bad one that might last a while. I didn't think she was going to pick me up after practice. I'd have to get The Walrus to give me a lift. My stiffness was actually getting worse as I moved around so walking home was out of the question.

I spared no mercy at practice, afraid that two days of being off would have us rusty for the series opener the next night against Columbus. We went through a long stretching session and calisthenics as a team before breaking up into group exercises. Pitchers, infielders, and outfielders all completed an intense fielding practice. A short round of BP went briskly, the pace enough to have some of the bigger guys gasping for breath. Pulling the cage off the field everyone got to face a couple of at-bats against live pitching. I challenged Three Way and Dirk to use this as their bullpen session, demanding that they bring their best stuff. The man not up to bat played his position in the field with a bench player rotating in for whoever's turn it was. Every at-bat was situational, if Jermaine led off with a single against Three Way he legged out his hit before returning to center, a ghost runner in his place. Good Hands would then have to read The Walrus's signals as if a game was being played. If we did a hit and run, Wal barked out "two, two, two" to let everyone know that the 'runner' was on the move meaning that infielders were supposed to rotate appropriately, turn a double play if possible, cover the base, and outfielders had to make throws back to the correct base.

Wampum made an error in right on a knuckling liner sprayed at him by Lord Al in Three Way's second inning. The game lasted three innings. Three Way gave up two hits, a walk, and one earned run. Dirk came within an out of a shutout before Andre tagged him for a two run homer. As a penalty, Gary and Dirk ran an intense sprint workout in centerfield as Jimbo put some of the bullpen guys through a session off of the mound. I tipped my hat to Herbie at 3:30 giving him the green light to do his thing. His eyes sparkled just a bit too brightly. It made me wonder if he knew about the illicit treasure stashed away in my locker. He shouldn't but Herbie was like that, he seemed to know everything that happened in this stadium. When my imagination got the best of me, I sometimes found myself thinking that he might be a mystical human manifestation of the park itself. Honestly, he was always here and five months into the season I still didn't know anything about his private life. Every time my head went there I remembered his antics every home game after the fourth inning and laughed it off. You'd have to be human to do that.

The Walrus wasn't happy about giving me a ride home. I guess he was still mad about Saturday night, not that I could blame him. I had put him in a bad position because Dirk had put me in a bad position. It had sure felt good earlier forcing Dirk to sprint until he puked. Wal and I finished changing at around the same time, the only two left in the clubhouse as was customary. We both stood, him waiting on me to ask him for a ride. I could tell he was torn about what answer he was going to give. The phone in my office rang saving him from telling me no. Without so much as a nod we parted ways for the evening. I moved to pick up the receiver to get told that I was losing my shortstop. I still didn't have a good replacement option, there was no way Abe would let me grab someone from Erie after I told him off last month. I did not want to have this conversation.

"Harry, I need you to ship out your shortstop. He's needed up here with the big boys."

"Abe, how pleasant. I was just thinking that we hadn't talked in a while. I've missed hearing from you. Rumors have been floating down here for a while that you were going to call Casillas up."

My reaction drained Abe of some of his glee. Loathing took its place. "I admit I was hoping I'd catch you with your pants down on this request."

"You do know we are a part of the same organization, don't you? We've got a real shot at the playoffs, going from worst to first seems like something you'd be happy about," I said.

"Oh, I'm ecstatic about that. Or I would be if it didn't mean that I'd have to put up with your prickish self for another year," said Abe. Why couldn't he have just taken a job elsewhere?

"Abe, we've never liked each other and I've been in this organization for years now. Don't gloat about my departure yet, I seem to have nine lives as long as Mr. Dombrowski is still around. What can I say, he likes my charming self."

"Not after last month. Playoffs or bust, Har. And I do mean bust. Good luck without Alex around, he's your best player."

"My best player...who I fought to have brought to the organization." I doubted that point would be scored properly in my favor. "Are you guys at home or on the road right now?" It wasn't the fake indifference of spite, I honestly didn't know given how caught up I was in things with my own team.

"Home with a game tomorrow against Toronto. I want Alex here by noon."

"Alright, I'll have him headed your way."

"Good luck Har. P.S. you need to have your team at the stadium tomorrow by one for a commercial shoot." and he hung up. I slammed the receiver down, gathered my things and made for the Pizza Papalis next door. If I was going to be forced to take a cab home I doubted there would be a meal for

255

me. A commercial shoot? Why hadn't they shot that today? Tomorrow was too important for such nonsense, my mood souring more. Chicago style deep dish pizza couldn't come soon enough.

CHAPTER TWENTY-NINE

I had called Alex after a delicious meal to tell him about his reassignment. I tried to call Wal but he didn't pick up and, despite a message, never got back to me. The Walrus was usually my method of communication with the team writ large dealing with scheduling changes. I had to call Rodney Young, the hitting coach, as Plan D after Jimbo and Three Way were both AWOL. Rodney, as stuck in his ways with regards to cell phones as he was with proper hitting stances, laughed at me and informed me that the only phone he had was the land line we were talking on. He assured me that he could have his son do it but the kid would probably ask for a bump in his allowance. Every coach has a contact list and I was relieved when the text came through to my phone. Gail probably knew how to send group texts but she had been holed up in the bedroom reading a smutty romance novel. Fabio, or whoever the guy was, probably got punished for lying when he was telling the truth too. I had hoped it might lead to make up sex but after eleven I gave up on that and had gone to bed so I could be up early.

Alex's car was almost as bad as Rusty Chevrolet, he didn't trust it to get sixty miles north to Detroit. After the last rental car experience Alex and I had, we both agreed that it might be best if I drove him. Given the timing of the call from Abe no teammates had the chance to say goodbye yesterday which I felt bad about. Most players use the minors as rungs on a ladder but Alex had really become committed to our success as much as his own. For some of the career minor leaguers that might not be so hard, but for a player who knew he had the talent to make it to The Show it was rare. From the conversation on Sunday night I knew the transition was going to be tough on Alex so I kept his departure a secret from the team bulletin last night. I wanted Alex's phone to blow up with congratulations and well wishes from his friends, his family, when he was caught up in the magic that was Major League Baseball. If he got them now, I worried he might not go. So here we were, into Michigan on that familiar stretch of I-75 heading north, just me and him. I had one last lesson to teach him before he went on to have a long professional career.

The Cadillac roared as I opened it up, ten cylinders delighting in the challenge of pulling the heavy vehicle forward. It was amazing, passing new model mid-size cars from The Big Three, my Cadillac was at least twice as roomy and had a real trunk to boot. Whereas now it is all plastic or aluminum, my baby was chrome and it sure shined in the summer sun. It probably weighed three or four times as much. We had about five miles until rural Monroe County gave way to downriver. I passed the turnoff to I-275, making my way towards the City at 85 mph. It was heaven. If Gail ever forgave me I really did need to thank her for this.

I slowed it down as we passed the Fort Street exit and I-75 turned north away from the Detroit River. We cruised just to the west of Gibraltar, Grosse Ile, Trenton, and Southgate before hooking eastward again through Lincoln Park and over the industrial fires powering the venerable auto plant, the Rouge River spilling into the Detroit River which was within eye sight again. "You're not in Toledo anymore," I said as the Marathon Refinery shaped our view to the left and the Detroit skyline loomed in the distance to the right.

We continued just north of the heart of the city. "I think you missed the exit," Alex said pointing at the back of a sign, ugly gray metal compared to the crisp green and white of the face. "It said Comerica Park, Ford Field, and the Fox Theater this exit."

"I know where I'm going. You aren't property of the Tigers until noon and we have some stuff to do before then." 75 ended the artificial zig zag through downtown and started north again into the suburbs of Oakland County. A hop onto 696 brought us to Woodward and our destination.

"We're going to the zoo?" Alex asked. "Isn't there something more important I should be doing now? I don't even have a place to stay tonight."

"I made a call last night and got you a week at my brother's. He is about 20, maybe 25 minutes from the stadium. Better yet it is free of charge. The son just went back to school so if you are polite that week will turn into the rest of the season, there is only ten weeks left at best. Now that you are making league minimum I would suggest purchasing a new car, between your earnings and the ten grand I gave you that should be more than enough to trade up from the junk you're driving now. Hence why I had you leave that back in Ohio."

"You didn't have to do all of this," Alex said sheepishly.

"I didn't have to, but it was the right thing. Besides, Gail is mad at me for our adventure last weekend so it was either help you out or endure an awkward evening. That is a pretty easy choice."

"Did we do the right thing? Maybe that money should be donated to charity." Alex was huge on charities, the whole concept fascinated him. I guess in Cuba everything was done by the government or illicitly on the black market. Of all the things to be impressed by in this country, it is amazing that charitable giving and concern for others was what stuck out. Maybe it was us, taking that idea for granted, who were truly the jaded ones.

"I already spent a sizeable amount of it. Don't worry, it was for the good of the team." I parked on the second tier of the parking garage, kids and summer camps bringing crowds out early on the weekday.

The Detroit Zoo is one of the country's best. Alex's hesitance gave way to enjoyment as we wound our way through the park. Outdoor exhibits featuring camels and wildebeests led to the otter and reptile houses. The path took a loop past the apes of Africa; baboons, rhesus monkeys, gorillas, and on to meerkats. Towards the back of the park we passed the expansive habitats for prowling tigers and lions, the males yawning at the onlookers as they waited for the morning feeding. Hulking rhinos threw dirt on themselves to keep cool. As we began our way back to the front the adult grizzlies and black bears slept while cubs in a separate exhibit wrestled in the pool. Zebras and giraffes did Africa proud while the warthog showed the less photogenic side of the continent. Taking the glass tunnel below the pool allowed us to come face to face with a swimming polar bear, a treat according to the volunteer working the exhibit. Peacocks, egrets, and flamingos were clustered together before badgers, wolverines and anteaters. Neither Alex nor I were as excited by the amphibian house as we were the reptiles, it is hard to top man-eating crocodiles and poisonous cobras and rattlesnakes. We stopped next to a giant bear fountain in the center of the zoo because I was unable to pass up the ice cream cart and no one was here to nag me about it.

The warm, dense August air made the penguinarium stink. Alex tried to make a pun about the odor being fowl which elicited a groan from me and a gentle chide from the exhibit worker that penguins weren't birds. That got a laugh which I immediately regretted as I swallowed a lungful of the rancid air. The Emperors were clustered at the top of the exhibit, some waddling and squawking to meet a social custom I didn't understand. The Macaronis, flamboyant yellow eyebrows curling back in a manner that would make Einstein jealous, were more active. A couple of them swam, bloated manatees compared to the nimble Rockhoppers darting by in the brown-gray water. I couldn't help but think that a human being would get dysentery by dipping a toe into that pool. My mind flipped back to our honeymoon again, the Japanese tourists standing out in Hawaii wearing surgical masks as a safety precaution. Gail and I couldn't stop laughing about how ridiculous they looked. At that moment, I'd have gladly taken one.

Before we got lightheaded, we left the Penguinarium for the last stop, the bird house. Since the last time I had been here, back in my days as a player, the zoo had added a butterfly exhibit onto the front of the aviary. Two layers of glass doors separated us from a lush garden that looked like it could have come from Central America. The volunteer at the inner door waited for a group to form, asking for the outer door to be sealed before granting us access. After a short spiel, the inner door opened and we entered. Sun filtered in hazily through a glass ceiling, the greenhouse effect adding to the purposeful humidity of the exhibit to create a sauna. The gardens didn't just look like Central America, they felt like it too.

The foliage was fragrant, quite enjoyable although I couldn't tell you what flowers were in there. Gail would have known. The arid Arizona heat made it difficult to grow much so Gail's garden was mostly imaginary, a best case scenario that was never possible. She'd daydream about all sorts of exotic flora, the power of fantasy can sometimes be more exact than reality and Gail knew her garden by heart. I guessed a lot of it was surrounding me today, I'd have to take her here sometime before the season ended. The volunteers were eager to point out the fact that 70 different species of butterflies were flitting around the open exhibit. They weren't shy either.

The giant monarchs floated by at waist level. Hiding on branches were brown ones, patterns like owls on their wings.

Every combination of primary colors imaginable seemed to be found here. The deepest blacks mixed with bright yellow, blue, or red, sometimes all three. The colors were striped, splotched, or circular. "We don't have as many butterflies in Cuba, this really is incredible, but it almost feels like home. My mom would love it here," Alex said. He let out a laugh as a butterfly landed on his arm, the pattern on its wings a majestic design that resembled a starry night sky. It innocently flitted away.

I led the way to the back of the butterfly house, passing through a heavy layer of beads and then another glass door to the aviary. We took our time to admire the regal plumage of the heron and the ibis. On several occasions, Alex found something he liked through the trees and made sure to point it out to me. "Skip, you seem a bit distracted," he said.

"Just looking for something," I replied.

"What? Maybe I'll find it for you."

"I'm looking for your last lesson. They used to have one...a ha!, over there," I said pointing, my voice carrying enough gusto to send a bird retreating from nearby.

"I don't see anything," Alex said squinting.

"There, just behind the stream on the ground."

"What's so special about him?" Alex asked.

"Just wait." A minute passed and all he did was stand there.

"Can you at least tell me what I'm waiting for? What type of bird is it? He looks like something you'd see in the backyard."

"I have no idea what kind of bird he is. Do I strike you as a bird watcher? And you'll know it when you see it. Maybe he likes an audience." A family came strolling by and I convinced them to stop to inspect the bird with us. The young son got restless but I held it together for two minutes until my feathered friend was satisfied that we were serious enough to put on his performance. With true showmanship he went into his act, hopping with style about four inches off the ground. I beamed and Alex cracked up which was enough to get another hop. The family moved on, staring at us like we were nuts. "That's what he does. He hops."

"You brought me all the way to this zoo just to show me that?" Alex said between laughs, out of breath.

"Well yeah, and you loved it."

"Of course but that doesn't mean I am any closer to understanding why you decided to show this to me. What deeper meaning could there possibly be in a bird whose only distinguishing feature is to hop?"

"Don't you dare listen to him," I said to the bird, "he didn't mean that." The little guy, bless his heart, looked like he wanted to stick out his tongue at Alex. "Honestly, he likes you a lot." My comment once again directed to the bird. He hopped again, in appreciation of my respect which caused Alex to lose it. He laughed for minutes. "See, I told you," I said with a wink that I thought the bird returned.

As Alex's attention toward me came back, I began with my lecture. "My father wasn't exactly a cool kid. Outside of me making it as a baseball player you could say that about

264

most of my family. They're tall but my dad, uncles, grandparents all look like the kind of people at home with a slide rule hanging from their pocket. Even my brother, after he was done firing guns for the Army found his way to the nerdy pursuit of engineering. My dad was a native New Yorker, didn't move out west until he joined the Air Force during World War II at 21. On his first date with my mother he took her to the Bronx Zoo and pointed out a guy who looks just like our friend over there. She got it, laughed hysterically just like you did. It was my Dad's way of testing her, see if she was truly able to understand him in a way that could last a lifetime. My dad was a hopping bird guy himself.

"These crazy little guys are all across the country, I used to visit zoos on occasion just to see if I could spot one and, in all of the big ones they're there. It's like a running gag, kind of a clue hiding in plain sight, that lets you know there are others out there just like you. See, that little bird, will put on a show for dozens of others today and none of them will care. Most won't see him standing there. Most aren't able to appreciate quirks. But some will, they won't just appreciate it, they will openly applaud it. How people treat fellow human beings isn't any different in that you are lucky to find a few who really understand you and those are the ones who you need to impress."

"So surround myself with good people. Got it," Alex said matter-of-factly.

"No, it is more than that, Alex." I paused, trying to arrange my thoughts as best as possible. "Why do you think that you struggled for so long at the plate?" I asked.

"Well," he sounded unsure, as if he had never considered the question. "My swing wasn't conventional and I could get away with that playing in Cuba but it caught up to me here playing in the States, against guys who were about to become the best in the world. I just had to make my swing more normal which I resisted for too long."

"No! You are taking the wrong lesson from that. You hit a drought, probably related to the fact that the Dodgers went out and filled your spot on the roster. All of a sudden you were looking at a dead end, for years. Disappointment like that would cause anyone to slump. That slump though was the window that others were looking for to run you down. It isn't supposed to be possible to hit with a stance like yours, they all said, and you listened. It was only after you let everyone else determine how your swing should look that it truly became unworkable. Imagine if I listened to every radio post-game show to hear people call in to say what a lousy job I'm doing. If I tried to please everyone I'd end up pleasing none of them.

"You were about to say the other night about how this team was family to you. We're family because we trusted you, or more accurately I trusted you, to be able to fix things yourself. I believed in you. And you proved me right. But don't think for a second that you have a normal stance, even with the changes you've made. You don't. Now that you are on the big stage, as soon as a pitcher makes you look foolish on a breaking ball or you don't manage to get a guy home from third with less than two outs the knives will be out again. Don't listen to them, they're the ones who walk by the hopping bird without noticing. The hopping bird hops, that is what he does and what he contributes to the world. Imagine if the hopping bird didn't hop when someone didn't get it, instead trying to impress like the ibis over there. The hopping bird can't be an ibis and you can't be normal. If either of you try to be what others want you to be, you'll fail and lose what makes you special to begin with."

"That sounds so simple but it isn't always easy to do that. Things are different here," Alex said.

"What is simple is never easy or we'd all be successful. This is your struggle. You haven't just adapted to the melting pot, you've erased any trace of the fact that you are a foreigner. You speak better Midwestern English than most of the people around here. When LL had a beef with you, you took a handful of punches. I'd have swung back hard. When he crashed into a wall because you stole his spot and it drove him to be reckless in the quest to prove himself, you were the most sympathetic guy towards him. You made friends with the entire infield in a couple of hours, because you needed it. You were ready to fight for Ducky and did fight for Dirk who wouldn't do the same for you. A lot of these are great things but they form a pretty convincing pattern that you struggle to define yourself apart from how others see you. That bird there doesn't give a damn about what the naysayers think and neither should you. You know what The Walrus wanted to call you when you first got here?"

"What?"

"The Hopping Bird. And you have to admit, you kind of looked like one when you swung. I hated it and told Wal so, thought that the history of this organization made a nickname like that more a burden, something that was impossible to live up to, than an endearing term. I'd like you to embrace that nickname now."

I parked the Cadillac on the curb on Montcalm as it had yet to be closed to traffic with the game still seven hours away. We were fifteen minutes late which I was sure Abe was counting. Despite my certainty, he wasn't waiting for us at the front entrance, just a lone attendant at the box office window. I popped the trunk and helped Alex pull his bags out. The last remnants of soreness from Sunday released with the exertion. I told Alex that I couldn't stay for an emotional goodbye since I was going to be late for stuff back in Toledo as it was. He didn't say anything, just wrapped me up in a strong hug. It may not be the manliest thing to admit but I was touched. As I shut the trunk and moved around the side of the car to the driver's side door I joked to Alex that if Abe has a problem with the bruises on his face to just add it to my shit list.

CHAPTER THIRTY

"How nice of you to show up on time," The Walrus said with a grin that I was happy to see. We were back on good terms it seemed. "Did you get Alex up to Detroit?"

"How'd you know?" I asked.

"Best friend's intuition. That kid meant a lot to you, figured you wouldn't send him off alone like the others. He probably earned it too since his face looked like De Niro's in *Raging Bull* yesterday. The kid's got a heart three sizes too big, helping to dig you and Dirk out of whatever it is that you guys got yourselves into."

"Yeah, we talked about that actually. And I'm the movie reference guy, that's my thing. You made two in ten seconds which I have to put my foot down about."

"I figured those were safe, everyone has seen them and who doesn't love *The Grinch*?"

"I've never seen *Raging Bull*," I admitted.

"Blasphemy."

"It's true."

"I'd tell you to rent it but it seems obvious that Gail has you cuckolded with chick flicks."

"Hey, watch it. You've lost so much weight I could probably take you."

"Naw, you're the one with the weak knee."

I punched Wal hard on the shoulder to make my point.. I finally noticed an audience, the team circled around the two of us. It wasn't particularly inconspicuous but I was caught by surprise.

"Alex got called up?" Trev asked.

"We didn't even get to say goodbye." Andre and Pigpen said simultaneously.

"I knew he was leaving," Dirk pouted in the background, just loud enough to make sure everyone heard how important he must be. No one cared.

"Well, thank you everyone for making it out here early today. I apologize for the late notice but your required attendance was only made known to me last night." I tried to tone down the speechifying, the talk with Alex still had me all fired up. "It seems we are needed to shoot a commercial."

"For TV?" Jermaine Willis asked. "What is it for?" Centerfielders, always interested in the spotlight.

"I don't know. I was expecting to see film equipment here. While we are waiting let's get more important business out of the way. As has been mentioned, Alex was called up last night to The Show, he'll be dressing for the Tigers tonight when they play Toronto. If you want to send him a message wishing him well, I'm sure he would appreciate it. Where's Brock Bisby at?" I couldn't see him standing behind Andre, he moved to the forefront.

The Walrus cleared his throat requesting a conference. "I think there is someone else who is ready to be the full-time shortstop," he whispered.

"Have the doctors cleared him?"

"I have. The kid has been fielding shortstop and left field with me early every day. He's ready. You wanted him to be passionate and now you've got it, roll with it. It'd be awful if you drove him to break his face for you just to keep him from playing a necessary part in getting this team to the playoffs."

"From one to Alex, where is he?"

"He'll never be Alex but the LL who was playing short at the beginning of the year is a pale shadow compared to the kid I've seen the past couple weeks. He's good, maybe damn good. Not best ever but he's capable. My only real concern is what happens if a ball comes up and in when he's batting."

"Damn it Wal, he's so fragile. They aren't going to be able to rebuild his face again and I am sure he's not at full strength."

"Har, that is his call. I'm just saying that LL is ready. Could it backfire? Sure. He has earned the right to have you take some risk on his behalf though. God knows I didn't expect to be advocating for him now but he has really become a team player the past couple months. LL was, honest to God, loading other players' bags with me Sunday when we were packing to get out of Lehigh. That is quite a change from the guy who tried to weasel out of everything we got to know at the beginning of the year."

"Get him some throws with Andre starting in an hour or whenever we're done with this stupid shoot."

I ended my conference with Wal and retook my position in front of the team. "Brock, make sure to stop by my office before the game tonight." If LL really was going to be my shortstop again Brock would have to be on standby.

#

"You aren't dressed. I was expecting everyone to be in costume," the director for the commercial said. I already didn't like the guy.

"It would be helpful if I knew what costumes we are supposed to be wearing. Hell, I don't know what the commercial is for," I said back.

"Ectoplasm, the new sports drink. We sent over a packet of information and instructions last week. It's supposed to tie in to the special uniforms you're wearing for tonight's game. You know, the *Ghostbusters* themed jerseys."

I looked to The Walrus for clarification, not caring if I talked down to the director while he was standing there. "Wal, what the fuck is this guy talking about?"

The Walrus actually blushed. Given his sense of humor what was coming was undoubtedly going to be embarrassing. "I didn't want to show you until it was absolutely necessary."

"Show me what?"

"Front office has us wearing special jerseys to commemorate the 30 year anniversary of *Ghostbusters*. They're pretty...awful."

"Hell, Wal, most of this team isn't thirty years old."

"Aw, they aren't so bad guys, you should have seen the *Chewbacca* ones we had to wear last year," Andre chimed in.

"Yeah, teh sux," said Lord Al. Teh sux? That sounds like something a teenager would text. If last year's jerseys had caused Lord Al's impressive vocabulary to devolve into gibberish I can't imagine how bad it must have been.

This year's jerseys were hanging in the front of everyone's

locker. As others hurried to change, I hesitated. If I had to use two words to describe this it would be teh sux. Who designs a uniform to look slovenly? The collar was meant to resemble a white t-shirt showing underneath a *Ghostbusters* get up. The center of the jersey imitated a thick black zipper with exaggerated silver teeth, reaching up halfway across the chest. A black patch sat over the heart, the movie logo replaced with MUD HENS in red script. The rest of the jersey was a tan brown, black spider web wrinkles and brown patches meant to be stains continuing the slob theme. The straps for the pack looped from the obliques to the shoulders. How fucking childish to have to play an important game against one of the best teams in the league in a kitschy novelty jersey that didn't evoke a lick of nostalgia. Putting the uniform on made me feel like Bill Murray, who wants to be *Venckman*? I tried to convince myself I was Harold Ramis instead but it didn't work. Bill Murray, sheesh. Maybe I'd lace the field with exploding clay animals. That or give me an actual pack, I'd debase myself for a real proton particle accelerator. The jersey didn't even have one patterned on. They put stains and made me look too stupid to zip up a suit all the way on the front but didn't give me a pack on the back. Black numbers that are too small, and in the wrong font, on tan just doesn't cut it.

When the team got back onto the field looking like a cast of a porn film where the exterminators all just happen to be in impeccable shape, a green screen was set up over home plate. "So where's the script?" I asked.

"There is no script," said the director. "You really didn't get the packet, did you?"

"Who did you send it to?" I racked my brain to remember the names of the guys in the marketing department and came up with nothing.

"We called here about a month ago and they said we'd have to clear it with the guys in Detroit. After sending a request, I had a conversation with, well I don't remember his last name. First name was Abe, the assistant GM. He made sure to stress that point. Seems he had taken a personal interest in the project," the director said.

"Of course he did. We'll, I'm a blank slate here, what were you thinking?"

"I don't know. I want it to be authentic, passionate. That's why I wanted to let you guys come up with the idea."

"Well, you had to have some plans seeing as there is a giant green screen over there."

"We need to incorporate *Slimer* somehow, he is the logo for the drink."

"I thought *Slimer* was used for Hi-C?" Three Way said. The veteran got a ton of surprised stares from the young guys. Wilting under the attention he said, "What? I've got a boy. When he was still using sippy cups it was just about the only thing we could get the rug rat to drink."

"HI-C was my favorite as a kid," said Trev.

"Snapple/7 Up bought the rights to *Slimer* for the launch of Ectoplasm. It is available only in the upper Midwest right now so we wanted to do an ad campaign that tied in with the anniversary of the movie and, if things go well, do a lot of promotion for the national launch when the third movie comes out in 2016."

"So, you want me to ad-lib while finding a way to include *Slimer* in the ad?"

"Not just you, hopefully the rest of the guys as well," said the director optimistically.

No one was stepping forward to volunteer. "Jermaine, what do you think? You sounded pretty excited about being in a TV commercial earlier." Jermaine made it a point to look anywhere but at me, it seems a centerfielder's thirst for the limelight goes away when he is forced to improvise. I didn't really blame him. "Trev? You get to do a commercial with Slimer. Bet your childhood self would have jumped at that opportunity." He politely declined. I wondered if Trev could be anything but polite. "Andre? Eh? Eh? I bet the camera will love you, Mr. Larger-Than-Life." Another rejection. I was done wasting time on this stupidity, time to do it myself. "Okay chickens, I'll tackle this alone. I will need you guys to stand together and say one line in unison, can you do that?" I had faith my guys could handle that task.

"Are we ready to go, then?" the director asked anxiously.

"I need a prop from my house. It's only a couple miles away so I won't be gone more than 15 minutes. Why don't you take some shots of the stadium while I'm gone. Those would come in handy, right." It wasn't a question.

"Action!"

"Hi, I'm Harold Freeman, World Series champion, 1984."
I made sure to show off the heavy ring. The million dollar
monstrosities they hand out now must be enough to give
someone carpal tunnel. "I love the game of baseball and have
been lucky to enjoy a long career as manager after I hung up
my cleats. I live for days like today, chasing a pennant but
even storybook careers have those days. For me, I need
Ectoplasm when I'm forced to dress like the Orkin man from
hell and make up a commercial on the spot because of the
capricious whim of an asshole boss." I took a swig, cherry is
the only flavor but it was damn good. I don't even like cherry.
"No *Slimer*, I don't want a kiss." I swung at air against the
backdrop of the green screen to knock *Slimer* out of the park. I
hoped I didn't get stuck with the cartoon animated version.
While I figured the guys at Industrial Light and Magic weren't
on this project, something halfway realistic would be nice. The
camera closed in on my face. "Is this over yet? On days when I
can't just be a baseball man…"

The camera swung to the team, "Today, we need
Ectoplasm."

"Cut! That was brilliant. So raw, evocative, edgy, real."

"Yeah, until you get fired," I said. Time to play the
Clippers. "Say, you guys got any more of this stuff? It really is
damn good, makes me hate Powerade more than I already
did." I finished chugging the bottle I used during the
commercial and was handed another. A lot of the guys on the
team requested another as well.

I retired to the locker room without shaking the director's

hand. I was in the zone, it was time for my team to do the same.

CHAPTER THIRTY-ONE

My zone had been rudely interrupted. While pre-game went fine, it had been a bear since the team returned to the clubhouse. I was on trip number 4 to the urinal in the past hour. Unfortunately, I wasn't the only one, stuck in the back of a long line. The stuff was like crack and we had all had way too much of it. "Guys, us old men don't have the bladder strength that you do. I need to cut," I said.

"You absolutely do not get to play the age card, Skip," said Good Hands. "I've got to patrol left field, how do I manage that with urine weighing my pants down? If you have an accident all you have to do is sit on the bench."

Jermaine was first in line. "He's got a pretty good point. That might be the difference between a steal of second and being out."

"This stuff isn't just tearing through old man bladders anyway. I've had so much it's coming back out like colonoscopy prep, only from the front," complained Trev.

"Yeah, I'm the ace and all but this is a different kind of number one stunner if you know what I mean," said Three Way.

"Dude, you mean Numba One Stunna, right?" said Jermaine. "You're way too white to use that, can't pronounce it right."

I laughed and almost peed myself. "Did you get that reference from a Hi-C bottle too? And Trev, what the hell are you doing getting a colonoscopy at your age?"

"Family history, doctor's orders," Trev said simply.

"Well I think that is the dumbest thing I've ever heard. Break the rules every once in a while, won't you? Don't tell the cleaning crew but I'm not going to make it waiting for all you guys, I'm peeing in the shower," I said.

I made it to a drain with seconds to spare, relieving myself in such a torrent that all I could do for the next two minutes is stand with my hands on my hips until it exhausted itself. Once I broke protocol, others got the courage to do the same. Every shower drain, urinal and toilet was used to find relief. "Easy, watch where you're splashing," I chided.

"Are you kidding? Of all the weird things going through my head while I pee in front of my boss and you're concerned with my aim?" Three Way said.

"Just be careful. And this goes for everyone, there will be absolutely no crossing of the streams."

After my bladder slowed my stream to a trickle and then a leak (it sucks getting old) and then a stop, I tucked myself back in and got the hell out of there before I got hit with an errant shot. LL was waiting, squirming to keep from popping. "Spot's open," I said.

"Can't. Shy bladder."

Huh, never would have guessed that one. "I bet you could make an exception right now."

After such an impressive showing in the bathroom I held onto Lord Al's board to let a moment of dizziness pass. The blood red eye of the Krampus stared back at me but I was too preoccupied to care. The disorientation abated and I returned to normal posture. Sixteen games to play and we had twelve squares showing glimpses of the gruesome scene below. Suddenly the incomplete Father Christmas didn't seem so comforting, my job hung in the balance and the odds were long. If the playoffs weren't a necessity before, the day that ad started they would be. Even that might not save me.

A low drumbeat became louder over the course of several minutes. I didn't have to leave the clubhouse to know it was now being banged outside the Washington Avenue entrance. It was nearly Gregorian in its consistency in tone, volume, and frequency. What the hell else was going to happen today? Talk about a strange week.

"Is that John Adams?" Ducky asked.

"Why would John Adams be here," I said. "Just stay focused on your start tonight. I'll go investigate." A couple days ago that type of statement would have gotten me a *Hardy Boys* buddy in Alex. A pang of sadness passed through me when I realized that I'd be sleuthing this one out on my own.

The clubhouse door opened and The Walrus came walking in with a bag of fresh greens from a grocery store somewhere. I didn't know there was one around here. "Hey Wal, what's the racket for?" I asked. I was suddenly keen on not having to inquire.

"Seems they called in the major leagues for this one. John Adams brought his drum over from Cleveland."

"Told you!"

"Ducky, what did I tell you about preparing for your start?"

"It isn't just the drum though. They've got a whole tribe out there. They're doing some kind of dance or ritual or something," The Walrus said.

"It's a rain dance," said Gary.

"We did put on quite a show the last time they were here," I said.

"Yeah, but those shitty new tech jerseys got trashed after that. Guess it happened to Tacoma or Portland out in the Northwest too. Majestic had quite a bit of egg on its face over the whole thing. Biggest flop since the Olympic speed skating debacle," The Walrus said.

"I don't think they are doing it for a repeat performance. Just a way to poke some fun at us."

"Well, we certainly are giving them that," said The Walrus as he gestured to the novelty uniforms we all had on.

"Those bastards," Gary said with complete earnestness. I had to rush to the office and shut the door before I burst out laughing.

John Adams wasn't let into Fifth/Third Field but there wasn't anything stopping him from taking a position on the plaza behind left where St. Clair meets Monroe. In fact, given the capacity of the Mud Hens park, he was probably closer to the field here, outside the stadium, then he was at Progressive Field during an Indians game. You'd think that I was used to the steady drumming by now, Adams has been doing it at Indians games for over forty years and I played probably a hundred times there. I didn't remember it being a lot to cope with then but tonight it overwhelmed me until I had a headache. We hadn't even gotten to first pitch yet.

I found reasons to continue to retreat into the clubhouse, hoping that people thought it was just the nerves. The last time I left the dugout involved more than a headache, the goal was to have them in and out during the game and I really hoped it went as planned, it would be quite the surprise. The installation guys greeted me with a blue collar "Hey bub" as I opened the clubhouse door for them. I gave a look around the clubhouse to see if anything was laying out, just in case. A couple of half-drank bottles of Ectoplasm that I was more than happy to let the guys take if it really meant that much to them. I told them to hammer or bang all they want, no one would hear them tonight. They were annoyed by John Adams too.

I went back to the field and exchanged lineup cards with the home plate ump, also the crew chief, Kelly Wright. "Mr. Wright, you only seem to come to town when the Clippers are here. Are you guys stuck like glue or something?"

"You know, I have done a lot of their games this season, come to think of it."

"You should bring that up with the Union, you've put in too many years to this game to deserve such punishment."

Kelly didn't laugh but his eye twinkled. "Easy Mr. Freeman, Columbus hasn't pulled any stunts quite like yours the last time I was here."

"True, but we go way back, you know I respect you. I figure every once in a while you like to be entertained is all."

"Hey, are you guys talking about me?" Dave Weedle, the

Columbus manager, asked.

"No Dave, we're not. You're too boring to merit much discussion," I said dismissively and began my walk back to the dugout. Ten games in two weeks to determine who made the playoffs, it didn't seem right for us to get along.

"What'd I do?" Dave asked Kelly Wright.

"Don't look so surprised. You're ahead of him by a couple of games in August, he isn't supposed to like you." Spoken like a true student of the game, Rex Stout could use some of those lessons. I'd have to ask The Walrus how our complaint was going. If the Commissioner's office shelved it until the offseason I was pretty sure it would get the dreaded pocket veto from neglect.

Ducky pitched well, giving up just two runs into the seventh. It was touch and go throughout, Columbus stranding 6 runners and hitting into two double plays. LL and Chuck turned a tough 6-4-3 on a ball into the hole. LL adjusted his glove nicely to backhand the ball as it hopped on him. Standing with a foot on the outfield grass he gave Chuck a good feed with zip even though he threw flat footed. LL's throws to Andre were crisp too, caught comfortably by the big first baseman in complete contrast to the fielding session we had on that off day in May.

Ducky made a nice pick of his own, starting a double play in the fourth. He got a runner at third on a bad sacrifice bunt as well. Since our talk, and the new pre-start routine that I wasn't invited to this turn, Ducky had become a plus fielder. For whatever reason, so had his breaking ball. Ducky's curve had turned into an out pitch as of late. That came in handy in the fifth when Ducky struck out a man with a runner on third and one out. I looked across the field to the visiting dugout, Dave was as gentlemanly as at the start of the game. Given the frustrating nature of his offense that night, I thought that was pretty good.

I had made a late change to our lineup card, quickly scribbling in Gary Wampum into the five hole and he didn't disappoint. Three hits including a double gave him four RBI on the night. We won 5-2 after Claudio Vega, Mendenhall and Grissom all were perfect in relief. Grissom got save number 35 on the year, another notch on what was a personal best season for him. If he did have mice at his house, they would be getting an extra piece of cheese. The weather was pleasant, not too muggy with temperatures in the low 70's at game time which cooled to around 65 by the final out. The stands were packed and our fans drowned out John Adams's infernal drum for most of the last couple innings. Four games back.

Most everyone had left. Wal sat in my office gabbing away about trivialities because I was a stickler for avoiding the elephant in the room. The surest way to end an attempt at tracking another team down in the standings is to begin talking about it. If you can remember how many superstitions I'm up to at this point, you've got a better memory than me. Gail would probably know, women remember everything especially when they can use it against you. Speaking of Gail, she was sitting in the first row behind the dugout, all smiles. It felt great that we were on speaking terms again but I'd be a fool if I thought she had sheathed the blade back to the hilt. When it came out again it would just be sharper, probably accompanied by The Look. Ah, relaxing after a victory and commiserating with a buddy about broads. If I just had a cigar in my hand. In fact, my real desire was to drive home to my girl and enjoy the rest of the night. Funny thing about guys, we talk tough but most of us are softies. That would have to wait until I saw Three Way's reaction. I was surprised he hadn't found it yet.

"So, I think I found someone," The Walrus spit out. He tried to say it casually but it was obvious it meant more to him than that.

"Oh, really? She's not in her 20's, is she?" I figured humor might make the subject easier.

"No, she isn't. Maybe with a Lifestyle Lift," he shot back sarcastically. After a moment for effect, "I'm interested in her for her money."

"Smart man. Us starters are probably doing okay in retirement but I can see how a bench player is stretched a bit thin by now. My pension can't go to just every player," I said offhandedly. That could be seen as a dick move but if anyone got me well enough to know I meant it in jest it would be Wal.

"I'm doing just fine, thank you much," he said with pride.

"How'd you meet her?"

"The internet."

"You didn't use *eHarmony* did you? Does that guy bug you or is it just me?"

"Just you. And I used *Craigslist*."

"I didn't take you for that kind of guy."

"You don't even know what *Craigslist* is, do you?"

"Not a clue. I'm kind of surprised you used the internet at all. But you have a smartphone too. I'm happy just to be able to use a remote control. What made you decide to take the plunge?"

"Well, Kim called about a month ago and wanted to give it another shot. I swear I would have done it but after I got off the phone with her I walked in front of a mirror and saw who I was turning into without her. I liked who I was looking at and it suddenly clicked that Kim had been part of the problem, not the solution."

"Well, I'm really happy-"

The office door swung open in a rush, hitting the stopper with too much force. I was sure a good size hole now existed where the handle had hit the wall. Three Way didn't seem to care about it, exclaiming, "What in the hell happened in the rehab room since this morning?"

"Surprise," I said wryly. "What took you so long to notice?"

"Well, I was eavesdropping on your conversation. Figured at some point I'd hear the story from this weekend. First you, Dirk, and Alex disappear for a day. Then you come back with you and Alex looking like you had gone twelve rounds with a prizefighter. This may shock you but it rouses curiosity."

"Don't eavesdrop, my business is none of yours."

"It is when it affects the team. Skip, we're so close to that championship we dreamed about. If there is something that might keep that from happening you better damn believe I'll be sniffing around," said Three Way. After a second he tacked on, "Now new equipment shows up that has to cost several thousand dollars mysteriously. As the veteran on this team and a captain, I'm smart enough to smell a rat. What's going on?"

"Don't look at me. No sympathy here," The Walrus said. I hadn't expected to be double teamed, and now that it had happened I didn't have a good reason why it took me by surprise. I was caught.

CHAPTER THIRTY-TWO

We moved to the rehabilitation area, I flipped a switch on the wall to ignite a new bulb. The darkness gave way to white illumination, bathing the room in a clinical glow. Out was the beaten up whirlpool that only leaked ice cold water and was too small. The men had done a great job replacing it with a state-of-the-art unit that sat off the ground, small legs making it easier to get in and out of when your muscles ached. It sat two feet deep, three feet wide, and 56 inches long. The rusty, jagged notches of the old unit gave way to sleek stainless steel and seamless welds. The new unit was connected to a water line, escaping from the floor accompanied by a small tankless water heater. Three Way gently ran his hands along the curve where the bottom of the tank met the sides, whispering something I couldn't hear. I'm pretty sure it was good though. He turned the hot water nozzle and purposely scalded himself, delighting in the fact that ice baths were now an option, not the option. "What did this cost?" Three Way asked.

"Enough. Not as much as the chiropractor who starts tomorrow. I had to agree to pay two months of revenue for his practice to get him to serve us exclusively until the end of the year. Don't worry, I didn't look for the cheapest guy. You've been sore all year Three Way, figured it was only getting worse as the season comes into the final stretch. I know Pigpen and Andre are dealing with some soreness and Lord Al swears he has sciatica. That's what the table over there is for."

"Har, where is all of the money coming from?" The

Walrus asked with concern. I let out a sigh and told them everything about Saturday and Sunday. By the end of the story they at least understood why I chose to do what I did.

"You guys have to promise to tell no one." I had now endangered two more guys with their careers. The fact that one was done at the end of this season and the other had already enjoyed a decades-long one, neither needed to worry about tomorrow, didn't comfort me.

Rat-a-tat-tat. A series of elated groans. *Rat-a-tat-tat*. More groans. This process repeated every 45 minutes throughout the early afternoon. The next set of cracks sounded more like bark popping in a fire than bb guns. "That must be Andre," The Walrus said. The chiropractor had sure been busy.

"He's probably wondering just what he got himself into," I said with a grin. "Have you scheduled a session?"

"No. My mom used to say that once you go to a chiropractor, you end up having to keep going back. It must feel good but I've made it this long without one. Something tells me that it is probably best to keep that streak intact."

"We're going to need extra stretching today. I saw a couple guys walking around earlier, looking like they had just survived an all-night rodeo if you know what I mean. I can imagine that spinal adjustments are subject to a bit of tightening afterwards."

"So that is why you haven't hopped up on the table?" The Walrus asked.

"No. After my knee I have a healthy distrust of doctors."

"Don't let the chiropractor hear you call him a doctor."

"Why?"

"They're just funny that way. Want to be considered legitimate medical professionals but maintain their reputation as being an alternative to formal treatment. My baby girl dated a chiropractor for a while. If I have to hear one more lecture on why vaccines are terrible for kids I might scream."

I thought about The Walrus's sentiment as Dr. Hanover stuck his beakish nose into my office without a knock. I would normally forgive the social faux pas but he then entered into a clinical discussion about how much work he had to do on Three Way. The whole spiel dripped with condescension towards our strength and conditioning program with complete disregard for the fact that Three Way had put in almost 2,000 innings in his career. Throwing 40,000 pitches at a level the average man could only dream about (ask Phil Mickleson whose tryout with Toledo is still laughed at) will make your body crack in unusual ways. Throwing overhand is perhaps the most strenuous physical activity in sports. If you have a man throw off a mound with his shirt off, you can see the biceps and triceps actually switch places. If a pitcher was not able to take the stress off his arm by transplanting it to his core he'd blow out his arm in a couple weeks. No strength program can halt that completely and it got my dander up to hear someone who didn't understand the demands of the sport lecturing about the signs of abuse it had created.

I cut him off telling him that Three Way would get all the attention he needs now. Hanover tried to warn me that too much too soon could carry with it adverse consequences but I told him off, encouraging the chiropractor to give Three Way a double session today and rescheduling with whoever was supposed to follow. Hanover said he had yet to truly understand all of the personalities on the team but he guessed that Dirk was not going to like that. I smiled and said I suppose he probably won't. Pushing Hanover back out the door he had so rudely entered I reiterated my previous instructions. I closed the door as Hanover began to object again.

Toby Mack got himself into as much trouble as Ducky had the night before but he wasn't able to get out so adeptly. The Clippers scored in every inning Mack pitched, including three runs in the fourth which forced me to get him. With over five innings to go, and all three of my most important set up men having pitched the night before, I had to dig deep into middle relief. Robert Tammeny, Robert Dillon, and Marquis Winston all got a chance to go over an inning in relief. Tammeny, who Lord Al liked to call Boss Tweed (he really did think he was clever), allowed an inherited runner to score as well as giving up an earned run himself to get through the fifth. Dillon gave up two earned to get five outs. Marquis allowed another earned run to get us through the seventh. I even had to let Charmin throw to righties and he surprised by making it through the eighth cleanly.

Luckily for us, the offense got to the Columbus starter, Ozzie Montoya. Wampum was still fired up from yesterday and collected three more hits. LL had two, including a double into the gap. Trev hit a home run and Andre got his 39th, without an ump saying otherwise. Dave didn't dip into his bullpen as early as I did, leaving Montoya out there too long. If this was the majors, he'd be taking a lot of heat for it in the papers tomorrow. I had the feeling that getting slammed on page 8-C of *The Columbus Dispatch* behind the Buckeye football preview wasn't going to bother him too much. It probably did bother him some that their advantage had steadily eroded throughout the middle innings until we took the lead in the eighth. Jermaine got a single with two outs and the game tied, stole second (to go with steals in the 3rd and 5th innings as well), and came home on a solid single to right by Good Hands. The Clipper right fielder, Matt Anthony, was playing shallow. He corralled the liner on two hops and fired a strike to home. Jermaine slid to the back of the plate, left leg expertly hooked around the beefy leg of the catcher to touch home with the tip of the toe before the swipe tag was applied. The safe call was greeted with disbelief by the Columbus bench and Dave had to play it cool to keep his catcher from getting thrown out. I never looked at the replay, I didn't want to know if their 'plaint was legitimate or not. The string of catcalls from the visiting fans that lasted until the final out made me think they probably had a point. Every good rivalry has some controversy. At the end of the night we won 11-10 and were three games back.

I believe the adage is that you aren't supposed to count your chickens before they hatch. In baseball, it is a long held idea, of which I subscribe to, that sweeps shouldn't be mentioned before the last out is recorded. Our fans didn't get the memo. Walking onto the field under bright afternoon sunshine, the stands were filled with 'Birdie Brooms' courtesy of the local hardware store. The kids had all figured out that they could make a racket if they held the brooms bristles up and slammed the handle into the ground or the back of the seat in front of them. After exchanging lineup cards I found Gail and Amber in their traditional seats, first row behind the dugout, glaring at me as they leaned forward and propped themselves up against the dugout roof. "I'm too old for this," Gail yelled. I wanted to say back that she didn't look it but I figured it would get lost in the din.

We got off to a comfortable lead, up 5-0 through four innings and I suffered through the rest of the game concerned every time I heard someone yell sweep. Columbus still looked hung over from the outrage of the night before, unable to muster more than 3 hits and only scoring on a solo home run for the game. We were now two games back, nine wins from completing Lord Al's board. It was a salsa celebration in our locker room, at odds with the mood of the visitors. Getting swept, and struggling to score, had created a superficial veneer of ennui around the Clippers. Or at least that is what Lord Al said when he came out of the clubhouse to find out why I was still inspecting the Clippers packing up their equipment in the visiting dugout, 45 minutes after the game had ended. We had an off day tomorrow and then played

Columbus in Columbus over the weekend. I was sure that the Clipper demeanor the next three games was going to be anything but ennuiish. Yes, I made that word up, and no I didn't tell Lord Al about it.

The salsa music jarringly switched to meditative New Age. "What the hell is that?" I asked Lord Al.

"After an extensive chiropractic session, Three Way has discovered a hitherto unknown level of serenity. It appears that he has chosen to share such sentiments with the team as a whole."

"He did look like he had just found Cloud Nine today," I said. Is that what Hanover was trying to warn me about?

CHAPTER THIRTY-THREE

"You feeling okay?" I asked.

"I feel great," said Three Way. He was no longer blissful, having a dud of a start will do that to an ace. "Honestly, the Doc-"

"Don't let him hear you say that."

"What?"

"Never mind."

"If that was supposed to be a joke I didn't get it. Whatever the guy did to me, it worked. It isn't just that I don't have pain, I don't feel anything at all."

"You're numb."

"No, not numb. I…am not fighting anything. My motion is smooth, easy. Too easy."

"If you need to fight something, the scoreboard should get you in a sour mood Three Way."

"If you want an eloquent explanation go ask Lord Al, Skip. I'm trying to tell you what's wrong. I feel terrible about this. It is like things are too right if that makes sense. I've been at this a long time, I don't remember it not hurting. Everything was calibrated to take that into account. Today I don't hurt. The pain wasn't a hindrance, it was the feeling I needed to tap into to get that little extra on my fastball. Without it, I'm back to pitching the way I was at the beginning of the year."

"I thought you were hurting too much earlier in the year."

"I was. Now I'm not hurting enough."

"You pitchers are an odd breed."

"You could have just asked my Mom, she's been saying that since I was born," Three Way said with a smirk.

"This isn't funny. I forbid you from seeing Hanover."

"Yes, mom."

"I'm serious."

"I'll never do it again. I'm keeping the whirlpool though. Don't you dare get rid of that."

Three Way had his worst start of the year in Columbus, 12 earned in six-plus innings. I let him struggle for longer than I should but I was hoping he'd get a 1-2-3 inning at some point and that would give him something to build on for next time out. It never happened and behind his stoic demeanor and bad jokes, I thought I detected a bit of worry as he handed me the ball with a man on first and no one out. It had been a consistent, shocking barrage. I thanked God that no one else had been affected so severely by Hanover. In fact, if you took the obvious, glaring black mark out of the equation, Hanover had the team playing spryly given the fact we were two weeks from Labor Day.

We won the next night, Dirk going eight strong innings, giving up an unearned run. Andre hit his fortieth home run, an achievement akin to hitting fifty in the majors due to the abbreviated schedule of the International League. It was a triumphant blow that if we were playing in an older stadium might have blown up a light tower, stacked probably 75 strong with industrial strength incandescents a la *The Natural*. I had decent power when I played, averaging 20 a year. My best home run went over the roof at old Tiger Stadium in left, bouncing off of Trumbull until it came to rest against the barbed wire fence of the Brooks Lumber Yard. As I stood applauding Andre round the bases I remembered that my recent trip to drop off Alex in Detroit was the first time I had been to the city and not checked to see if the familiar red and white building was still there. With today's stadiums defined by the toothbrush lights, halogens that sat high above the field and numbering perhaps twenty, as well as open views of city skylines, there was no good way to measure the nature of home runs today. They measured it at 515 feet but it didn't feel anywhere near as special as Reggie Jackson's bomb in the '71 All-Star Game. For all the great things about modern ballparks, one of the worst features of today's architecture is to rob us of such scale. I cheered harder to try and make up the difference.

Before the game started I had scanned the crowd for any sign of Braden and another round of hired muscle. On occasion I looked towards The Walrus or Three Way it was obvious that they had similar sentiments. The outs kept coming, easily, until I told Dirk that he wouldn't be needed in the ninth. It had been his best game of the year, I hoped he was trying to make up for the loss in Lehigh but I should have known better. He didn't fight not getting a chance for a complete game, saying, "You told others." He must have noticed their uncanny interest in the crowd as well. "How can I prove to Detroit they made a mistake in calling up Alex if I don't win? If you are going to steal my big payday, that is all that matters to me now." I think he was truly offended that, a week after he lost us a game because of gambling and endangered the lives of his teammate and coach, we'd still be concerned about it his next start.

The guy owed me his career and he was still wrapped up in himself. Worst part is that he would get his shot at the bigs the next season and stick. Of course he ended up playing for six teams in eight years so I guess no one else could stand him either.

We lost the next night, giving Columbus a series win at the worst possible time. Even so, we had gained two games on the Clippers over the week and sat three back in the standings with four more against each other to end the year. We entered the eighth with a 2-1 lead but Mendenhall let the lead slip away. It was just his third blown save of the year, still the lowest in the International League for set-up men. It hit him hard. Alex would have known what to say to make him smile, the rest of us weren't so lucky. The best thing about baseball is the fact that tomorrow isn't just another day, tomorrow is an opportunity to soothe disappointment.

I left for the stadium the next morning, trying to outrun Gail's pestering about supporting Trev tonight. She had first mentioned it during a breakfast of toast and poached eggs. I nodded my head and said "Sure, sure" in as convincing a manner as I could muster. It must have worked because all she said was how exciting it was. This must be how it feels when husbands forget their anniversaries. For the next hour I racked my brain to try and figure out why Trev merited special support today and I could come up with nothing. It would have been easier if Gail didn't give the subject the *Seinfeld* treatment. It seemed as if tonight's mystery event was the most important thing ever, so important that she actually said nothing about it. Maybe she did know that I didn't have a clue and was just torturing me on purpose. She liked those kind of games. Whatever, she had made this year the best of my professional life by going through it with me. It had been the perfect adventure, just like she had said she wanted that first night we had together in the apartment. That gave her license to be annoying at times.

Walking into my office, a heavy cardboard box sat on my desk. I was relieved to find out that inside was a more formal wrapping, topped off by an elegant, lacy bow. A tag said it was for Andre, they had gotten that award etched quicker than I expected. Laying on top of the box was a note asking me to present it to Andre tonight. For as ridiculous as the birdie brooms and *Ghostbusters* jerseys were, the organization did a lot right. For a brief moment I got sentimental.

A knock at the door broke the feeling. It was followed by Trev sticking his head into the office, "Hey Skip, up for throwing some BP today? Wal is feeling a bit dizzy."

"Dizzy?" I asked.

"Yeah, Doc says his blood sugar is too low."

"Oh, dieting as hard as he has been will do that to you. Get that man some juice."

"We tried to offer him some Ectoplasm but he wasn't

interested. We got that stacked by the pallet now in the back room, they were serious about keeping us stocked with the stuff. Wal didn't want any, said it would cause him to pee away any sugar he put into his body."

"Not if he drinks just a bottle. We all got in trouble having half a dozen. You say we got stocked with more? That could be trouble."

"Easy, nobody gets more than one. Guys put me in charge," Trev said.

"Of course they did." If there was anyone who could instill temperance in regard to that stuff it would be the Bible thumper. "Wal likes Frostys, send someone to Wendy's."

"Brock Bisby is on it. So, about throwing? I really don't like the machine."

"I'll be out in a minute. Oh, Trev, you have my support tonight."

"It isn't really me that needs it." I prayed that he would elaborate since I still didn't know what the hell was going on. "She's been practicing really hard so I am sure she'll nail it." A ha! That was it, Amber was singing the national anthem tonight. I smiled. I had raised hell with the marketing guys until they finally found a spot with her doing vocals for an eight man instrumental group from Jamaica. Something told me that the choir girl from Ohio would mix disastrously with Bob Marley wannabes. I didn't dare say that out loud.

"Hey, easy there, big guy." I had made sure that the whole team was standing along the baseline as if we had just been introduced on Opening Day. Trev's broad frame was shaking, not really a leaf, more a mature oak tree. "She watches you perform in front of a crowd every day."

"Yeah, but that is different," Trev said.

"Not so much. Hell, she had to sit through a ball nearly caving in your chest. Don't for a minute think it is easy to be able to do nothing but give support while we're out there. There is a certain helplessness in being able to only watch the ones we care about. Being a rock is what she needs right now."

The horns came to life first, softly, and slowly, something that barely resembled the familiar notes of Francis Scott Key's masterpiece. Wal was standing on my other side, "So this is what it felt like to sit through Feliciano's abomination. No wonder Ernie Harwell nearly lost his job over that."

Bass guitar and drums melted in with the horns which only served to make things worse. The octet didn't even look the part, attired in small-brimmed hats, deeply tinted sunglasses, golden leisure suits that glittered around thick black lapels, and neon green ties set with an exaggerated Windsor knot. "Is this the '50's?" Wal grumbled.

"I guess no one told them that ska was outdated half a century ago," I tried to whisper.

"Is it ska or calypso?"

"It sure isn't reggae. Does it actually matter? We're dating ourselves just by having this conversation."

"I think that's an unfair assessment, Sir." Lord Al paused at the word, knowing I didn't like to be called it. "It was ska and calypso that, combined with the diaspora, brought

301

Jamaican culture into the mainstream. Even if you are not properly acquainted with the excellent harmonizing of the genres, the influence as music marched to rocksteady and reggae is undeniable. What we are listening to was a seminal influence on British rock n' roll. Without it the British Invasion might never have occurred. Just imagine you are a young Mick Jagger, exposed to the new sound-"

"Okay, we get it. It is still an abomination of an anthem and it is going on forever," I said. An unexpected blast from the horns, tower of power style, drowned out the rest. They died into another soft rhythm as the crowd began to become restless. Amber had so far just stood there for over a minute, not looking at anyone. Her pose seemed to convey confidence, not shyness, and as the horns died down she began a strut from the plate, through an aisle cut into the positioning of the band, to the microphone. As she opened her mouth to let out the first note, the band gave another blast of the horns into a number that sounded at home in a Havana nightclub in the age of Sinatra. Who taught these guys the anthem?

As soon as 'O say, can you see?' came from Amber's emblazoned red lips, the crowd had ears only for her. Her voice was strong, hitting the notes true. The band, whatever genre they were, ceased to matter. Through a solemn statement about bombs bursting in air and the rockets' red glare the audience began to buzz, expecting Amber to kick it up a notch into the finale. The meek, indifferent girl I still saw her as could have never exposed the world to the voice that followed. With appropriate energy Amber bragged about our flag still waving and belted out how the United States was the land of the free and home of the brave. Whitney Houston couldn't have done it better. In fact, a fireworks display on the level of the Super Bowl may have only detracted from Amber's performance. The last note rushed from Amber's lips, her eyes remaining closed as her head hung, spent. The dopey band was off, finishing their anthem abomination a good ten seconds too late. Silence hung over the crowd until the need to applause overwhelmed them. A standing ovation, punctuated by whistles and cheers, went on for minutes. The adulation washed over Amber and her head finally rose, eyes opening wet with tears. The mascara running down her cheeks couldn't hide the fact that Amber was a woman, and a damn fine one at that.

A cheer came raining down from the crowd, "Encore! Encore!" Somehow it didn't come across as a demand, more like a collective pleading. Amber's blackened cheeks flushed a bright red. She looked adorable. I patted Trev on the back.

"That's my girl," he said with pride. "I told you she'd knock it out of the park, pun intended."

"We have to work on your humor. You'd think the trips to the comedy club would rub off."

The crowd didn't sit down, the applause continuing until people's palms began to hurt. I don't think anyone wanted to be the first one to quit clapping though. Amber's face got redder. "Ok, ok," she finally relented. "I'm sorry but the anthem is all I have planned." That seemed to be acceptable to the crowd and the band started again. They were drowned out with boos until they got the hint. Poor guys, they thought the crowd's reaction included them. Embarrassed they began to slouch toward the gate behind home plate. Their awkward exit went mostly unnoticed as Amber began from the beginning, acapella.

Amber ended her second rendition with more of a flourish than the first. Pulling the microphone from the stand she was free to show a performer's flair. She combined her demonstrations with a photogenic smile, and a seductive strut, the first I had noticed it. There were no fresh tears as the stadium came to life with more applause. Amber carried the high of the spotlight now, her face radiating with true beauty. I tried to imagine her finding such a thrill at a local dive bar or her first opening act for a national tour. I couldn't picture Amber happier than that moment.

Trev must have been thinking the same thing. He gave me a look, swallowed deeply, trying his damndest to put on a boyish grin. It didn't work as he stepped out from our line and made his way to Amber. She saw him coming, running to him and jumping into his arms. Trev's head and neck disappeared during their embrace behind a wild mane of golden brown hair. Amber hadn't dropped the microphone and the speakers popped with muffled static as the microphone rubbed against Trev's uniform. A private conversation came across as just popped p's and hissing s's.

Trev set Amber down, dropping to a knee. It took some time for her to understand what was about to happen. Both hands went to her mouth. Trev showed no nerves picking up the microphone to ask Amber if she would marry him. Amber didn't give Trev a chance to pull the ring from his back pocket before she was back in his arms. There was no amount of hair that could hide the tenderness of the kiss that followed which I took as a yes. Once the embrace had run its course a deep crimson touched both of their cheeks. Trev now reached for his back pocket for the ring, coming up with a squashed bag of sunflower seeds. The crowd laughed as he threw those to the side with a sheepish grin. A second attempt produced what Trev was looking for and he slipped it on Amber's finger in a modest manner which contradicted everything that came before it.

"I had no idea they were so serious," I said to The Walrus.

"Seriously? I didn't make it more than a couple of days without running into them somewhere in this park trying to steal a couple of kisses."

"Steal kisses? How old fashioned."

"I am old. And Trev is way too straight laced for much more than that."

"So they never?"

"Does it really matter?" The Walrus asked.

"No, I guess not. I didn't know Trev was the kind of guy to take such a risk. Even if they were closer than I realized, it has only been a couple months. That type of courtship rarely makes it."

"Courtship, and you called me old? Truth is, no one knows what makes a good relationship last. Hell, sometimes they break after 25 years like mine."

"I didn't mean to bring that up," I said.

"You didn't. I did. I don't know if it will work out but I do know one thing for sure."

"What's that?"

"You will never be able to say that Trev only plays by the rules again."

I suppose not. Andre's presentation would have to wait until tomorrow.

CHAPTER THIRTY-FOUR

Griff Vernier's year was still going strong. Even with Three Way's impressive record (just two losses since the end of May), Griff was a shoe-in for awards season as the best pitcher in the International League for 2014. Luckily, as the schedule fell we didn't see Vernier in this series. Indianapolis didn't offer much resistance with their other starters. We scored 25 runs in the three games; Gary Wampum led the team with 9 RBIs, Trev and Lord Al second with 4. I was able to rest the back end of my bullpen and several of my important starters. Andre enjoyed a day off, I kept LL out of two as I was still worried about the strength of his jaw.

Three Way had made sure he was stiff for his start, almost too stiff. After a terrible bullpen session I was walking on pins and needles as he creaked all the way to the mound before the first inning. The troubles of the start in Columbus stayed in the home bullpen. Three Way's fastball cranked back up to 94, something I thought was an impossibility at the start of the year given his age and injury history. "You look better today," I said with a grin as I took the ball with an out in the eighth.

"You already banned me from the chiropractor, if I threw another dud I figured the whirlpool was gone too. I said I was keeping that, a real God send."

I laughed. "You can keep the whirlpool."

Columbus played in the division as well, sweeping the last place Louisville Bats. We were still three games back of the Clippers with seven to play. Lord Al's board was down to

5 open squares, everything now filled in except what was in Father Christmas's bag. I made sure to tease him that his statistics must be rusty, five of seven might not get us in. He assured me I was full of it, or I think that is what he said. Before I met Lord Al I didn't know words existed that could opaquely inform someone they had shit running out of their ears.

We switched opponents for the next three after a day off. Columbus took two of three from Indianapolis at home (Vernier's start being the only blemish for the Clippers). We took the first two games against Louisville comfortably. It had been quite the homestand so far, 5-0 with 34 runs scored and 14 allowed.

The last game of the series was similar to the first two, we jumped out to a comfortable 5-1 lead after four innings and put things on cruise control. I tried to let TP pitch the ninth but he gave up a home run to the right-handed clean-up hitter for the Bats with one out. Statisticians may hate the fact that a three-run lead qualifies as a save but the rule exists and I turned to Stu Grissom to nail down the series. Coming into a game in the middle of an inning isn't the norm for a closer and resorting to it has turned out badly for me at times in my career, pitchers are creatures of habit. Grissom had never shown any aversion to the job before, I had done it two or three times early when the back end of my bullpen was so shaky. In a stunning turn of events, Grissom gave up four runs before he got out of the inning. Grissom's Goons (his name is similar to a former Red Wing enforcer) were moribund as they moped in their traditional seats out by the bullpen, fake black eyes and missing teeth only adding to their somber looks. It was a crushing loss and the second blown save from the back end of the pen this week. We entered into the final four games of the year, a two game series here followed by two away, needing to win all four to make the playoffs. Somehow it didn't seem right to tell Lord Al that his board was short by a square. I wrote a note that would soon get lost in the mess that was my desk to remind him about it after we pulled off the sweep.

With four games left and an off day in between each abbreviated series, I was able to set up my rotation with some flexibility. Every game was a must win for us and I was lucky to have my ace set up to pitch the first game. Dave Weedle surprised everyone when, perhaps in a sign of panic, he decided to throw the returning John Targas against Three Way.

Columbus radio was patchy by the time it got to Toledo. Local stations, or those coming from Detroit and Cleveland, were my normal first choice. I suffered through the static to see if people were discussing Dave's move. It had indeed generated controversy during the coveted lunch hour program. Targas, the Columbus ace, had been dealing with an oblique strain and there were many who didn't want him pitching at all until the playoffs due to the recurring nature of the injury. Others were sure that Targas could be used in this series but only if needed in the final game. I turned off the radio as I finished my bologna sandwich (I'm a man of simple tastes) with a smile on my face.

Weedle looked like a genius as Targas set down the first six of our batters in order, perfect through the second inning. Three Way resembled his form from the Indianapolis game, not the aberration the last time he faced the Clippers. The Columbus centerfielder and leadoff man Dante Johnson turned a squibber down the third base line into an infield single but that was it for three innings. Pigpen threw out Johnson trying to steal second and the next eight went down in order. Mark Koliba, Lucas Thune, Matt Anthony, Todd Flint, Manuel Ortiz, Jack Haberstam, Tony Scarrapoli, and Buck Flores were no match for our veteran ace.

We had the first scoring threat of the game with two walks, one by Chuck and the other by LL sandwiched around a shallow flyout by Pigpen. With men on first and second, one out, Jermaine stepped in for his second at bat. I called for the sacrifice bunt, something that would make Bill James and Sabermetricians howl in protest, to get both men into scoring position with two outs and my best hitter in the box. Jermaine took the sign from The Walrus, called time and turned to look into the dugout as if to say, "Really, dude?" I returned the silent question with a silent answer, a smile and a nod. Jermaine adjusted his gloves in an exaggerated manner as a protest that I was sure would tip off the opposing bench as to my plan. As Vargas delivered a fastball, knee high, Jermaine pivoted and laid the bat head across the plate. Todd Flint was in at third but Lucas Thune was tied up at first holding the runner. The pitch was a good one to bunt and Jermaine made the most of it, pushing it past the pitcher on the right side of the infield. Thune was caught by surprise, leaving the first base bag in a panic, cutting off the charging Buck Flores. Thune scooped up the ball but had no one to throw to Targas wasn't able to cover first in time, beat to the bag by Jermaine. The farmer's son could only stand there and watch the sacrifice turn into a single. The bases were loaded with one out.

Good Hands couldn't pick a better time to live up to his billing, all that stood between us and the early lead was a fly ball. Good Hands liked to go the other way and the right fielder, Matt Anthony, has a great arm, leading the league in outfield assists but I was sure Chuck could get to the plate before the ball. Anthony took two steps in, giving up the fly ball over his head if Good Hands could get it there. After getting ahead in the count 2-1, Good Hands took the bat off his shoulder, firing a line drive to right. The ball, if left to rip into the outfield without interruption, may have reached the wall on the fly but it never got higher than eye level. Anthony took two steps towards center and came running in hard to intercept the seamed bullet. He caught it and went through his footwork to get everything on the throw that he could as Chuck took off for home.

If there had been controversy a week ago when Jermaine tested Anthony, there was none in this game. The throw came back to the infield almost as fast as it went out, low enough to be snagged by the cutoff man just as it was taught, but firm enough to make it to Tony Scarrapoli on the fly. Tony caught the ball and turned up the line to brace for a collision. Chuck didn't try to hook slide. The collision was one sided, even standing still Scarrapoli gave no ground, his protected chest acting as a brick wall. Our diminutive second baseman hit and bounced backwards ass first, like he had just run out of bungee cord in the carnival game. Our crowd was silent, speaking volumes. Anthony gave Scarrapoli a salute and a smile from right with gusto. The call in our favor from a week ago was still on the Clippers' minds. To make things worse the Clipper cheering section began singing Uptown Girl by Billy Joel. The two had been dubbed the Uptown Connection in Columbus, Anthony to Anthony, very tony. Get it? Hate it? No one ever said the Clippers were good at puns.

We had carried play early but it was still scoreless, if the Clippers were in good with the baseball gods it was usually at this point that momentum switched in their favor. Three Way held his ground. The Columbus bats stayed quiet, a two-out single in the fourth by Thune ended the inning when he tried to stretch the play into a double and make up for his fielding mistake the inning prior. Added to Dave's unusual managerial move, the Clippers were pressing as if they were the team that was three games down in the standings.

Targas was not in game shape due to being rushed back from injury, his rehab entailing a couple of weeks of bullpen sessions. The stuff that had made him one of the league's best pitchers shone in the first and second, began to fade in the third, and gave way completely by the time the heart of the order came up for a second time. Andre, Trev, and Lord Al went back-to-back-to-back, the first time I had seen that as a manager. What came later put into perspective how big of a feat it was.

A double in the fifth by the powerful third baseman, Todd Flint was the last good swing the Clippers got off Three Way. Flint went to the gap the other way, stunned that his blast caught the top of the high wall. His wavy brown hair, probably too short to be considered a mullet but ratty none the less, served to highlight the shake of his head. A thick pull of spent tobacco flopped from his mouth like cud as he yelled to the third base coach about how he got all of that one. His disbelief was so thick it settled in creases that his goatee and surrounding stubble could not hide. The temps were in the upper 50's and crisp, if the game had been played under the humid swelter of night earlier in the summer he would've been right.

We tacked on two more runs against the Clipper bullpen in the seventh to lead 5-0. Three Way cruised after Flint's double, a final line of eight scoreless innings. He finished his start strong, striking out the side against the bottom of the Columbus order. Buck Flores, whose nickname properly inferred that his defense was money but exaggerated his offensive prowess, took a cut at a breaking ball out of the zone. The roar of ten thousand in the crowd heightened to a fever pitch at the urging of the normally reserved Three Way. Clapping his left hand against his mitt, he screamed a primal celebration from the mound to the foul line walking off the field, muscles tensing and jerking, feeding on the spotlight.

Columbus scored one in the ninth. Vega reverted to his old wildness without the game on the line. He put a man in scoring position without courtesy of a hit and the DH, Manuel Ortiz, brought him home. One win down, three to go.

CHAPTER THIRTY-FIVE

Dirk was money, pardon the pun, again the next night but it didn't look good early. He gave up a run on three singles in the first including an accidental squib shot off the end of the bat of Lucas Thune that beat the shift. A stab at third by Trev on a line drive from Todd Flint drew a high pitched squeal from Amber that cut through the dugout roof to my ears below for the first out. A double play followed to limit the damage. Dirk threw 24 pitches in the first inning and faced five batters. The next five innings he would take on 16 hitters, only one above the minimum (a walk to Buck Flores with no one on). No inning went above 13 pitches. A lengthy at-bat to lead off the top of the 7th by the catcher Scarrapoli ensured that Bobbsey would have to give way to the bullpen for the last couple innings. Before I took the ball, Dirk stranded the walk, ending the inning with his 7th strikeout of the night, all swinging and most on his changeup which had particularly impressive bite considering the cool weather.

The Columbus starter, Ralph Kidder, started off the game strong, yielding two base runners in the first four innings. He nursed the one-run lead into the bottom of the sixth before any signs of trouble. Good Hands led off the inning with a walk, taking a full-count pitch just off the plate, his head craning forward and inspecting the ball until it made it to Scarrapoli's mitt. Kidder bent at the waist in exasperation when the call went against him and a chorus of carps filtered onto the field from the Clipper dugout. Tim Ietta didn't change his mind. I knew I liked that guy. It was the right call. Scarrapoli had framed the pitch, the elbow on his catching arm inching away from his body to inconspicuously pull his glove back over the outside corner. Andre followed with a soft single that only fell in because Matt Anthony had to play near the warning track in right to respect Andre's power.

When Dirk was in trouble, Trev stepped up and got him out of it. Now that Kidder was in a bind, the Clipper defense bailed on him. An error by Haberstam at shortstop squandered a tailor made double play ball, loading the bases. Scarrapoli was charged with a passed ball with Lord Al at the plate, tying the game at 1. Kidder couldn't compose himself, walking three straight batters to reload the bases, and bring in two more runs. In the bottom of the eighth, a reliever was stung by another Columbus error leading to an unearned run. We won 4-1, halfway there.

With our last off day coming before the trip to Columbus, I told the team to get away from everything for 24 hours. Lord Al was spearheading a field trip for the blue blood types on the team to a PGA Tour event in Akron. I was jealous, like most baseball players I was able to carry my talents into a pretty nice swing away from the field and, having grown up in a warm weather state in Arizona, I got a fair bit of practice at it. If I wasn't lost in a movie, golf had always been a close second choice to escape for three or four hours. I tried to keep my disappointment from my face as I got to spend the day in the Mud Hen clubhouse with The Walrus, Ducky, and Three

Way who had just wrapped up a long session in the whirlpool. He suffered addiction regarding that thing.

Since Ducky had come clean on the mound in Lehigh about his dreams, something close to PTSD, and how they were affecting his ability on the mound, Wal and I had structured the day before his start to keep him calmed down. The theory us armchair psychologists had so brilliantly come up with was that Ducky's pre-game jitters were triggering the episodes. Herbie had helped us out, setting up a fire pit on 'Ducky nights' as he called them. Tonight there was no Herbie and no pit. "Hey Wal, you see *Groundskeeper Willy*?" I asked.

"No, I heard he tweaked his back during his goofy dance routine yesterday," said The Walrus.

"Finally got bit on the last game of the year? Sucks but that was bound to happen. Herb's too old to be doing that stuff," I said.

"Just imagine if he twerked," said Three Way.

"I'd rather not. You know how to start a fire?" I asked.

"Is the Pope Catholic? I'm the father of a cub scout. Fires and derby cars I've got on lock down."

"Thank God. I can't remember the last time I got a fire started," I said. "The environmentalists have made that nearly impossible back home. Once I took the kids four wheeling out in the desert and got a hell of a fine from a rather crusty ranger for it. You can imagine what they do about fire pits. Then the boys got to middle school and they were only interested in chasing girls. It was my daughter ironically that tried to get us to go again. Never happened. Outdoorsy stuff really wasn't a

Freeman family tradition."

I threw Three Way my keys to the groundskeeper's pen. He pulled his own set from his pocket and jangled them with a smile on his face. "You honestly think I don't have the run of this place by now?"

"You really are a crafty veteran." Three Way threw my keys back to me, belt high. "Quit thinking like a pitcher. I'm too old to bend down."

"Sorry," Three Way said sarcastically. "I'll remember to keep it at the chest next time."

The Walrus and I had our own job to do, trekking up the aisle to the concourse. We followed it until the third base line turned into the left field line. We made a right when we could look out onto St. Clair, filled with cars because of some show at the Seagate Convention Center that I was too busy to know about. My knee was tightening up already, it sucks getting old, so I handed my keys to Wal and wished him luck. "This looks like a job for a third base coach."

"Hey, I'm your bench coach and don't you forget it." The Walrus climbed the stairs that led to the back of the scoreboard, disappearing inside. It was his turn to pick the movie, I had asked earlier during our manly microwave dinner what he had chosen but he had declined to respond, taking another bite of his patented cashew salad. I hear it is the arugula that makes the difference. The speakers came to life first, flashes of trailers getting cut off as Wal skipped to the title menu. A score that I didn't recognize played, repeating every 30 seconds or so as Wal waited for the scoreboard to warm up. The field was bathed in color and, soon after, my best friend joined me for the walk back to our impromptu campsite. "What'd you pick?"

"The only choice I had," The Walrus responded.

"The only choice?"

"Yeah, *Raging Bull*."

"Are you sure that's a good idea? I believe that being punch drunk isn't much different than taking a baseball to the noggin," I said.

"Oh shit, I didn't…you don't think?"

"Too late now," I said with a laugh. "So this really is a must-see movie?"

"Is the Pope Catholic?"

"That's Three Way's line."

"You'll like it. It isn't particularly uplifting but it speaks to the thrill of the fight quite well."

"Don't."

"What?"

"Try and turn movie night into a commentary about our season. Just let me enjoy the story."

"Well hell, Har. I would've just brought some of your b-movie schlock with half naked girls and paper thin plots if I was concerned with finding something whose "story" you'd enjoy."

"I have impeccable taste in movies."

"So that's why Gail was more than eager to get you out of the house for these get-togethers?"

"I can't help it if the two of you don't have good sense for quality cinematography."

Wal was right, I really did need to see that movie. If Ducky was concerned with the subject matter he never said anything and my Southwestern queso was a hit. Mr. Diet himself went back for seconds which I teased him about. Three Way and Ducky both asked what my secret was. I tried to lie and tell them that Velveeta and Pace microwaved together wasn't difficult but they called my bluff. I finally caved and admitted the truth, telling them about my Grandma's Arapahoe neighbor who took years to perfect a queso recipe because he was sick of losing to The White Man at the annual chili cookoff. It was quite the controversy when it was entered that first year. They called me a liar just like Gail had. Maybe my life really was so interesting as to be unbelievable. I had a feeling Gary Wampum wouldn't have questioned it.

As the movie ended, the DVD player automatically flicked off and the scoreboard turned to a royal blue. The first time we did this, I was dumb enough to make the trip up to the small control room in back of the screen and turn the machine off. With experience came wisdom and now I knew we had fifteen minutes before the board would shut off on its own accord.

"So, are we finally going to sleep outside?" Ducky asked.

"No."

"You say that every time."

"It's too cold." The Walrus nodded in agreement.

"Before it was too hot. I figured you'd think it was perfect tonight."

"It may have been too hot, or I'm not interested in sleeping outside. You wake up with bugs in your mouth."

"Beats breathing in the smell in the clubhouse."

"Ah, the clubhouse isn't so bad, not since that goose was set free," said Three Way.

I started from a light sleep at 4 AM to hear a steady downpour that had not been in the forecast. I almost woke Ducky up, just another reason not to like the outdoors.

The next morning a heavy fog lowered the ceiling of dark gloomy clouds until Toledo looked like a scene out of a Dickens novel. A cool night had turned into a frigid morning, at least by August standards. It took until close to 11 AM for the thermometer to climb into the fifties, a late afternoon clearing made a valiant attempt to get us to sixty degrees for the high but failed. A good day to travel. I was not ashamed to throw a sweatshirt over my uniform as I watched that night's game from the dugout. What transpired was enough to warm me up. The Clippers starter, Dean Sanders, was hit early. Andre singled in two in the first and homered in the second as we batted around. After two innings we led 7-1 and Ducky was good enough, with the help of four innings from the bullpen, to let us coast to an easy win, 12-4.

We had hit 86 wins for the year, meeting Lord Al's goal. It was good but not good enough. Tied now atop the West with Columbus, our record trailed the other division leaders, the Rochester Red Wings (91 wins) and the Norfolk Tide (89 wins). That asshole Lloyd Jackson was still leading off for the Charlotte Knights who had just won game 88, locked in as the wild card team. 88 wins was the best record in International League history for a non-division winner. Lord Al came to me grumbling about our rotten luck, something about this year being a statistical black swan, a five sigma event. I had no idea what that meant. I did know the grueling marathon of a season would be remembered, or forgotten, by what happened in the last game. We savored getting three-quarters of the way to our goal for all of 15 minutes before hitting the showers and returning to the team hotel.

"Trev, one last time for this regular season, do the honors," I commanded.

We locked hands and prayed to God over a baseball game. The pre-game ritual sounds stupid when you talk about it outside of a locker room but inside, it would be hard to find something more appropriate. "The Kingdom, the power, and the glory are yours, now and forever. Amen." Normally that familiar worry about the vanity of praying for the benefit of myself would creep into my head. September 1st, 2014 was not a normal night. I had the team focused, the solemnity of prayer zeroing them in on the task at hand. It was time for the resident orator, Lord Al, to stoke the fires of competition.

"They call this game the American pastime. Perhaps it is fitting then that the only thing standing between us and a Division Championship, a banner, a flag that will fly long after we are gone, is ourselves. Why is that fitting? Because this country is a story of average men doing great things. America is the story of Henry Knox, a bookseller who became a general, toting cannons in a grand excursion across the Appalachians from Fort Ticonderoga to Boston to expel British forces, a feat thought impossible. Andrew Jackson, the hero of 1812 called a log cabin home as a child, so did Lincoln. Joshua Chamberlin who saved the Union Army in the Battle of Gettysburg was a school teacher, when the war ended he would go back to being a Dean.

"This isn't war, it is a game, the national game. For 365 days a year we toil in relative anonymity, working without fanfare for the chance to take all of the hard work, the entirety of the preparation, and stand apart, no matter how brief. That work, the doubts and fears, the dreams and aspirations, it was all for this moment. C.S. Lewis defined love not as a feeling of affection but instead a steady appreciation for the best in the life of another. I believe in earnest that the bond forged by the men on this roster is the sincerest manifestation of love. So pure that a product of a Dominican barrio, an ace preparing to extinguish the flame of his career, and a manager whose northern star is eccentricity, can transform into an amalgamation far superior to the sum of the worth of the individuals that comprise it. That love will shine tonight, once again pulling us through the trials of our shared experience. Tonight, as a team, we cease to be ordinary, to be mundane. Tonight we become something more than our best, more than minor leaguers, more than fallen men. Tonight we become champions." Game time.

CHAPTER THIRTY-SIX

"First pitch at 6:05 PM." The packed house roared. Ozzie Montoya received the ball back from Scarrapoli after splitting the plate with a fastball at 96 mph. I had never seen Columbus's number four starter throw that hard. I walked over to Rodney Young and asked, "Is there some tape on this guy that I haven't seen? Where did that come from?" Rodney assured me that he was as surprised as I was. Since the break we had enjoyed a 10-2 record against Columbus, tonight that wouldn't matter. Montoya, who we had shelled a couple weeks ago, set us down 1-2-3. Jermaine struck out on three pitches, late on the fastball each time. Good Hands tried for a bunt but the ratty third basemen, Todd Flint, charged bare handed and threw off balance with a perfect strike across the diamond to nip him by half a step. So much for the shaky defense that had characterized the last couple games. Andre hit a fly ball a mile but it traveled up more than it did out. Dante Johnson camped under it in center waiting for the ball to come back down for the third out.

Brett Swansey was our fifth starter but he had proven to be more reliable as of late and that meant more to me than his slot in the rotation. Unfortunately for Swansey, that meant he was going to have to grind out a win against a buzz saw. Just as Columbus had appeared a different team in the field, they proved to be more potent at the plate. Tonight was essentially a one game playoff, Columbus had already collapsed and choked away a sizable lead in the standings. Now that the specter of the collapse was a reality, the pall that had made them hapless, bumbling buffoons lifted. Its energy was replaced by a desperation laced with the drug of the possibility of atonement. Dante Johnson led off the bottom half of the inning by slapping a single past Trev who was in at third to watch for the bunt. Dante stole second on a 1-0 count, fearless running in a fastball count, and made it after a good jump. Pigpen didn't stand a chance. The left fielder, Mark Koliba, moved Dante to third by selflessly grounding out to Chuck for a 4-3 putout. With a man on third and less than two outs, Lucas Thune walked. Swansey had been careful pitching to the powerful left-hander, nibbling at the edges and falling behind 2-0. I made the sign to Pigpen to give the unintentional intentional walk at that point, fearing a home run. My decision was too cute by half when their clean-up hitter, Anthony, doubled in a run. Calling time at second base he turned toward the Columbus dugout and gave that same stupid salute. Thune wasn't fast enough to score from first, men were at second and third with just one out. Todd Flint cussed again as a deep fly ball died on the warning track, a sac fly and one RBI rather than a three-run homer. Haberstam hit a sharp ground ball, unfortunately for him it was right at his counterpart. LL threw him out with ease.

After one, Columbus led 2-0.

Trev came back to the dugout angry at himself for not being able to get to Dante's leadoff single. I tried to calm him down, being even with the bag you can only ask a third baseman to take a step and a dive before the ball is by him.

Trev played the ball perfectly, it was just out of his range. In truth, it was out of anyone's range to the wide side of the bag. The mild mannered third baseman stalked out of the dugout to leadoff at the plate in the same mood as he came in. My words had meant nothing.

Trev swung wildly at the first two pitches from Montoya, both breaking balls out of the zone. He was out in front of the 0-1 pitch by so much that his helmet fell off as he tried to slow his swing. Montoya went back to the same pitch to try and get strike three but Trev laid off. He laid off another breaking ball 1-2 and the count went full when Montoya overthrew a fastball causing it to hit the ground in front of the plate. Both Ozzie and Trev asked for time after that, collecting themselves. Trev fouled off five consecutive full-count pitches before drawing a walk on the 11th pitch of the at-bat. As he trotted down to first a buzz, the familiar buzz of a rally, rolled through the dugout.

Lord Al singled up the box, his swing as graceful as the eloquence of his vocabulary. Wal looked in from the coach's box by third base to see if I wanted my number six hitter, Gary Wampum, to attempt a sacrifice bunt. I signaled negative, trusting my guy to swing away. Gary did just that, driving a ball into the ground that Haberstam had no trouble turning into a double play. LL couldn't get Trev in from third and the inning ended with us still trailing by two. The Walrus didn't say anything as he came off the field but I knew that he was in favor of playing it safe.

Tony Scarrapoli led off for Columbus in the second, a tuft

of dark chest hair spilling out of his jersey where the top button was left open. Scarrapoli was not a power hitter but his display of testosterone proved a fitting companion to his swing this time. A 2-1 Swansey fastball ended up in the standing room only section on the concourse in left.

After two, Columbus led 3-0.

We failed to threaten in the top of the third, a two out walk to Jermaine was erased when he was caught stealing, a rarity that season. For a stretch over the summer, he had stolen 25 consecutive bases. I met Jermaine at the top step with an enthusiastic clap to the back and my best "'Atta boy,'" knowing that we had to take chances against Columbus's best punch. I hoped we could keep it within striking distance early, hanging around on the road in an elimination setting had a way of paying off by the end of the night.

Swansey returned to the mound for the home half of the third and promptly allowed two base runners. I went to get him, turning to Three Way on short rest. As far as I knew, Three Way had never come out of the bullpen in his career, it seemed fitting that in what was potentially his last game I asked something new of him one more time. "Just when you think you've seen it all," he said as I handed him the ball.

"Yeah." Nothing more needed to be said. Three Way had thrown his arm out for me all those years ago in Durham, he'd step up to this challenge without hesitation.

Three Way went through the Clippers 4, 5, and 6 hitters. Anthony popped up behind home plate. Pigpen discarded his mask, dropping it by his side, allowing it to snag in his cleats and trip him. The ball found Pigpen's mitt as he was crashing to the earth, the ball rolling in the stiff catcher's glove precariously until Pigpen squeezed it shut. It wasn't graceful but he avoided an error and we avoided giving the Columbus clean-up hitter a second life. Todd Flint's grounder was stabbed by Three Way, showing why he was the best fielder on the staff, but resulted in only a fielder's choice when Thune took out Chuck at second before he could try for a relay to first. Chuck flipped almost a full rotation, landing hard on his lower back. Chuck got up limping, the team doctor and me rushing out to check on him. While Chuck was being attended to I made sure to work the second base umpire hoping that it might get us a close call later on. When play resumed the DH, Manuel Ortiz, flew out to center where Jermaine hauled it in on the run five steps before the warning track.

After three innings, Columbus still led 3-0.

Three Way's ability to shut the door put our team back on an even keel so to speak. Good Hands led off. He took a fastball down and away to right, flicking the bat head softly so that it produced a wobbly line drive over the head of Buck Flores. The Clipper defense shifted against Andre, moving the third baseman into short right field, playing for the giant to pull. Montoya did not pitch him that way, keeping away with breaking balls. With a 2-1 count I saw Andre wink towards Good Hands before emulating the left fielder. The swings between my 2nd and 3rd batters looked as if they were happening from two sides of a mirror. Andre's result, coming from the left side, floated past where Todd Flint had just vacated. Good Hands made it to third easily since Haberstam was slow to remember to cover for the vacant third basemen. Andre, the lumbering leviathan, held with a single. Trev scored Good Hands on a sac fly, the throw from Koliba in left sailing over the cutoff man allowing Andre to tag up and advanced to second. Lord Al struck out on a steady diet of fastballs, Montoya realizing he had gotten too attached to his breaking stuff. Into the fourth now, he was still hitting 96 mph. Wampum was up next, a dead fastball hitter. His eyes lit up on a 1-0 pitch over the middle of the plate, whipping a hit into the corner that allowed Andre to score. LL failed to score Gary, Columbus clung to a slim lead.

Three Way continued to be perfect in relief, setting down every batter he faced through the seventh. Montoya was not as good but the aid of two double plays allowed him to match Three Way with zeroes on the scoreboard, more important considering Columbus had the advantage.

Chuck led off in the top of the eighth facing a new pitcher for Columbus, their setup man, Dallas Bohenic. The reliever had walked only 4 men in 64 appearances on the season. Walk number five could not have come at a worse time, a free pass to our number nine hitter. Chuck had improved offensively in the second half of the year but his average was still anchored at around .240 with little extra base power. The Clipper fans, who had been quite vocal in support early on when the club was off to a fast start, seemed to know that the leadoff walk was going to prove costly. Boos streamed down from the stands, the frustration reigniting the nimbus clouds that had blown Columbus off course the past month. Bohenic's demeanor slumped as Jermaine dug in.

Being the leadoff hitter, Jermaine never swung early in the count. His job was to let the bench see the opposing pitchers stuff by working the count in the first inning. Those habits always carried through for the rest of the game. Jermaine averaged 4.8 pitches per at-bat, the most on the team. Switching his M.O., Jermaine swung at the first pitch, a get-me-over fastball. The action surprised Bohenic, his eminently hittable pitch getting tattooed for a single to left.

The Walrus looked in to me to see if the sacrifice bunt was on this time. I tried to play the percentages, scout's honor, and Good Hands failed to keep the ball fair on two separate attempts. I kept the bunt sign on, this attempt popping up past the catcher, nearly to the backstop. The foul bunt with two strikes resulted in the inning's first out. Good Hands was despondent as he returned to the dugout, a brief flare of anger as he slammed his bat back into its spot in the rack. This was normally the time where Alex would be there to offer a comforting word. It put a smile on my face to see LL be the first guy over to Good Hands, whispering a joke into his ear that elicited a smile. It was a small moment but a powerful reminder how special this team had become. If we were going to make the playoffs it would involve something out of the ordinary.

Andre took ball one causing Bohenic to step off the mound and call Scarrapoli out for a conference to discuss the important next pitch. Returning to his position behind the plate, Scarrapoli didn't bother to put down signs. With a man on second, the Columbus battery was doing everything they could to keep Chuck from tipping Andre off. Wal looked into me to get our signs, his eyebrows arching at me when I finished going through the sequence. With Bohenic's slide step, the double hit and run was on. The 1-0 pitch was a fastball that tailed back over the inner third of the plate, too juicy to make it to Scarrapoli's glove. Andre laced a single into right, scoring Chuck with ease. Jermaine hit the bag at second and made the turn for third. Wal threw up the stop sign, arms raised high above his head but Jermaine didn't look up. Anthony charged and came up with the ball before Jermaine had even touched the bag. Jermaine was fast but he wasn't that fast.

Anthony was caught by surprise when Jermaine didn't slow down, awkwardly trying to restart his throwing motion after he had begun to pull up. He didn't get everything on the throw home. Jermaine didn't slide, lowering his shoulder to collide with Scarrapoli, the road gray uniform streaking like a silver bullet. Jermaine barreled into Scarrapoli before the ball got there and this time the Columbus catcher took the brunt of the collision. Jermaine hit him with too much speed to get the worst of it. The ball whizzed through the mash of limbs to the backstop and Jermaine fell forward, his palms slapping the plate. He scored from first on a single, running against the best outfield arm in the league, to give us the first lead of the game. It was unorthodox, a perfect summation to the year. Andre took second in the fracas but didn't get any farther. Heading into the bottom of the eighth we led 4-3.

The next six Columbus outs didn't produce a Joe Carter moment. That didn't stop them from lasting forever, each pitch becoming the length of an at-bat, each AB turning into its own inning. Mendenhall gave up a one-out single but a strike out and a weak foul fly that LL made a nice play on wasted the runner. LL caught the ball running away from the infield, over the shoulder, sliding to avoid the railing that he was closing in fast on. His spikes kicked up the loose dirt, generating just enough friction to slow him to a stop before he came into contact with the barrier. I let out a sigh of relief, I had been sure he was going to wind up headlong into the stands again. Wal had actually grabbed my hand in suspense, quickly letting go after the catch was made and he realized what he had done. "And you were the one chastising me for being too afraid to play him," I said.

Walrus changed the subject, "Do you think anyone...you know, saw?"

With a laugh, "No, your secret's safe with me. You should tell your new flame about our bromance though. Gail came to grips with it a long time ago."

"Bromance? Look at you dropping some modern slang."

"I'm serious. Getting involved with a baseball guy is an acquired habit."

"How about we win tonight and then we'll talk about how we're secretly gay lovers?"

As so often happens, a great defensive play shows up at the plate. LL led off the top of the ninth with a home run. With a half inning between us and the playoffs, we led 5-3.

The final out came with no one on. It was a pedestrian ground ball to second base. That may not sound exciting to the reader but it was pretty damn special to our club. Men streamed out of the dugout and from the bullpen to create a pile of humanity just to the left of the mound. LL was stupidly somewhere in the middle. Being a wise veteran of the game, I was smart enough to stay away from it worrying about friendly fire to my shortstop's jaw.

The pile reached critical mass before disbanding. Someone I had never seen before began throwing Division Champion gear at me and others; a hat, t-shirt, bracelet, bandana, God knows what else. Without asking for it, a cluttered pile of merchandise was stacked in my hands reaching from my belt buckle to my chest. It drew a grimace from the mystery gifter but I didn't want any of it, dropping it in a heap at my feet and walking towards the crowd of men that now more closely resembled my team. With the exuberance out of the way, hopefully I could manage a staid handshake line before media tore me away and they found the champagne in the locker room. I crossed from foul territory to fair when Andre yelled, "Get him!" Uh oh.

Jermaine was the fastest one, cutting off my escape route by getting behind me. I had no choice but to brace for the horde, much to the delight of my staff who were whooping and hollering like they were 20 again. Andre clasped me in a tight bear hug to quell any resistance I may have had. With ease, he hefted me off the ground, my legs dangling meekly in the air. I felt hands grab at my calves and bend my knees, support following soon after. The support shifted until they were comfortable and I teetered for a moment until I found my balance. Andre let go, stepping back with an enormous grin on his face. "Looking good, Skip." I was on the shoulders of others, a first, and it was as good as you'd expect it to be.

"Who's carrying me?"

"It sure as hell isn't me," I heard Three Way say.

"It's us," came two voices who I knew immediately to be Trev and Pigpen.

"Why didn't you do this before? This is kind of cool."

The Clippers dugout staff had been smart enough to put plastic tarp across every square inch of the visiting clubhouse. The pop of corks were the prelude to an hour's worth of pagan revelry. Enough alcohol sprayed onto each player and coach to get you drunk by osmosis alone. More made it down our throats until a good buzz was the least of our issues. Sweat, blood, dirt, and booze fermented into an unholy aroma that couldn't be washed away. One cheap drunk, I don't remember who, threw up on the bus ride home which set off a couple of others. Maybe someday we'd be embarrassed about it.

The small gathering of families and loved ones that had parked outside the player garage awaiting our triumphant return home were not so accepting. "God, I thought you were old enough to keep out of trouble without me around," chastised Gail as I wrapped her up in an embrace after stumbling out the bus door. She didn't pull away when I kissed her on the mouth, I don't know how. I almost got a slap for trying for some tongue. "Ugh. Men."

In '84, during our run for the championship Tiger greats like Al Kaline and Willy Horton had regaled us with stories about the crowds that streamed to the airport to meet the team plane after the Tigers beat St. Louis in 7 games in 1968. The plane taxied in to the terminal to the roar of thousands. In hindsight, it was a very good thing that our state of inebriety that night was not exposed to similar throngs.

CHAPTER THIRTY-SEVEN

If this was a Hollywood script, our triumph over Columbus which capped a second half to remember forever would be the end of the story. Maybe a handful of filmgoers would ask what happened in the playoffs, but most are happy to go home on a high. In real life, the next four weeks is what people remember a team for and I am sorry to say that our season did not end with me hoisting the Governor's Cup. The last tiles on Lord Al's board got filled in sometime during our ignominious return that night. Sitting in Father Christmas's sack was the International League trophy. I had asked him later in the week, before our first round series with Charlotte, whether he was being presumptuous. I'm sure I've already mentioned how that is a superstition of mine. His response was classic, perhaps because it was so unlike him. "Maybe. So what?"

The best of five series went the distance. It would have been over sooner if I had not needed Three Way that last game in Columbus, having him for two starts instead of one. Then Ducky pulled his stunt in Game Two, finally getting his revenge on Lloyd Reynolds after Lloyd called him a pussy again. Ducky did not have the best arm on the staff but it became superhuman for one pitch. The fastball hit Lloyd where it was intended to, the upper back. We were all shocked when Lloyd's histrionic display of pain wasn't just him being an obnoxious jackass. The diagnosis came later that night from the hospital, Ducky had given him a broken shoulder blade. I

336

suppose if you get ejected from a playoff game you should make it count.

The Ectoplasm advertisement began running the day after we made the playoffs. It didn't take long for Abe to get wind of it and he made it clear that I wouldn't be asked back for the next season. I told no one, it would be hubris to think that my impending departure could be enough motivation to change fate. The championship series against Rochester ended in six games, Three Way's last start honorable, but not enough. He gave up one run in eight innings on the road against the best team in the league. We failed to score a single run to keep the wild ride going. It may have been a loss in the record books but I can't remember a gutsier performance in his career.

Abe fired me that night, I had to clean out my office the next day. Gail offered to help me but I politely declined, choosing to do it myself. I needed an entire trash bag to hold the junk that littered my desk. Months' worth of coffee stained receipts, issues of *Baseball America*, scribbled notes, lineup cards, a letter from the Commissioner's Office explaining why the appeals investigation was being delayed again; they were going to bury it. Then there was all the other bullshit that I piled high to give the appearance that I was important. It was all removed to let me pen a letter of recommendation. I was surprised to hear that Abe had accepted my advice and hired Three Way as manager for the Mud Hens for 2015.

The box filled with what was left took up a seat in the back of my pink Cadillac. It sat for the rest of the fall by the door of our tiny apartment. The market must have been bad because our month-to-month lease drew no ire from the landlord. I crammed the duffel bag of illicit cash, what was left after paying Hanover as agreed and sending out under the table bonuses to the players, into the farthest recesses of the Caddy's cavernous trunk. Concern crept into my mind about how to keep from declaring it for income purposes. At some point someone would ask how I had come into it and the truth coming out would make the résumés I had sent out to a handful of minor league teams as worthless as toilet paper.

I ended up deciding on the most logical option, to think about it later. Gail had never seen the leaves change color so we took a tour of northern Michigan. The second week of October is peak color across the Upper Peninsula and our trip made me regret never seeing it during my playing days. I-75 wound north and west for four hours after we passed Detroit until the lakeshore town of Mackinaw City burst from the wooded hills. A ferry across the deep blue of Lake Huron took us to Mackinac Island where we stayed on the upper floor of the Grand Hotel. We enjoyed a beautiful sunset over the Mackinac Straits from the building's iconic porch. I held her hand as she sat next to me. "You know, old people do this," I said.

She mock gasped. "Did you just call me old? I'm going to have to wash your mouth out with soap."

"The truth can be a real bitch."

She leaned in and bit at my ear lobe, "I dare you to make me show you how young I still am."

"Mmmm. I may have to take you up on that." After we

made love that night she dozed off and I laid in bed awake thinking that it was supposed to be the other way around. As the hands on the bedside clock continued to spin around the face I lazily floated into a light sleep.

I was up early the next morning, strolling through the quiet streets while Gail slept in as she was wont to do. There were no automobiles here, forbidden to keep the island's old school charm, allowing for a peaceful walk along the water's edge. Clopping hooves from the draft horses provided a steady rhythm to the passing of vacation homes, bed and breakfasts, and storefronts. The Grand was on the western end of the island, the Mission Point Resort the east, and the docks and main drag settled in between. When I hit the far edge of the stores, under the white walls of the old fort, I turned around. For a nice fee I borrowed a driver for three hours to be our personal chauffeur. He took us all the way around the island, about seven miles, allowing us to stop and take pictures in front of several of the landmarks. Gail laughed at me for using an actual camera but she'd probably agree that it takes better pictures than her iPhone if she was forced to. Soon she found herself borrowing it to take pictures of the waterline, fascinated by flotsam of all things. You never know what a desert girl will be interested in.

The driver stopped our cart in front of a long trail of steps (over a hundred before I stopped counting) that took us to the highest point on the island. We stood on the lookout at the bustle below, framed by blue water and the color of the trees. "It's perfect," she whispered. "Did we miss this for all those years with you gone?"

"No. We had a damn good life that was so blessed that it is still getting better."

"I love you," she said squeezing my hand. We headed back down the stairs to the cart, continuing to the old military outpost. We toured the interior of the fort, enjoying the view of the park and the statue of the French explorer, Marquette. Late afternoon had us sample fudge from Reba's. Eating our way through town, buying clothes from the stores and dressing up in costume at the old time photo shop gave way to me surprising her with a massage and spa at the Lilac. I rented a bike to do some more riding, all my knee could handle, followed by a tour of the haunted theater. I'm not too proud to deny it.

"Have you ever seen a bridge like this?" Gail asked.

"No, it is more impressive now than the view from the ferry." The five mile long suspension bridge that connects the Lower and Upper Peninsulas of Michigan is a true feat of engineering. At the crown we had to be 400 feet above the water, a view I relished but one that had tickled Gail's fear of heights.

"The bridge is so rough."

"It's grating, so the thing can sway in the wind, expand and contract like the Golden Gate bridge in San Francisco. If it couldn't do that, the thing would crack under the stress." Northern Michigan could be quite unforgiving according to the accounts of some of the locals we had met. "You can see through the grating so don't look down."

"Holy fucking shit," Gail said. We made it in one piece.

US 2 took us along Lake Michigan west where Gail stopped me on occasion to explore. She wanted me to make the trek down the steep valley to the Cut River but I refused. Then she went without me, forcing me to deal with the pain in my knee to catch up. There wasn't anything down there so I made sure to bitch the whole way back up. Some scenic outlooks of Lake Michigan drew our attention and we stopped in Escanaba, a population of maybe 15,000 which was, amazingly, a big deal for the area. Gail was fascinated by the docks, cargo freighters coming and going from all down the St. Lawrence Seaway. I got a kick out of winding through Iron Mountain, a large brick building painted with a logo for Izzo and Sons on it, the roots of the famous college basketball coach. Michigan State, ol' Gibby's Spartans.

Crystal Falls weren't much but the Bond Falls were. A photo of us standing in front was an instant favorite and new wallpaper on her phone before the end of the day. Gail dragged me through the Lake of the Clouds in the Porcupine Mountains, a five mile hike that had my knee barking by the time we finished. The photo got changed the next day on the top of Brockway Mountain, the rustic outpost of Copper Harbor framed by Lake Superior now that we were on the northern most point of the peninsula. To the south we looked over foothills of magnificent reds and yellows. The loop back south had us stop at the Eagle Harbor lighthouse and we bought a loaf of fruit bread that was phenomenal from a bakery attached to a Catholic monastery. Gail taught me to text, I sent Andre a photo of me with a porter inside the actual Keweenaw Brewing Company, a couple blocks from the Franklin Square Inn of Houghton where we stayed overlooking the Portage, a university sprawling out to the east.

"This vacation thing isn't so bad, you know," she said not so subtlely as we headed back to the east along our loop on US 41 and M-28. Superior had better lookouts and some pretty towns, Munising being my favorite. Pictured Rocks took both our breaths away. The cold northerly winds couldn't dampen our spirits, standing on the lake shore looking up at the cliff face formed by millennia of gales and waves. Looking out across the largest freshwater lake in the world, it didn't look much different from the views I had seen of the Pacific or the Atlantic. "Babe, this has been everything I hoped for, can I ask for one last favor?"

"Name it," I said, not in a mood to disappoint.

"Can I go to a baseball game with you, not to watch you play, I mean, but to have you sit with me and just be a fan?"

"Really? I never took you as much of a fan."

"I wouldn't have married you if I wasn't at least somewhat interested."

"There's only one problem."

"What's that?"

"The season is over. Majors too."

She handed me her phone, an email up on the screen. LL had saved us two tickets (player's comp) by the third base dugout for Game Five of the World Series. The Tigers were ahead in the series and hoping to close it out at home so they didn't have to travel back to Atlanta. "Is this real?" I asked.

"Of course, silly. I hear Trev and Amber are going to be there too."

I got us a room at the Crowne Plaza on Jefferson, the view of the newly renovated Cobo Hall and the Detroit River was impressive. Gail was sure it was too high. I didn't tell her where I had made reservations for dinner. The water was gray, it was cold for October. The first nip of winter that we had been lucky enough to escape in the UP (where it was now snowing according to the weather) had made it south. I left Gail alone for the afternoon, trying to get rid of the cash that was left over. Honest to God, Gleaner's Food Bank wouldn't accept all of it. I had to haggle with them to take $50,000 in bills, finally asking with a dumb look on my face, "If I am really a drug dealer, how would I launder money through your organization." I still had $75,000 left over when an idea hit me. They were glad to take it.

"Where are we going?" Gail asked as I parked in the garage attached to the Renaissance Center.

"You'll see, have you heard from Trev and Amber?"

"Amber sent me something five minutes ago saying that they are waiting for us." We snaked through the maze of ringed walkways that loop through the main tower of the RenCen concentrically (I think that's the right word at least).

The ring I was looking for curled up and stopped in the center of the tower but it had been years since I was in here and I hit a couple of dead ends. "The architect of this place should have been shot," Gail snipped. She was late and the subject of a surprise that I wouldn't tell her, two pet peeves of an otherwise wonderful woman.

"There it is," I said casually like I had always known where I was going. The escalator took us to another ring that led to a small platform with two elevator doors. A good-looking black girl, who was dressed sharply, pressed the button to call a car. The wait wasn't long but it was long enough for Gail to figure it out.

"Oh no, you didn't, did you?"

"I have no idea what you mean, dear. Trev, Amber, how have you guys been?"

"Great," Amber said bubbily. She was speaking for both of them.

"Excellent. If my wife doesn't kill me, I may need to spend the night at your place."

Gail noticed the sign on the dais that the black girl was standing behind, "The 76th floor, Harold? Do you remember the Space Needle?" Our first child, Gail didn't find out until after I had left for Spring Training. She had spent the entire spring trying to find a way to catch a flight to see me to tell me in person but I was caught up in the season. She began to show, too stubborn to tell me on the phone, or wait until the All-Star Break. We had a series in Seattle in early May, a lot closer to Phoenix than Detroit, and she flew in to surprise me at the airport. It was a hell of a surprise and we spent the weekend attached to the hip outside of when I had to be at the old Kingdome. That was the first time I learned of her fear of heights. We were swept by the worst team in the league after we had jumped out to a 35-5 start. I teased that she was a bad influence. A part of me probably believed it, another superstition.

"You liked it when you were up there." The bell chimed and the door opened. I pushed Gail in and crowded into the six person car towards the back. "You'll like this too. Just have to keep you from passing out in the glass elevator." I was lucky that she had mellowed as she got older, there was a time that this would have been too big a deal for any doghouse to contain. As the car ascended toward the sky I heard a couple of weak gasps from her. When the car reached the top I got a hard kick to my leg. I probably deserved that.

The hostess seated us at a table towards the center of the restaurant. The paleness left Gail's cheeks slowly, through appetizers. By the time entrées came, she had tenuously adjusted to her surroundings. The noise from the wind on the glass caused an intermittent creaking that kept her from being fully comfortable.

"So, Amber, how are the wedding plans coming along?" Gail asked in starts, as if still waiting for something awful to happen. I was pretty sure the top of the tower wasn't going to fall into the river, she wasn't.

"It is so overwhelming, picking a date was easy as Trev has to have the ceremony in the offseason. We couldn't imagine a more joyous time than Christmas. Right now the date is set for Saturday the 26th, 2015."

"That's a great first step. Oh, I'm so excited!" With that, Gail forgot she was 800 feet in the air.

"It gets harder though," Trev said.

"You've got to watch out for the Krampus." The girls didn't get the reference, annoyed. Trev smiled but he was too afraid at what the repercussions might be if he laughed.

"Weather is always a problem that time of year and it can be so cold," said Amber. "My family is from around here which is where I originally wanted to have it then I thought about Trev's parents who spend the winter in Florida. We'll have teammates coming in from all over anyway so I'm thinking a destination wedding, maybe on the beach."

"That's...wow. Have you thought of just doing something small?" I said. Gail and Amber both looked at me like I was crazy. Those two had really gotten too close this past year.

"We did something small and I've regretted it ever since," Gail said.

"Wait, you have?"

Gail ignored me. "You only get to do it once, go big girl."

I didn't get the hint about my opinion's worth. "Isn't the point of a wedding to celebrate what comes next? Happy wives don't go back and watch their wedding videos, do they? I thought that is what happened when you got divorced. A wedding is just a day, the real magic is walking into a house for the first time or having a child. Planting a tree together and how she looks beautiful even after you smear some dirt on her cheek. Creating an artificial fairy tale isn't important, forging a bond that allows two people to grow into something better is. What was C.S. Lewis's definition of love, Trev?"

He looked like he wanted to be anywhere other than sitting in front of a plate of chicken carbonara, the center of this conversation. "What?"

"C'mon, I know you listened to Lord Al's talk the night we won the division."

"Oh." He gulped, "C.S. Lewis said love isn't extreme affection, instead it is a steady, constant care about the wellbeing of another." He added meekly, "Or something like that."

The table was uncomfortably quiet, Trev and I taking a bite of our food to try and break the silence. Amber began to cry. "I don't know what to do."

"Oh honey, everyone thinks that. Just go with what will make you happy. Do what will make Trev happy. You two are the only two that matter," cooed Gail. She was serene above the table but I got another swift kick below. That just made me scarf down my food faster. Trev followed suit.

We left the women to talk by themselves, walking around the outside glass taking in the view. "The last time I was up here, this place spun around."

"Yeah, why'd they stop?" Trev asked.

"Don't know. Maybe it broke."

"How would you replace a motor this high up that is big enough to turn a restaurant?"

"That is the type of question that proves we were meant

to be baseball players rather than engineers."

He laughed. "Yeah, guess so."

"Hey Trev," I paused. "Smile. You're in love with a beautiful girl. This is supposed to be an exciting time and, for better or worse, you will never know for certain about the future. Just appreciate what you know today. If you do that every day the rest will take care of itself, warts and all."

"I'll try to remember that."

"Have I steered you wrong before?"

He looked down at his finger, feeling where a ring was destined to go, "No."

"No, what?" said Amber as she snuck up and grabbed Trev around the waist from behind.

"Done talking about wedding stuff?" Trev asked, avoiding the question. The kid was going to be a good husband one day.

"For today. There are 460 more days to fill with it." Amber gave a devilish smile.

"What are you two looking at over here?" Gail asked, surprisingly tranquil about being so close to the edge.

"Look at you. I knew you'd be fine once you got up here," I said.

"It is quite a view."

"Yeah, Detroit was quite the city."

"*Sheldon* couldn't live here."

"Huh?"

Amber burst out laughing. "No, Gail, you're right."

"What the hell are you two talking about?"

348

"See the wheel and spoke pattern?" Gail asked. "That's a no-no for *Sheldon Cooper*, you know that show you watch, *The Big Bang Theory*."

"I thought you hated that show?"

"Hate? No. It is stupid though, dorks having sex like rabbits. But you find it charming so I have picked up a little bit over the years."

"You only pick up something that trivial if you truly like it. I knew I had good taste in film. All this ribbing I get and you've secretly adored it this whole time. Even my habit of quoting stuff."

"Don't flatter yourself too much there, dear." She wrapped her arms around me, "You've rubbed off on me a little. I turned you from a knuckle dragging caveman into something approaching respectable. I win."

I looked towards Trev, "You can still get out."

We got to the stadium an hour before first pitch and were still almost late to our seats, stuck in hellish lines to get through security. "Glad they don't have that in Toledo," Gail said, sentiments that everyone else agreed with. I was a bit disappointed that we had to hurry to our seats. I had been given the tour of Comerica Park before but I wanted to do a walk around for the others, including a picture or two perhaps with the statues in left. Gail asked if I wanted a hot dog or a beer to which I replied that I was content. Dinner had been filling, pasta with a heavy sauce that was still settling in the pit of my stomach. An usher shepherded us to the first four seats off the aisle of the sixth row. We could spit onto the corner of the dugout, nestled down close enough to the field to avoid the winds that rolled through the concourse.

Gail joined us after Kid Rock threw out the first pitch and the anthem. The speakers blared Eminem, enshrining my opinion that white men can't make rap appealing either, as the Tigers took the field. She carried a Diet Pepsi and a scorecard. "What's that for?"

"I'd like you to teach me how to keep score."

"You're adorable, you know that?"

The game was a pitcher's duel, if you ignored the eternal television time outs the pace was fairly quick for a playoff game. The Tigers put up one in the third and that stuck as the only score in the first two hours and twenty-five minutes. It was an easy game to keep score. I got to teach Gail how the positions are numbered. She asked why the shortstop was six and the third baseman five to which I honestly said I didn't know. She asked why you go right to left on the infield (except for the shortstop) but left to right in the outfield. Once again I said I didn't know, just because. She didn't like that answer. She really didn't like it when I said that there is no established way to keep score, it is an individual's preference. She couldn't get past the lack of rules, even as I tried to discuss the fact that keeping score was just a means to an end, to record what happened, and nothing more.

Up one in the ninth, the Tigers manager subbed Alex into the game for defensive purposes. The move drew wild cheers from our group which garnered a couple of rude looks from some of those sitting around us. Alex was as crisp at short under the bright lights as he had been for my squad. He made a nice off-balance charge to get the speedy Braves shortstop with one out. No amount of defense could keep Atlanta from tying it a batter later when Justin Upton hit a solo home run over the home bullpen in left. From their last out to new life in one play, no other sport can swing momentum so quickly. The game went to extra innings. I was excited at the possibility of seeing Alex get the chance to bat. A scoreless tenth nearly ensured it.

The Braves were held off the board in the top of the 11th, Alex due to hit fourth in the bottom of the inning. A double by the Detroit catcher led off, the winning run in scoring position with no one out. A line drive was picked by the shortstop for the first out. The Atlanta manager decided to walk the next batter, setting up a double play possibility. Gail asked me why he wanted to do that and I told her that the only run that mattered was at second, if he scored it was over. By walking the next man, a double play was possible, a plus, without being worse off. That and the Atlanta manager had Alex pegged as a patsy.

Alex's stats the past two months, in limited at-bats, hadn't been bad. I knew the visiting squad had gotten this wrong. Suddenly an old memory crashed into my conscious, Sparky Anderson yelling to Gibson that Goose Gossage and the Padres were pitching around a man to get to him. I got up and made my way down the aisle to the railing. The first pitch was a strike, Alex's swing in similar form to how it was last time I

351

saw it but unable to catch up to a 99 mph fastball. It seems all the bullpen guys threw that in the majors now. A brief silence came over the crowd as Alex asked for time. "Hey Bird!" I yelled. He stopped adjusting his gloves at the sound of my voice. Some goofy clap soundtrack came over the speakers to rev up the crowd to which they reacted like lemmings. Alex's eyes found me and he stood out of the box waiting for the noise to die down. I saw the umpire bark at him to get back in the box but he was waiting to hear me speak. Alex raised his hands above shoulder level, palms down, to tell the crowd to quiet. Slowly, his gestures took hold and the sound of silence rolled across the crowd like the Wave.

"They pitched around specifically to get to you Bird. They think you've got nothing. He," I was now pointing at the pitcher who had turned to stare at me, "thinks you can't hit him! Prove him wrong." A small cheer came up at my outburst, 45,000 people watching me now as I slunk back to my seat. Alex stepped back into the box. The next pitch was low. I turned to see a stadium employee talking with the usher at the top of the steps to our section. Another ball. They were coming down towards me now. I stopped looking, eyes now glued to the field. I felt a tap on the shoulder just as the pitcher released the 2-1 pitch, a fastball that Alex connected with.

At the crack of the bat, the security guy forgot about me. I heard him let out a yell as he tracked the ball through the night sky. The crowd, already standing, erupted into a frenzy. Before the ball landed over the wall in left the party was on, the Tigers were World Champs for the first time since my team had done it 30 years ago. I wondered if Wal was watching somewhere. Alex's hands clenched into fists above his head as he came around first. By second base he was pumping his fist as the winning run crossed the plate. There was no hesitation to join his teammates at home this night, jumping onto the plate and enduring a plethora of slaps and punches as adrenaline forced him to jump again, and again. He didn't look like a hopping bird at all, he was a hopping Tiger.

I turned to the security guard, "Yes?" He didn't hear me nor did he care. Gail wrapped her arms around me and planted a kiss on my cheek. I could get used to this baseball crazy chick indeed.

It felt like all of the Detroit area had come downtown to celebrate in the streets. People teemed in the lots between the Stadium and the Fox Theater, across Grand Circus Park, back towards Greektown, even down Woodward for blocks. It took a long time for our group to walk through the throng. Gail was cold, even after taking my jacket, but the line for the People Mover, which we took over earlier, was not going to dissipate for hours. I decided to leave our vehicle at the garage. Gail and I said goodbye to Trev and Amber, me wishing them luck and Gail promising Amber that they would be talking soon. It was just us again, walking west towards our hotel.

"Do you know the routing number for our bank?" I asked.

"Not off the top of my head. Why?"

"Can you fish a check out of your purse, please?" She did, handing it to me as I pulled out a card from my pocket. I dialed the number and put the card back, the phone going to my ear as I opened up the checkbook. "I'm looking for George." A wire transfer would be done by the morning.

"What was that about?" Gail asked.

"Remember that story you didn't believe me about, Dirk's gambling?"

"Yes," she said hesitantly.

"The vacation we've been on was paid for with those winnings. What was left I put on a long shot bet. I tried to get rid of it to charity but they wouldn't take it so I laid odds on the longest shot I could find."

"And what was that?"

"That Alex would hit a home run. Guess I'm just not meant to be rid of it."

"You're serious? How much did you win?!"

"Enough that I don't want to hold onto it."

Gail laughed, "Mr. Freeman, you are incorrigible. How do you expect to keep a job in baseball publically humiliating your employers and gambling on the game?"

"I figured you'd be happy. It seems to me that you enjoyed the last adventure we went on."

"I did. Very much so, actually. What did you have in mind?" Gail asked.

"I have it on good authority that the butterfly gardens of southern Mexico are quite beautiful."

www.ingramcontent.com/pod-product-compliance
Lightning Source LLC
Chambersburg PA
CBHW020353260626
47156CB00007B/2091